DEAL
with a
DEMON

Text copyright © 2013 Celeste Easton
Originally released as a Kindle Serial, April 2013
All rights reserved.
Printed in the United States of America.

Published by Montlake Romance
PO Box 400818
Las Vegas, NV 89140

ISBN-13: 9781477807668
ISBN-10: 1477807667
Library of Congress Control Number: 2013904920

DEAL
with a
DEMON

C E L E S T E E A S T O N

This is for my support system.
Without you I am nothing.

Episode One

Chapter One

She'd left her fucking gun in the kitchen.

Nic Wright opened her eyes and kept her breaths calm and even, as if she were still sleeping. Her back was toward the bedroom door, but she knew without question someone stood there, watching her.

Your weapon can't help you unless it's next to you, genius.

And she'd left herself vulnerable—unarmed, asleep. An unwelcome thought of her parents ghosted through her mind.

No time for those thoughts. Some sneaky bastard had crept up on her, and the only weapon at her disposal? The stupid demon handbook she'd been reading that had lulled her to sleep. It would have to do. She wrapped her fingers around the worn edges and waited for the creeper to get closer.

If Drew had shown the smallest inkling of responsibility and returned her calls, she wouldn't be in this situation. But no. Her brother, the meth head and constant pain in her ass, had disappeared without a trace, and his apartment looked like a satanic cult had moved in.

She couldn't hear the footsteps on the carpet as the person moved across the room, but she could feel a shift in the air, a sense of the room getting more crowded. The mattress sank as the person knelt down. Male for sure—too big to be one of her brother's junkie girlfriends. Not her brother either. Drew would have hopped in and smacked her in the back of the head.

She firmed her grip on the book and waited, the taste of adrenaline salty on her tongue.

When the stranger leaned in, the scent of rosemary and smoke drifted down to her, like he'd come from a gourmet bonfire. The alluring aroma wouldn't deter her, though.

Closer, buddy. A little closer.

The bed creaked as he loomed over her, and she flashed into action, flipping over and swinging the book up in a sweeping arc. The bound edge connected beneath his chin, knocking his teeth together with a snap. She popped up into a crouch and drew back with both hands for another blow. The hardback was nothing compared to her Ruger nine millimeter, but she used it with the same intent. She dealt the next hit to the side of his head. He careened back onto the floor where he lay, motionless, his arms and legs stretched out spread-eagle.

Knocked out. She smiled for a second, then her heart stuttered and she wanted to kick herself.

She had just coldcocked the most gorgeous man she'd ever laid eyes on.

What the hell was a guy who looked like *that* doing in her brother's shit-ass apartment? And what if she hadn't heard him at all? She could've been dead by now.

And who knew how long he would be out?

She ran for the kitchen and grabbed her gun from her duty belt on the counter—

Wait. How'd he get in? She glanced at the door. The dead bolt was still locked. Drew lived on the third floor. Did the beautiful man climb up a ladder and through a window? He'd come in from the hallway, so not through the bedroom window, but maybe one of the others? The fire escape reached the kitchen windows...no. Impossible. There was no way a man his size could have climbed up the fire escape without the ancient, rusty thing crumbling into a pile of dust.

There'd be time for answers later. Right now she had bigger issues, one of which could wake up at any minute. She stopped to listen, and the apartment was all quiet. He'd come alone.

She dashed back down the hall, her nine ready in her hand. Her victim didn't stir, but she could see his chest moving with each breath he took.

Well, at least I didn't kill him.

Out of arm's reach, she knelt down for a closer look. His temple was split and knotted where her last hit had landed, but the rest of his face was fine. Better than fine, in fact. A smooth brow and sculpted jaw completed by a perfect mouth. For some ridiculous reason she wanted him to lift his dark lashes to see what color his eyes were.

He wore silver rings on a couple of fingers, and his black dress shirt had the sheen of expensive fabric. His jeans were snug, leaving little to the imagination, and as she wondered about their contents, he stirred. Her stare flew to his face.

Ice green. Frost-covered emeralds, her brain noted. His eyes were a glacier.

"Well, that hurt a bit." His voice matched his appearance: wicked, rich.

Her cheeks flamed and she scuttled away from him.

He reached up and rubbed at his temple. "No need to run off quite yet. At least allow me to introduce myself."

He sat up and Nic got stalled by the deliberate, predatory way he moved, as if he were a jaguar waking from a catnap—ready to pounce on her if she bolted. She stayed frozen in a half crouch.

"I am the help you requested." He offered her a smug, feline grin. "You Called for me."

She noticed the way he'd drawn out the word "called," like it had a double meaning. The weight of her gun bolstered her shaky confidence. "Are you a friend of Drew's?"

"I doubt it."

He was tall with the tight, bold frame of an athlete, but the tattoos and shiny jewelry didn't match up with the quarterback image. Neither did the shoulder-length blue-black hair. He reminded her of a rock star—not of the pop, pretty-boy variety. More like the kind associated with screaming guitars and bra-tossing women; the type who dressed in leather pants and sexed up the groupies backstage with a bottle of liquor in one hand and a death wish in the other.

Then it hit her. This guy was some big-time drug dealer's henchman; one look at the jewelry and the pricey shirt said it all. Had her brother gotten into trafficking to support his habit? Maybe there was a chance he'd been kidnapped and they'd sent a representative to collect a ransom. No wonder Drew's loser best friend, Jimmy, hadn't wanted to talk over the phone when she'd called him. They were probably watching him too. "How much money do you want?"

"I'm not here for money."

His smile made her wonder what else he might accept for payment. Could he be part of the cleanup crew there to make sure no evidence had gotten left behind? "Who do you work for?"

He laughed, flashing straight, white teeth in a crooked grin. "I don't work for anyone except you."

Huh? "Why are you here?"

When he rose to his feet so did she. He was a full head and shoulders taller than she was and almost twice as wide.

He held his arms out toward her, palms up. "I am First Born of the Asmodai, eldest son of Asmodeus, and a Prince of the Nine Hells. I am the answer to your seeking. I am Helper. I am Arden." At the end of his speech he bowed low over his knees.

Nic giggled. Then the giggling turned into laughter. Maybe it was the stress over Drew, or the fear, or the precise formality of his delivery, but she laughed until tears stood in her eyes. Her brother had gone crazy, this man in front of her too, and she was on the fast track to following them both.

"Not exactly the response I am accustomed to," he said between his teeth.

"Sorry." She swiped the wetness from her cheeks. "I really don't know how you said all that with a straight face. I bet whoever you work for loves your sense of humor."

"I work for you."

His dry delivery was spot-on. Maybe his employer picked him for his acting ability. "OK, really, how much money?"

"Stop asking about money and explain yourself. You're the one who Called *me*."

"I didn't call you."

"You did."

The charade didn't amuse her. "All right, buddy, you've had your laugh and now it's time to get real." Nic aimed her

Ruger at his head and marched over to search him. She'd call the cops once she knew he wasn't armed. Of course then she'd have to listen to the local PD guys rib her about being a rent-a-cop, but oh well. Maybe they could get answers out of him.

Her hand met hard muscle as she felt around his chest and ribs. She'd frisked people before, but none had made the hair stand up on the back of her neck or warmth flood her veins. She did a quick pat down of his legs and tried not to linger on his inner thighs even if it meant she missed something. "Where's your weapon?"

"If you're done stroking me, I'll explain."

His words stopped her short and she pulled her hands back. He was very nice to feel, but she didn't want him thinking she'd noticed. She also didn't want to give him or the jerks who took her brother any other reasons to laugh at her. "Fine. Say whatever it is you and your buddies cooked up to spoon-feed me, and then we'll start talking about why you're really here."

"I told you. I'm here to help you."

"Sure you are." No matter how serious his expression, she didn't buy it. What kind of drug dealers did business this way?

"OK. Maybe we should start over." He sighed and crossed his arms over his chest. "You called for help."

"I said I didn't call—"

"Wait." He held up his hand to silence her. "The book you nailed me with. What was it?"

"I don't see what the stupid book has to do with this."

When he stepped toward her all her senses fired up and for a minute she lost focus. He looked vicious, and his dark handsomeness hid—she was sure—a deep penchant for violence. He picked the book up from the floor.

"What could a book have to do with your little game?"

"This is not a game." He flipped the book over, and when he read the title he laughed, his emerald eyes sparkling as he looked up at her.

Nic ignored the little jump from her stomach. "What's so funny?"

"Go figure." He chuckled and one corner of his mouth tilted up in a smirk.

"Would you please tell me what the fuck is so amusing?" Her thin patience was all but exhausted and she edged nearer to popping him one in the nose.

"Do you know who wrote this?" He turned the cover around to face her.

"*A Purposeful Existence*," she read. "*A Mortal's Guide for Demon Assistance*." Some tiny nugget of memory tugged at her brain, but she pushed it away.

"And the author's name?"

The name was long and foreign looking, and when she tried to pronounce it, he laughed. "Az-mo-dee-us," he said, enunciating the syllables as if he were teaching it to a toddler.

She bit at the inside of her lip. Hadn't he mentioned the strange name when he'd given her his bullshit intro? "Is that who you work for or something?"

He laughed again. "Hardly. Asmodeus is my father."

"Very funny." Nic didn't know how far his act was supposed to go, but judging by the goose bumps on her arms, it had reached the punch line. "Your father is a demon who writes books? Yeah, OK. Your joke stopped being hilarious about two minutes ago."

"This. Isn't. A. Joke." His smile took on a feral look and she figured he must be tired of the game too.

She stared at the author's name. Something about the book...

Then she remembered. The book had jumped at her. She'd been standing just inside the doorway to the bedroom, her discoveries in the apartment and her desperation brewing a toxic soup in her gut. When she'd asked out loud for some answers, it had flown across the room, end over end, and landed open at her feet.

Her gaze jumped from the cover to her visitor's face. She remembered reading a passage about "Calling," but it must have been right before she fell asleep because the memory was hazy.

Wait. Wait one fucking minute. Could the book have put a spell on her or something? If it could fly across the room, what else could it have done?

But one thought stood out in her brain like a lone grave on a cemetery hill—Summoning a Helper, the last section she remembered reading. Could she have really done that? Had she summoned a demon to help her find her brother?

No. Nope. No. No way was she going to buy any of it. Before she'd set foot in Drew's apartment earlier, she'd been sane. Now? Well…sanity was as absent as her brother.

She looked up at the man standing in front of her. The demon part fit one hundred percent. She'd never seen a mortal man his equal in the looks department. Was he what demons looked like?

Yep.

Was she completely deranged?

Yep.

"Let's start over," she said.

"Good idea. Wish I had suggested something like that." Nic glowered at him, but he continued. "I am First Born of—"

"You can skip the son of Asmodeus, nine hells part. I believe *you* believe what you're saying, but I'm not an idiot regardless of what those assholes you work for think." His eyes grew colder and his smile thinned to a tight line as she went on. "I figure you're their cleanup and collect crew, but I think you missed your calling. You should be out in Hollywood breaking starlet hearts and smiling for the cameras instead of running errands for some big, slimy drug—"

He yanked a dagger from his boot and she jumped away, lifting her nine and leveling it at his forehead. Why didn't she check his goddamned boots?

"Calm down." He rolled his eyes and shook his head. "I'm not going to hurt you."

"Yeah, that's what all the bad guys say right before the woman's guts end up on the floor."

"Why are you so stubborn?"

She bridled. "You don't even know me. How dare you call me stub—"

His eyes never left hers as he sank the blade into his palm and down into his wrist. When he pulled the knife back out, the skin on the sides of the gash lifted open. His smug expression didn't change when dark blood ran from the wound, over his wrist, and dripped onto the carpet. He held the hand up toward her like an offering.

Time to go. Her best option would be to ease out of the bedroom and make for the back door...

The flow of blood from the wound stopped. How did a cut so deep stop bleeding in half a second? He'd almost cut completely through his hand. That wasn't possible—

Then the cut began to seal up, the split skin coming together in a seam. The lines of his gray tattoos closing together in precise alignment.

Her breath was the only sound in the room, wheezing in and out of her in a stuttered rush. She couldn't look away.

The mark from the slice faded and faded until his palm appeared untouched.

"Now. Can we move on?" He slid the knife back into his boot and crossed his arms over his chest.

"How did...how did you do that?" She tried to force her brain to catch up. Doubt had wedged itself firmly in the front of her skull. Did this little prank include special effects or had she been drugged? Maybe the descent into total lunacy began with disturbingly real hallucinations. Total psychotic break.

"We regenerate."

Panic held her like a vise. Her heart thumped so fast inside her chest she feared it would explode. "Who are you?"

"My name is Arden. I am demon, and I am here to help you."

She stared at him. He smiled, and the change it brought over his face sealed the deal for her because only one word could describe his grin: evil.

And right then, that moment of knowing something evil was in the room, she turned from disbelief to dismay, and then to resignation because her mind couldn't follow the events of the last ten minutes unless she allowed for the supernatural. A tiny kernel of rationality remained in her mind and she tucked it away. She might need to cling to it later when he told her Santa Claus was real too. Of course, at this point she had checked out of the reality motel altogether. What would another fantasy hurt?

"OK, Arden, I'm Nic and I guess I need your help." The words rang funny in her ears, but if she was going for absolute nut case, she might as well embrace the ride.

"I wouldn't be here otherwise." He adjusted the cuffs of his shirt. "So what's the story?"

His casualness irked her. Why was she the only one having trouble with the situation?

Regardless of her cluttered thoughts or her better, more rational, judgment, she told him about Drew disappearing and about how she had found the apartment—even included her brother's nasty relationship with crystal meth. He laughed when she pointed out the crude red drawing on the ceiling above the bed. When she showed him the stunning array of occult paraphernalia lying around the bedroom, he mumbled something about amateurs.

Nic did not want to go back into the spare room. The first indication of how low Drew had sunk had happened when she'd looked in there before. But she needed something to shut up Arden the Demon Delusion. "This isn't the worst of it."

"Show me."

——

Arden paid very close attention to the sway of her hips as he followed her through the dark apartment. She was a remarkable specimen regardless of the drab uniform she had on or the handgun tucked into the back of her pants. Small framed and toned like a runner, she wasn't his usual choice for fucking. He normally went for females with lush curves and long blonde hair; in earth-speak: porn star.

Nic. The perfect name for such a scrappy little thing. Maybe a nickname? Her brown hair was short and close-cropped in the back but longer in the front, and when she turned back to glance at him, it fell over half her face like a masquerade.

But, the nerve of her to brain him with his father's book. She'd moved so fast, giving him no time to react. Then she had the gall to demand answers of him, accusing him of being some drug pusher's lackey? Judging by the chip on her shoulder, he'd guess she hadn't been kissed enough. This project would be his last, but he would make damn sure he took care of *that* problem as soon as possible. And if he had the chance, he'd use his Gift on her to get her naked beneath him. Shit, he'd use it just to know how she tasted.

He stepped into the room behind her, and before she flipped on the light, his night vision afforded him a disturbing view.

The room had been worked by a professional.

The floorboards had been scrubbed raw and there were signs scraped into the wood in primal slashes. Jars with murky contents and bundles of dry, rotten flowers lay in compass points inside the arc of candles.

And in the center of it all, dominating the floor and stretching the length of the room, was a huge chalked circle with the symbol of his father's Master drawn inside.

"What does the star mean?"

"It's not a star," he said. "It's a pentagram. Someone used this room as a gateway."

She nodded and pushed her hair off her forehead like she was checking for fever. Sometimes humans reacted that way to seeing his kind; they think they're the victim of some bizarre delusion. Her earlier dismissal of him had led to him having to cut himself. He hoped she was on board now because he didn't want to have to show her another example of reality. Her smoky eyes shone with the light of a human teetering on the edge of madness. Another display like the one he'd given before might push her over the edge. He needed her lucid if he wanted to have any chance of getting to the bottom of this mess. "Any idea how long ago this happened?"

"I was here two days ago, but none of this," she motioned to the display, "none of this was here. Drew's journal said something about a ceremony."

"I need to see the journal. Go get it."

Anger flashed in her eyes. "Don't order me around."

"Do you want to help your brother?"

She chewed on her bottom lip. He saw her internal debate in the way she kept looking between him and the mark on the floor. This was a female not used to being ordered around. He could fix that easily enough, but it might be more fun to watch her bend to his will. Nic might provide him more joy than he'd had since before—

Nope. Not going to think about the past. His chance for a different life stood in the corner of the room deciding whether or not to do as he'd asked. Maybe he needed to change tactics. He offered her an innocent smile. "The journal might help."

She narrowed her eyes at him and he saw suspicion brewing clouds in her gaze. He wondered if he'd be able to use his Gift on someone with eyes like those; the storms she stirred there might be stronger than his talent, which only made him want to try it on her more.

Before he got the chance, she marched out of the room. Two seconds later she returned, a tattered leather journal in hand.

"Most of what's in here is gibberish."

He couldn't resist running a finger across the back of her hand when he took it from her. "I'll be the judge of what's important."

She snatched her hand away and glared at him from under the fringe of her hair. "Just read it and tell me what the fuck's going on."

Oh, he was going to enjoy making her mouth say the word "fuck" to him. It would be more like begging him for it but...

He pulled his wandering thoughts away from his crotch and back into the head on his shoulders. He flipped through the stained pages to read the last entry in the book.

"Well?" She'd moved away and leaned against the door frame.

Sorro. Shit. Seeing that demon's name in the brother's journal did not leave much room for a positive outcome. How did Sorro get out of the Fourth in the first place? And what could he possibly want with a living human?

He should've known it was too good to be true. To meet the requirement of the Incubai King, he thought all he would have to do was use his Gift to get her to submit, and then convince her to go with him. Now it was all fucked. He'd have to go home, back to the pointless existence he'd been living, and sit and wait for another opportunity.

Of one thing he was certain: he'd make it a point to find Sorro and show him what happens when you inconvenience an Asmodai.

He tossed the worthless journal on the floor and turned to her. "There's nothing I can do."

"You're not going to help me?" Her eyes had almost changed color—like a winter river.

"I'm sorry." He wasn't. "I'm not getting involved." True. If Sorro had taken her brother, he was a goner and nothing could be done about it. A demon didn't get named after an emotion like grief if he led people to happy endings.

He hated the thought of not getting what he'd come for. Hated the fact that his first Call in six months, and a chance to put the final piece in place for his change to Incubus, was a total waste of time. Who knew how long he'd have to wait for another opportunity? And he didn't want to wait any longer, but this situation wasn't part of his plan. Too messy. "I'm afraid you're on your own."

"I thought you were supposed to be some kind of demon knight in shining armor. What happened to your Helper bullshit?"

"You know, you really are lovely when you're fired up."

"Don't you dare change the subject." Nic moved closer and pointed at him. "Why can't you help?"

"If Sorro has taken him, there's nothing I can do."

Her stone glare reminded him not to underestimate her. His sore temple was a throbbing reminder of her capabilities, but he was still wholly unprepared for the way she chose to make her point.

He stared down the barrel of her gun and chewed at the inside of his cheek to keep from smiling. He hadn't even seen her reach for her weapon. She was full of surprises, this one.

Arden knew he needed to tread lightly or he'd end up with a hole in his head. The shot wouldn't kill him, but the recovery time would be substantial and he'd wasted enough time already. "Let's not get carried away."

"I'm not getting carried away. I'm simply making myself perfectly clear." Her hands were sure on the weapon's grip and she smiled.

"Point taken. Now, would you kindly lower that thing and let me explain?" At first she hesitated, but then just switched her target from his head to his chest. Well, that was a little better—a chest shot would be a lot easier to heal.

"You're going to help me find my brother."

"I'm trying to tell you, it's not going to happen."

"Why not?" Although her eyes shone with livid determination, he saw sadness there too.

Her devotion intrigued him. If her brother was such a loser with no goals except his next fix, why was she so bent on finding him?

And how could he use it to his advantage?

He decided to play it out a bit and see where he could lead her. "Your brother has been taken somewhere you can't go."

"What?"

"Sorro has him."

"Who's that?"

"A very nasty demon. Doesn't play well with others."

"Where did they go?"

"Probably to the Fourth."

"What in the hell is the Fourth?"

"It's not 'what' in Hell. It's 'where.'" He had only ever been as far as the Second, and it wasn't a trip he was eager to repeat. And the Fourth level? He didn't even know how to put it in words she would understand.

"So, Arden, you're telling me my brother has been taken to Hell?"

Hearing his name come from her mouth made a chill run up his neck. "Yes, but there's nothing you can do about it."

"There damn well better be something *you* can do." She stroked the trigger. "And you should start doing it. I'd hate to put a bullet between those eyes."

He needed to think of something quick. He had a feeling she wouldn't hesitate to back up her words. She struck him as the kind of female who would shoot first and ask questions never.

"There is a way, but I don't think you'll like it." He knew very well how to do it, but there was something about this mortal that stirred his protective side. She was wearing a uniform and holding her weapon like she'd had plenty of training, so he knew she was capable of taking care of herself. Still, the desperation coming off of her made her vulnerable, and if he took her Below, everyone down there would smell the fear on her. It would make for a very gory, bloody, and volatile situation.

It would also make for an impressive solution to his boredom. Plus there was the added benefit of getting what he wanted.

"I don't care where I have to go. I have to get Drew back." With a tired sigh she lowered the gun until the barrel pointed at the dirty floor. "He's my responsibility."

There was his key. She needed him. Perfect. "You can't go."

"Why?"

"Because…"

"Because why?" Her moment of vulnerability must have passed because she was back to displaying the chip on her shoulder.

He needed to play this very, very carefully—use her own weakness, her own pride and stubbornness against her. "Because you're afraid, and you can't come with me if you're scared."

"Are you fucking serious? I'm not scared."

"You are. I can smell it."

She crossed her arms and narrowed her eyes. "You can't smell fear."

"I can, and I'm serious. If you have even a trace of the smell on you, it would be bad."

"Bad like how?"

"Are you familiar with the term 'eaten alive'?"

She pointed to the embroidered logo on the chest of her uniform. "If you hadn't noticed, I'm kind of a professional. You know, the kind trained to deal with emergency situations and stuff." She waggled the gun at him and rolled her eyes.

She had no idea who she was dealing with. He was First Born and a Prince of Hell. Perhaps she needed another lesson.

He stepped toward her, the heat of his power building inside of him until it became the tip of a hot iron in the center of his chest. When her gaze collided with his, he held the contact until he saw her lips part and her eyes film over with a glossy sheen. He had total control of her now and could take whatever he wanted from her.

The arm holding the gun slackened, but he noticed she didn't lose her grip on the weapon. He would have to be cautious. He moved in closer, brought a hand up, and placed it on the side of her neck, never losing contact with her eyes. She flinched at his touch but didn't move away. Her skin was warm and smooth beneath his palm. Stray spikes of her hair framed her face. She smelled like tea with honey and her gray eyes were full of hardened stone. So many options came to his mind of the things he could do with her. Or *to* her.

He leaned a little closer and inhaled her scent. The light perfume of her fear was like a drug to him, pulling him, lighting him up from the inside out.

"Nic."

"Mm?"

He could take her right here on the filthy apartment floor and she would love every minute of it. And he would too, for that matter. He rubbed his thumb along her jaw and saw the heat in her eyes grow. He wanted to kiss her. Badly. The need pulsed through him. He drew her close until he could feel her breath on his lips.

And right then, right before he had his first taste of her, someone decided to start pounding on the apartment door.

Chapter Two

Arden cursed. He wasn't sure who he hated more at the moment, the person outside who was now beating on the door even harder, or himself for losing control. He had gotten so wrapped up in his intended target, he'd almost forgotten why he'd put her under in the first place. With his spell on her broken, he stepped away from her and back to reality.

Nic shook her head and he knew she was trying to clear the cobwebs he'd spun with his Gift. Without maintained eye contact, the effects wore off right away and she'd be left only with the thought she'd had right before he'd taken her under. He hadn't even gotten the chance to see how far he'd be able to go.

Her fingers flexed on the grip of her firearm as the knocking continued. She looked up at him and frowned. Her lips—the ones he'd been so close to tasting—parted, a question swirling in her stormy eyes. Then he saw the moment of indecision dissolve from her expression and he knew, just by looking at the set of her shoulders, she'd closed herself off again. He would have to work on breaking those walls down.

He offered her a serene smile, which she answered by narrowing her eyes and putting her hand up in a *stay* gesture.

Really? Did she think him a pet? He didn't even pause before following her out into the kitchen, trying to ignore the fact that following at her heels made him feel like her lapdog.

Oh, he was going to enjoy breaking her.

The subtle shift in light shining through the single-pane windows told him dawn couldn't be far off. He watched Nic creep toward the door. She took position on the left and nodded him over to the other side. He wasn't too happy about being ordered around, but he saw her plan and took up the other corner.

The door rattled in its frame from the pounding visitor. Nic stepped up and leveled the gun at where the person's head would be. Arden grasped the knob and bobbed his head at her once, then flung it open.

The person outside wasn't expecting it and fell onto the kitchen floor in a messy pile. Before their guest could get up, Nic had the barrel pressed against the back of the stranger's neck. Arden was impressed with how fast she had moved.

"Uhn—what the fuck?" Male. Human. And squirming under the weight of her knee in his back.

"I'm the only one who's going to be asking questions, asshole," she said. "I'm the one with the gun."

Arden smiled. Under regular circumstances, her aggressiveness wouldn't appeal to him. He preferred submissive bed partners. All of the women he used knew his status and would never dare to boss him around. But with Nic? He could picture her soft mouth making demands of him as he pressed inside of her.

Maybe allowing her to think she was in control would be to his benefit…and his pleasure.

"Nicolette? Is that you?"

"Jimmy?"

The man uttered a sound of relief. "Oh fuck, you almost gave me a heart attack. I thought you were one of them. Can you please move your gun? It's kinda digging in back there."

She stood up, letting her weapon rest at her side. Arden didn't know if he should reveal himself yet, so he stayed silent, fading back into the shadow behind the open door where he couldn't be seen but could watch unobserved. Nic obviously knew the male, and Arden wouldn't interfere unless it stalled forward progress.

Nicolette. Beautiful name. He wondered how her parents—

Focus, idiot.

"OK, Jimmy, you need to start talking," she said.

Arden could smell the man from five feet away. He reeked of garbage and sweat.

From his spot in the shadows, he saw Jimmy roll over and shuffle into a sitting position. "Take it easy. I got over here as fast as I could."

"Don't care," she said. "When was the last time you saw my brother?"

"I was here last night. Drew called me and said he scored some sweet shit. He invited me over for a sample. But when I got over here, there were some weird-ass dudes here with him."

Nic shot Arden a pointed look. Time for the big reveal. He pushed the door closed and stepped out of the shadows.

"Hi there, Jimmy," he said.

Jimmy took one look and skittered across the floor like a crab. "Oh shit! He's one of them too, isn't he?"

One of them? The male had seen demons before. This situation became more complicated by the second. He wanted answers.

"Nic, don't you see what he is?" Jimmy pressed his back against the refrigerator, and the scent of his fear intensified.

"It's OK. I know who he is." She glanced at Arden. "I need you to tell me who he works for and where they took my brother."

Jimmy stared at Nic, bug-eyed. "Fucking hell, you don't know shit."

"I know you and Drew got messed up with the wrong people and now you're here and he's…gone. Who were you two getting the supply from?"

She still thinks I'm some drug dealer's errand boy. Hadn't she learned anything from his demonstrations? Perhaps he would have to *show* her his capabilities.

He stepped over to where Jimmy huddled against the refrigerator and knelt down in front of the stinking human until he was at eye level. The heat of his power brimmed inside his chest. When he leaned in for the capture, the junkie's constant twitching stilled and his eyes glossed over. Jimmy was his to command.

"That's better, Jimmy. Everything is fine. Everything is cool."

"Everything's cool," Jimmy repeated.

"Tell me what happened when you were here with Drew."

"I was here with Drew."

Arden was tempted to sneak a smug smile at Nic, but he didn't want to break the hold he had on the man. "What happened?"

"I came over 'cuz Drew was having a little party."

"And?"

"When I got here, there were these two dudes sitting on the couch. They kinda looked uptown, know what I mean?" Drool dripped down Jimmy's chin. He might have wiped it away if Arden told him to.

He didn't. "What else?"

"They looked like they were hustlers or something. I figured that's who had the dope."

"Next?"

"Drew and me got off and it was awesome stuff. Those dudes were laughing at us, but then they got all serious. They had whacked-out names too. One was called Sad or something, and the other guy was Flip."

"Flic?" Arden asked.

"Yeah, Flic. They made us go in the spare room and it was all done up like some witches had been living in there or something. Then they started singing."

Here it comes.

"They were singing loud and dancing around and Drew was laughing. He was looking all creepy, like he didn't know if he should burst into tears or start screaming, ya know?" Jimmy was deep in the spell, but his fear was here and now; Arden could feel it ramping up his power. He had to be cautious. If the human got too worked up, he'd never get the whole story out of him.

"Easy, Jimmy, easy."

Jimmy swallowed and went on. "The three of them were getting crazy and the room started shaking. I was freaking out and yelling for Drew, but it was like he couldn't hear me. Then this light started coming out of the floor, and the wood was cracking and boards were popping up."

Arden knew the answer, but asked anyway. "And then what?"

"They all got blurry, like that light was swallowing them up, like it was eating them. I was screaming and screaming because I knew the light was bad, but they never heard me. They started spinning around and the light was spinning. I couldn't see Drew anymore. The floor opened up and those three went down in it, and when the boards fell back into place like nothing happened, I took off." A single tear tracked down the male's cheek and the scent of urine filled the kitchen.

Arden let go of his spell and backed away, disgusted. Jimmy had pissed all over himself.

———

Nic had come to a conclusion: she was dreaming all of this. Jimmy wasn't sitting on the floor stewing in his own urine. The gorgeous man with dark hair and emerald eyes was not looking at her. She was asleep. She'd been reading that stupid book, and her price to pay? The most realistic nightmare she'd ever had.

If this were dreamland, though, would she be able to smell piss? She took a deep breath.

Yep, still there. She blinked. Arden was still staring at her.

And if her mind had snapped—the most likely scenario—why did the whole situation ring so true?

The drawings on the bedroom walls, the giant pentagram in the other room, the knife slicing through Arden's palm and the wound reknitting, Jimmy falling so far into a trance that he'd wet his pants; compelling evidence when she thought about it.

OK, let's pretend all of this is real. Drew, as part of some desperate, drug-induced frenzy, decided to further his education by jumping headfirst into Satanism. He played around with all those books, fucked up, and called up something dangerous. And those dangerous things somehow convinced him he could get everything he wanted if he tagged along with them. But why would her brother believe it?

One word—well, actually, two: methamphetamine psychosis.

But that didn't explain why *she* was starting to believe it. She'd never done a drug in her life besides caffeine, and she'd always used decongestants for their intended purpose; *not* cooked down with toxic chemicals and shot into a vein.

She tucked her nine into the back of her pants. Was this her new reality? Demons existed and one of their Princes was standing five feet away looking at her like he'd just proven a huge point.

And Jimmy? A junkie for sure, but as deluded as her brother? More than likely. But he'd been with it enough to get out while he could—

Wait a minute. Drew had been sucked into another dimension and his so-called best friend had run out on him? "You took off? You stupid fucking junkie."

She leaped on Jimmy and snatched him up by the front of his soiled shirt until he was half-standing. "You watched my brother get sucked into the floor by two demons and you ran?"

"I was scared shitless," Jimmy said. He shook his head a couple of times as if to clear things up. His eyes lost a bit of their feverish gloss. "You think because you're a stupid rent-a-cop you wouldn't do the same?"

She had a strong urge to put a bullet in his head so she wouldn't have to listen to him whine, but she let go of his shirt. Drew's friends were really stellar. She gave Jimmy a shove and he stumbled back into the fridge.

Nic retrieved her duty belt from the filthy green countertop by the sink and put it on. The two men in the room remained silent as she slid her weapon home into its holster at her hip. Maybe they both knew she needed a minute.

Two days ago, she'd had a fight with Drew over money and rehab. After the first five unanswered calls, she'd figured he was only pouting. By the next day, his continued silence had worried her enough to rush over like a good sister and check on him, only to find him worse off than she could've imagined.

But the topper on this cake of a day? The blow her belief system had taken. She wasn't religious; she was practical. Now? The proof was all around her. When she turned to face the men, the most forceful example of the evidence stood across the dirty linoleum with his arms crossed over his chest and a smug look on his face.

A sliver of thought floated to the surface of her mind. She looked away and reached down to fiddle with the snap over her extra clip. What had happened in the other room? Her memory fuzzed over, but she remembered Arden's warm palm on the side of her neck and the sight of his face *way* too close for comfort.

Of course, she didn't really have the luxury—or the inclination—to think about that right now; she had too many other things to deal with. None of which were going to take care of themselves.

"OK, Jimmy, I'm not going to shoot you, but don't make me regret it." She stomped over to Arden and glared up at him. "And you...you're going to help me go get my brother."

His head tilted to the side and he raised his eyebrows in surprise. "Is that right?"

"Yes, and you're going to do it now."

"Even if I decide to help you, we don't have enough people to do the ceremony properly."

"You're going to have to make do with what we have." She turned to glare at Jimmy. "And you're going to help too, idiot."

"Why the hell do I have to help?"

She marched back over to him and in a flash her Ruger was at his temple. "You'll do it because I'm the one with the gun."

Jimmy nodded, but kept his mouth shut.

"There's only one small problem with your plan, Nicolette." Arden's use of her full name startled her. It also made her body temp rise by about ten degrees.

"I don't see anything wrong with my plan."

"I haven't agreed to help you. And don't bother with your gun, it won't work on me."

She rounded on him, and the satisfied look on his face made her want to crack him in the head. Again.

"I have to be motivated to assist you. It's kind of how this whole Helper thing works."

"What kind of motivation are we talking about?" By the appearance of his crooked grin, she wasn't going to like it. In her limited exposure—movies and scary stories—demons wanted either your soul or...

Sex.

And someone—some*thing*—like him...he reeked of sex in his tight jeans, and it glowed in every facet of his gemstone eyes. His swagger, his confidence; all signs pointed to "yes."

If she were one hundred percent honest with herself, it made her heart sprint to think of him wanting her. But she would never agree to it; couldn't *let* herself agree, even though the thought still brought warmth up from her toes to the crown of her head. Guys who looked like him didn't go for girls like her.

"There has to be a reason for me to take on your problem. We get Called up here when someone is really desperate, but there has to be a bargain. We are demons, after all."

"Don't do it, Nicolette."

"Shut up, Jimmy." She sighed. At this point, her old reality twisted into something she no longer recognized, and what choice did she really have? "OK, what's the bargain?"

Chapter Three

Nic couldn't agree to what he was asking. "No way."

"That's the deal. Take it or leave it." Arden leaned back against the counter. Even from across the room she could see the sparkle in his eyes.

She wasn't surprised. He knew how much she needed his particular kind of help, so she should have guessed his price.

No way. But...damn it.

She peeked over at him and mulled it over. Her brother was in the hands of some horrible monster and this could be her one shot at saving him. Drew was her responsibility.

And it would be an absolute lie to say she wasn't curious. The demon Prince was *very* nice to look at, and the way his shirt fit led her to believe there was a nice body involved too. She eyed the curve of his lean muscles. When was the last time she'd had something like him lying in her bed?

Never something that nice.

She was going to kill Drew for putting her in this position when she got her hands on him. If only there were a way she could trick Arden into helping without having to pay up at the end, she'd be—

An idea popped into her head. She might make it out of this, but she needed to buy some time to get a handle on the plan forming in her brain. "I'm going to need a minute."

"Of course," he said with his perpetually sensuous grin.

"Watch Jimmy."

"Of course."

Jimmy had fallen asleep while the deal was offered up. Arden's parlor trick must have been powerful if it put a meth head to sleep. She was thankful he hadn't heard the gritty details of the bargain.

Nic walked back to the bedroom and closed the door behind her, leaning against it for support. If she hoped to get this right, she needed to tap into some of her inner calm. She closed her eyes, took a deep breath, and when she opened them back up, she spotted the book written by Arden's father lying on the floor next to the bed.

She sat down on the mattress and flipped through the pages. Something she'd spotted earlier—before she'd fallen asleep and her life had zoomed off the charts into utter chaos—about the summoning of a Helper, something about the Call itself.

There wasn't a table of contents so she skimmed, skipping over pictures and charts until she found it.

Her one memory of the words blinked inside her head. The words themselves had begged to be read aloud. Like the letters and sentences needed to be heard to be appreciated. That, in itself, was probably some kind of trick too. Damn demons.

She flipped another page and found it. The footnote was impossibly small and difficult to read. Having gotten to know a bit about the author's son, she figured the snippet was something they didn't want to print in large type.

Nic had to squint to read it:

The Call for Helpers is akin to the sweet song of Spring, alluring, a signal of new life to come. But along with its beauty, the Call has an opposing force, as all in nature has an opposite. If the song sours, as if the first warm, sun-filled day of that delightful season is threatened with a rain shower, the Helper will find him or herself in misery. The mortal has the power to turn the Call into a bitter-sweet dirge if he or she can convince the Helper their assistance is no longer needed. To do so, the mortal must address the Helper by their true name. Then, like the last sad leaf of Autumn falling from the sleeping tree, the season will change, and the Helper will return Below.

"Bingo."

Someone knocked on the door. She laid the book back where she had found it, not wanting to arouse suspicion when she was supposed to be agonizing over her dilemma.

"I need your decision. The ceremony must take place before sunrise."

Arden. She steeled herself. If she could get him to play along, she'd figure out his true name somehow, and once Drew was home safe, she would use the name and be done with the whole mess. Simple enough. "OK, come in."

"What's your answer?" He shut the door behind him and approached her. When he got close, she could smell the strange scent of rosemary again. Under any other circumstances, she would be intrigued by it, but—

Who was she kidding? He smelled amazing.

She took a step back. "Let me get this straight. You came here to help me, right?"

"I got the Call, yes."

"And you're agreeing to help me on the condition that I give myself to you?"

"That is what I said. Weren't you paying attention?" She shot him a glare and was further irritated when his smile only got bigger. "Easy, killer," he chuckled. "What I mean to say is, I'm offering you my assistance. In return, you will be mine."

"And your support is based on my need?"

"Yes."

"So, it would follow that you would be helping me get my brother back." She chose her words with care. When trying to get one over on a demon, caution seemed vital, if not mortal. "If I agree, you will take me to Drew and help me get him home?"

She waited and watched impatiently as he debated. Did he suspect something? Her lip was still sore from biting it earlier in the night, but she chewed on it anyway.

"I will, but only if you consent to surrender to me."

Surrender? She wasn't falling for his tricky wording. "Not until after we've brought Drew back. Once I'm sure he's safe, then I'll have sex with you."

His eyes turned frosty, but the look didn't make her think of cold. In fact, it made her very, very warm. It also made her doubt her reasoning. She wondered if she alone would be enough to tempt him. A man with his looks probably had a whole harem at his disposal. But why would he go to all the trouble just to get in her pants? And in the end, if she couldn't get his true name out of him, all she had to do was have sex with the beautiful demon. What could it hurt?

Nic looked right into his flawless eyes. "Deal?"

"It's a deal," he said.

Arden kicked Jimmy again. "Wake up."

He was about to attempt a crossing ceremony with this idiot as a pilot and there wasn't a lot of time to train the human. It would be a miracle if he and Nic didn't get lost in the Abyss. At least she appeared to understand the gravity of the matter.

As soon as he'd agreed to her deal, she went to work. In no time, she had gathered all the things they would need. He was thankful the ceremony site was intact. It would make this easier for all of them. The gateway had been opened once so it would be simple enough to open it again.

But this time he'd be going Below with a mortal. Of course, the mortal he was helping had no idea what she had actually agreed to; he would help if she gave her life to him. It was the final thing he needed to make his transformation. The other tasks had been total cake in comparison. All he had to do now was get her down to the Fourth and turn her over to the Emissary who would take care of the rest. Then his days of sitting around the house waiting for a Call while he practically died of boredom would be over. The greatest part of all of it would be the moment he became full demon and the weak human half of him was stripped away. For good.

He caught a glimpse of her in the other room. She looked a bit like a Trickster with her petite frame and pixie-like nose. Her hair kept spilling onto her forehead and she shoved it back with a frown. It seemed like a waste to have something as delectable as Nic around and not take advantage of the situation.

He made up his mind on the spot. Before he gave her over, he would know the pleasure of her flesh. Once satisfied, he'd dump her and be born again as an Incubus.

But neither was going to happen if he didn't get Jimmy up off the kitchen floor, so he kicked him again for good measure.

"Hey, man, stop it."

"Wake up."

Arden made eye contact, and before Jimmy had time to realize what was happening, he was trapped. "Jimmy, I'm going to need you to do exactly what I tell you."

"'Zactly what you tellmee," Jimmy said, his words slurred from the effects of Arden's spell—too many trances in too short a time.

"Good. I'm going to give you a book and you're going to read it word for word, all right?"

"Wordfer word…alllright."

"Now, let's go in the other room." He kept his gaze locked with Jimmy's as he backed out of the kitchen.

Arden jerked his chin at Nic for her to follow them. He saw the determination glinting in her eyes and raw lust pulsed in his veins. Would the same fire burn there when he entered her for the first time?

No. No distractions.

Candlelight illuminated the room, and the dancing flames made shadows run across the floor. Arden was careful to position Jimmy outside of the circle. He handed him the book. "Once Nic and I are in place, you can start reading."

"I can start reading—"

"No," Arden said. "Do not start reading until we're in position, you twit."

"I'ma twit." A drop of drool crested Jimmy's bottom lip and slipped down onto his chin. "Twit."

He needed to stay focused. If he kept the man under for too long, his mind would be broken—as if it weren't broken enough already—and he didn't want to risk having to leave the apartment to find some other sheep to coerce. The time wasted might provide Nic with the opportunity to change her mind and he refused to let that happen. She belonged to him now.

Without breaking contact with Jimmy, he took Nic's hand. Her palm was damp. Good. He liked having her on edge. It would make her surrender so much sweeter when the moment came. "All right, Jimmy. Start reading."

The candles in the room blazed with energy as Jimmy droned out the archaic words, the junkie's face lit by an unnatural amber glow. Arden kept his hold on the man so he wouldn't fuck up the reading.

The air in the room shifted. They were nearing the portal.

"Whatever happens, Nic, don't let go."

The sucking feeling started at his ankles. She must have felt it too but her grip on his hand didn't tighten. Her ignorant dismissal of the situation irritated him. It wasn't every day a human got the experience of being vacuumed off the face of the earth, and she acted like it was no big deal. Once they got to the other side, she would see how much she needed an attitude adjustment.

The air in the room compressed. A tremor entered Jimmy's voice as Arden fought to keep his eyes locked on target. "Doing great, Jimmy. Keep reading."

The pull on his lower half intensified. If Jimmy messed up now and mispronounced a word, Nic would explode into a million pieces and would float forever aware in the

Abyss. Alone, the crossing would have been simple, but this time he was taking a *living* human with him. It had been done before, but now he needed to make sure the package arrived intact. He had to keep contact with Jimmy until they were safely on their way or things could get ugly.

The boards of the floor beneath them shook and split apart, throwing splintered wood into the air. The walls of the apartment rumbled and the flames on the candles flared like blowtorches turned to full blast. He squeezed Nic's hand when the edges of the room started to blur and twist out of shape.

The great tug of the crossing bore down on him as if the weight of the earth itself tried to push them through the portal. He wanted to turn his head to check on Nic but didn't dare take his eyes off the junkie.

He shouted for Jimmy to keep going and saw the obvious too late; fear had consumed the frazzled addict, and his reading had slowed and stuttered. He knew by the change in the room that the reading had gone far enough for the gateway to be opened, but he needed to make sure his prize made it across with him, so he spun and snatched Nic into his arms, locking them around her like a tourniquet right as the floor dropped out beneath them.

The gateway was a vortex of blackness. A cacophony surrounded them like all the sounds that ever existed were being broadcast at one time, in fast forward and at full volume; it was deafening.

"Nic!" He yelled so she would hear him above the chaos. "Hold on."

She buried her head in his chest and covered her ears. He switched his hold so he could get his arms around her;

they would be landing any second and he didn't want her damaged. He had to deliver her in one piece.

He held her against him and smiled. Nic would never see the earth again.

Episode Two

Chapter Four

The noise. Nic couldn't breathe for the sounds filling her ears. Screeching chaos and unbearable static so loud she knew her ears had to be bleeding.

Then there was a pop, like a kid's ruined balloon, and then utter silence. Her heart jumped inside her chest.

One minute she'd been standing in her brother's apartment, the next she'd been sucked into a maelstrom in the arms of a demon Prince. She forced her eyelids open—keeping them closed made everything worse.

The discolored landscape, blurred by the water in her eyes, spun around and around, rushing toward them at a hundred miles per hour. She was sure the landing would be death. She would be crushed by the force of the fall.

Forty feet, thirty feet, then twenty, and a scream lodged in her throat. She closed her eyes against the spiraling tableau.

The descent morphed again—the insane approach slowed, slowed, then stalled six feet above the ground. After a nanosecond's pause, they fell the rest of the way. She landed on top of Arden on an expanse of fresh-cut grass.

The impact shoved the breath from her lungs. She gasped, managed to get some oxygen down, and then blinked. And blinked again.

It looked like...a park? *In Hell?* "Where are we?"

"Fallen Park," he answered.

Lush rolling lawns of emerald green spread out around her, cut down the center by a cobblestone path. Tall trees stood like sentinels along the path, waving their verdant leaves at her like a hello.

She glanced up at the sky and saw something she would never be able to erase from her brain. The colors were wrong—as if someone had done a bad adjustment on a television set and sucked out all of the blue but turned the reds up. All the way up. Even the puffy clouds crossing the sky were stained pink from the crimson sunlight. A chill iced her blood.

She was still lying on top of him and could feel his hard body against her. Nic pushed his arms from around her and rolled away. She clambered to her feet, turning in a circle to take in the view. The park was laid out with such precision; the trees were all the same height and width—like they had been cloned from one another—and there was no one else in sight as far as she could see. She got so caught up in the landscape that she ran smack into Arden and found herself staring right at his broad chest.

He didn't even flinch. "Enjoying the view?"

Sort of. "No." She took a step back. His closeness unsettled her more than the pink clouds passing overhead. "Now that you've been so kind as to deliver me into the pit of Hell, I'd like to get going."

"You might want to change your tone," he said. "You're not on home turf here."

"I'll take that into consideration." She gave him her most plastic smile. "Which way to the demon's lair?"

A muscle in his jaw twitched. "I got you down here in one piece."

"Am I supposed to fall at your feet for the favor?" She *was* grateful, but there wasn't a chance in Hell—literally— that she would tell him. Still, the fact remained she needed his help. "Look, I'm a little disoriented. All of this came at me pretty fast."

Something—some shadow—darkened his expression for a fleeting second and then disappeared. "Right," he said, shaking his head. "Let's go then."

He mumbled something else she couldn't hear and stalked away. She followed but took her time about it just to be a pain in his ass.

At least it was a nice ass to follow.

And the path made her wonder what was so bad about spending eternity in Hell if it was like this. Everything looked so serene.

She figured they were nearing the edge of the park because the trees thinned out and the path widened. Next to the end of the walkway was a massive statue. At first she thought a trick of the weird red sky had rendered the sculpture with false color, but as she got closer she realized the figure was carved from glittering green stone, or the world's—underworld's—largest emerald. Arden didn't even glance up at it when he passed, but she couldn't help but gape. Especially when she got close enough to see what it was.

The base of the statue rose above her head, and standing on top was a man with a cane. The detail carved into the face and the clothing was like the trees in the park—precise and beautiful. He wore a frown on his brow, but the look in his emerald eyes was sad, weary as if he had seen something horrible happening right in front of him. The expression made her throat constrict with inexplicable sympathy.

She broke away from the sculpture and kept walking. The park bordered on what appeared to be a very affluent neighborhood, the homes sprawling affairs surrounded by high, elaborate fences. Through the gates of one, she saw workers tending a rose garden in full bloom. The next gate was open and the drive curved up and away from the road to end at the foot of a gargantuan fountain spewing water into the air.

She realized she was lagging behind and jogged to catch up with Arden. He had stopped at the next drive. "How much farther to your place?"

"We already passed my house. This is our destination." He drew his arm out in a flourish as if he were presenting her with a game show prize. "My father's house."

The other gates she had seen so far were toys in comparison; this one had to be over twenty feet tall. At first glance it seemed the two halves came together to form a giant angel wrought in black iron, but when she looked closer, she saw it wasn't an angel at all. The sleek curves were meant to fool the eye. She turned her head to the side and the figure reappeared. The deceptiveness of the gate set her on edge; like she would never know what was real or illusion.

Arden walked over to the stone wall on the left. He pressed his palm to one of the bricks and it slid upward to reveal an electronic keypad. He punched in a sequence of numbers and the massive gate parted. Its hinges creaked and she jumped.

"Easy." He smiled as he came up next to her.

Her stomach flipped over his crooked grin. "I'm not going to randomly shoot someone." He was too handsome, in an unsettling and fascinating way. She really needed to stop looking at his face.

"I know, but you are armed and jumpy." His grin widened and he placed his hand on her shoulder. "I wouldn't want you offing a gardener or something."

Where his hand rested, a flame ran over her skin. "Give me a break, would you? I don't do well in unfamiliar surroundings." When he laughed, she added, "It makes me feel like I'm not in control."

"I can imagine you out of control…" His words trailed off and he looked away.

"What's that supposed to mean?"

"I would love to see what happens when you really let go."

A blush crept up her neck as his words sank in. Thoughts of surrendering control to him swirled in her head. She remembered the feel of his hand against her neck, those cold eyes…

What was she thinking? She had a brother to save and here she was fantasizing about a demon—who looked like a rock star and stared at her as if she were a meal, with eyes like cool arctic water and lips made for pleasing…

A demon. *Arden is a demon.*

She started up the driveway without him, needing some distance. She made it about ten feet, then was grabbed from behind. "What the—"

His lips crushed down on hers. She was too stunned to move at first, but then wriggled to try to free herself. His hands gripped her arms and pulled her in while his mouth dismantled her shock. She wanted to resist, *really* wanted to, but gave in, arching into the hard mass of his body. His soft tongue trailed across her lips. She tasted spice and fire. Her body responded to his with a flare of heat. When his lips left her mouth to blaze across her cheek and down onto her neck, she whimpered.

"Nic." His voice danced over the delicate skin of her earlobe.

She couldn't manage to speak, and when his arms circled around her, she didn't think she would be able to stand without support. His breath whispered along her collarbone and she got lost in the moment.

Until he snatched her nine out of its holster and tucked it into his belt. "I don't think you'll be needing this."

Motherfucker.

His eyes had changed to a hard emerald green like the statue she'd seen in the park.

Her own words came back to taunt her—*a demon nonetheless.*

She stared at his back as he walked up the drive away from her. If she'd had something in her hand, she gladly would've chucked it at the back of his head. And now she was standing alone on the flawless flagstone driveway, weaponless, in the First Level of Hell. The differences between herself and her surroundings lay plain.

The drive split the vast front lawn into two halves. Like the other estates she'd seen on the way, the landscaping was impeccable; it looked like what she would expect to see around a vast English mansion—something the monarchy might have outside of the city. The sprawling enormity of it dwarfed her, and in comparison she was inconsequential.

She gritted her teeth. Her nine and its heartless steel had become a security blanket for her, a cold protector against any threat. Without it, and facing the looming stone house in front of her, it was as if she were a teenager all over again—awkward and vulnerable.

Drew. If she thought about her brother, maybe it would put the straight back into her spine. It worked enough to get her feet moving again, but she felt the emptiness of her holster like a heartache.

Arden reached the foot of a wide staircase leading up to the front door. She had almost caught up with him and was fully prepared to take her Ruger back by force, regardless of the fact that he might outweigh her by eighty or ninety pounds of pure muscle.

At the last second he was saved by the butler, who appeared from a massive set of double doors at the top of the stairs.

All the things Nic had ever learned about good manners went flying out of her head when she got a look at the diminutive servant. He was a head shorter than she was and green; not the shade found in a kid's paint set, more like the juice left over in a jar of olives. He had a broad face with smooth skin, except for the smattering of scales on his forehead and the nasty scars running up one side of his face as if he had been smacked repeatedly with a hot iron. The scarring made him seem feral, but his tiny yellow eyes were warm. Her thoughts of physically repossessing her gun were forgotten when he smiled at her.

He looked from her to Arden. "Good morning, Master."

"Hey, Remy."

"Sir?" Remy straightened the sleeve of his black uniform jacket.

"Oh," Arden said. "Remy, this is Nic."

"Good morning, mademoiselle," he said with a bow.

She bobbed a curtsy to him and felt ridiculous.

"You'll have to excuse her, Remy," Arden said. "She doesn't do well in unfamiliar surroundings."

She shot him a glare that would have melted rock. He wouldn't say something like that if she still had her weapon.

Remy cleared his throat. "Miss—?"

"Wright. Nic Wright."

"Miss Wright, if there is anything I can do to make your stay here more comfortable, you have but to ask," he said.

It was on the tip of her tongue to ask for him to get her a new gun, but before she could, he stepped aside for them to make their way into the house. When she glanced back over her shoulder, the butler had disappeared like smoke in the wind. She wondered if he would be an ally in hostile territory should the occasion arise.

The entry was more stunning than she expected. From the outside, the mansion seemed so British-country-estate that she figured the inside would be wood paneled and stuffy. Instead it was open and modern. A wide marble staircase dominated the space, rising a full story before dividing and leading off to opposite ends of the house. The light that spilled in through the tall windows cast a rosy glow on the white marble floor. Although she was in Hell, the color seemed so soothing.

She looked off to the right, and through an open door she spied a library. Across the foyer was another room but the closed door kept its contents hidden. She figured the mansion had a lot of secrets she would never know about.

The smell of food drifted to her from somewhere within the house, reminding her she hadn't eaten for almost twenty-four hours. Her stomach growled like a muscle car.

"Hungry?" Arden had the nerve to laugh when the rumbling continued.

"No. My stomach doesn't like the company." She crossed her arms over her middle and fought the urge to punch him. He might have her gun tucked into his belt, but it wouldn't help him if she broke his nose. "I'm not hungry." Her stomach protested by growling again.

His eyes narrowed. "Sounds like you're lying," he said. "Look, I'm going to go to get some food. Follow if you want."

He strode away, beneath the stairs toward the back of the house, and she scrambled to keep up. Her stomach applauded the gesture, but her stubbornness rejected the idea of following him around like a needy abandoned kitten.

She caught up with him behind the stairway, in an atrium of sorts. The creamy marble cut a polished line between tall, thriving plants that ran the length of the corridor. It smelled damp and earthy and full of life. The contrast between all the greenery and the red-tinged light coming through the windows had the same calming effect the pinkness of the foyer did.

She thought it time for some answers but didn't really know where to begin, so she picked a neutral topic. "How old is this place?"

"It was a gift to my father for sticking by his Master's side in the Great Fall."

She stopped beneath the canopy of an enormous tropical plant. "Are you talking about when the angels rebelled against God?" He couldn't be serious. *Could he?*

"We call it the Fall." Arden halted his march to answer her.

"Your father was in on that?"

He cupped a purple flower on the plant beside her and his eyes grew distant. "He was one of the few who stood with Lucifer when the shit hit the fan upstairs."

"But that was…" She trailed off. "Didn't that all take place before mankind was even around?"

"Yep."

That meant he was…"How old are you?"

"I'm about one hundred and thirty-six."

She reeled. The man didn't look a day over thirty. "You don't look—I mean, how is that possible?"

"We don't age like humans, and time moves…slower down here."

It made sense. What better way to draw out punishment for sinners than to make time a slippery thing? But how had he spent all of his time? "All that time…don't you get bored?"

His gaze snapped up from the flower and she saw the gleam of hard emerald in his eyes when he answered. "Yes, Nic, I do." He let the bloom drop and ran the back of his hand over her cheek. "But I have a feeling you're about to make things more entertaining."

"You're a demon." She said it aloud in hopes her traitorous body would take the hint. No such luck. Heat spread out from his hand and coursed through her.

"Yes."

"Aren't you supposed to be bad?"

He leaned in and whispered in her ear. "I am bad. And you're hungry."

His breath ghosted over her neck, and her stomach fluttered before answering with a rumble. When he chuckled, she scrambled to cover her embarrassment. "I'd rather find my brother if you don't mind."

"If you starve to death, you won't be any help to him. Come on," he said, grabbing her hand. "Let's go see what's for breakfast."

Chapter Five

If it weren't for Arden's hand holding her in place, Nic would have turned around and bolted. Not that she had anywhere to run to, but the thought was in her head all the same.

Aunt Margie had kept a beautiful, if modest, home. So had her parents. But nothing in Nic's past could have prepared her for Arden's dining room.

The size was almost overwhelming and she had to clench her teeth to keep her jaw from dropping open. The biggest table she'd ever seen was positioned alongside a glass wall with a spectacular view of the gardens behind the house. The floor was a swirling and spiraling mosaic of green marble, which complemented the dark, ornate woodwork of the furniture.

Opposite the doorway they'd come through was another entrance. Before she could get herself under control, it opened and two huge men walked into the room.

The first was older. She could tell by the hint of gray in his black hair and the cane tapping the floor in time to his walk. Arden's father, she guessed. He looked so...normal. Weren't demons supposed to be hideous and fearsome? He also seemed familiar, but her brain was too busy with sensory overload to process where she'd seen his face before.

The second one was a real stunner. Built like a linebacker with the face of a male supermodel and shoulder-length golden hair. The two were talking and stopped short when they looked up and saw Nic standing with Arden.

The room grew silent and she bit at the inside of her lip to keep from fidgeting.

Arden set his hand at her waist. "Father, Chase, I'd like you to welcome our guest." He pressed her forward as he made the introductions. "This is Nic Wright."

She realized the linebacker had to be Arden's brother because when they got closer she saw the resemblance between the siblings despite Chase's blond hair. And the similarities between the three men were astounding.

As they all stood staring at one another, the quiet settled in until she didn't think she could handle standing another minute without bolting.

The older man cleared his throat and flashed a smile. "Please excuse our shock, Miss Wright, but it's not every day we see a human standing in our dining room. I am Asmodeus."

He took her hand and instead of shaking it, he planted a kiss on her knuckles. Nic thought it was a sweet gesture coming from a man who was supposed to be a big, bad demon. He had beautiful emerald eyes just like Arden's and his grin reminded her of the crooked one she'd seen on his son's face.

"It's nice to meet you—um...Your Majesty." The words fell out of her mouth in an awkward heap, but she didn't know how else to address a demon King. And when he smiled again, she realized why he looked so familiar. The giant emerald statue in the park. It must have been crafted by a true master because it was an exact replica.

"Let's do away with the formalities, my dear. You can call me Asmo and I'll call you Nic, all right?"

"Fine by me...Asmo."

"Splendid. Now, allow me to introduce you to my son Chase."

When Chase took her hand, she couldn't help but grin. He really was good-looking but in a prettier way than his brother; there was no edgy demeanor or sarcastic smirk, and although their faces were practically identical, Chase's was friendlier, less chilling.

"It's a pleasure to meet you, Nic." He didn't release her hand, just stared.

"You can let go of her now." Arden's tone was cold.

"Excuse me, brother." Chase dropped her hand. "I figured her for another of your pets."

Arden stepped from her side and stopped about three millimeters shy of his brother's face. "You do not want to get hurt in front of company, do you?"

"Like you could hurt me," Chase said. He didn't budge an inch. His fists were clenched at his sides.

"If you refer to her that way again, I'd be happy to show you how wrong you are."

Arden was sticking up for her? And about to come to blows with his brother over it from the sounds—and looks— of things. But she really didn't need anyone to speak for her.

"Excuse me, gentlemen," Nic said. "I know I'm only a human, but I *can* speak for myself." She wasn't even sure they heard her, because neither one seemed ready to back down. The room was graveyard still and dead quiet.

And her stomach interrupted the silence with an angry growl.

Chase was the first to move; it was subtle, but the corners of his mouth began to twitch, and then a slow smile spread across his face. Then Arden began to laugh and Asmo joined in too.

Nic didn't know if it was possible to be *more* humiliated, but having three demons laugh at her was about as low as she could go.

The brothers shook hands, still laughing, and moved toward the table. She wasn't sure where to sit, but Chase helped by pulling out a chair for her. Asmo took the chair at the head of the table on her left and Arden seated himself on her right. Chase sat down across from her. The normalcy of all of it amazed her. If she didn't already know she was wide-awake, she would have believed herself dreaming. Again.

The table was so full of food, she could barely see the mahogany surface. There were silver platters covering most of the table, and one had strange purple fruits that she had never seen before. Her stomach gave up its weak rumbling and screamed for her to have at it.

When she glanced down at her place setting, the array of silverware confused her. There were five forks, two knives, and three different spoons, all in silver that gleamed as if it had been polished within an inch of its life. The plate, shaped like a stop sign and almost as big, was made of what looked like stone. In the center, a folded napkin.

At least I know what the napkin is for. She unfurled it and put it across her lap.

The other diners dug in, but she didn't know where to start; too many choices and some of the options she didn't even recognize. Did they eat fish heads for breakfast down here?

Arden leaned over and whispered, "Need a little help?"

"Uh, yeah."

"Do you like cherries?" he asked.

"Yes."

"Try the purple things. They're called tempress fruit. You'll love them." He smiled and slid the platter closer to her plate.

They reminded her of plums, only smaller, shinier. She piled some onto her plate, picked a fork at random, stabbed one, and took a careful bite.

Her mouth exploded in the sweetest rush; like eating cherries and grapes covered in honey.

"Here," Arden said, handing her a small bowl. "Try them with cream."

She speared another one and ran it through the bowl, then took a huge bite. If she thought she liked them before, the cream sent her over the edge.

"Good?" he asked.

"That is honestly the most amazing thing I've ever eaten." She took another heaping bite.

"You've got some cream on your lip." He reached over with his napkin and dabbed her mouth. A mischievous grin spread across his face and green sparks danced in his eyes like light through crystal.

"What's that smile for?" Her insides heated, but not from embarrassment. Something about the light in his eyes seemed downright sinister.

He bent to her ear and spoke for only her to hear. "I was thinking about how your mouth would taste right now."

Nic cast a furtive glance across the table and was relieved to see Asmo and Chase engaged in their own conversation. If they had heard, they made no sign of it. She could feel

Arden's stare lingering even before she looked back at him, and a chill trembled up the back of her neck.

The man was *too* gorgeous and without a doubt danger-ous, but she was drawn to him—a flailing star pulled ever closer to a supernova and the unknown possibilities of its black heart.

He settled back in his chair, but the cold fire didn't leave his eyes.

Damn. She needed to focus. Her brother was down here somewhere and she needed to get to him as soon as pos-sible. These were the people—demons—who were going to help her, and she had to stop getting caught up in her hormones.

"So, Nic," Chase said around a mouthful of food, "how did you get unlucky enough to end up with my brother—ouch! Why did you kick me, bro?"

"Don't talk with your mouth full. It's unattractive and rude," Arden said.

"You don't have to get violent. I was only asking a question."

"Swallow, then ask, you bonehead."

She almost choked on a bite of pancake. They acted so *normal*—so brotherly—with the name-calling and bicker-ing. Maybe she really had lost her mind and this was the big-gest, baddest psychotic delusion in history. But the taste of food on her tongue and the sensation of the chair beneath her had to be proof otherwise, right?

Right.

Chase made a big show of chewing and gulping his food. "Better, First Born?"

"Don't call me that." Arden dropped his fork to his plate and it clattered against the stone.

"I'll call you whatever I—"

"Boys." Asmo didn't even glance up from his cup of coffee. Then to Nic he said, "You should see when all seven of them are here." He rolled his gem-like eyes. "You'll have to excuse my sons. I'm afraid I let them run a bit wild." Asmo kicked back in his chair. "So, to phrase Chase's question more politely, what brings you to our home?"

"My brother was kidnapped...sir—uh—I mean, Asmo." If she had been able, she would have kicked her own shin under the table for stumbling over the words. She couldn't help it. The demon King had been kind to her so far, but he was still intimidating as fuck.

"Kidnapped?" he asked.

"Yes, at least that's my best guess." Even though Asmo hadn't moved from his relaxed lean, it almost seemed like she was being interrogated.

"By whom?"

"Sorro," Arden answered for her.

At the mention of the name, the demons around the table grew silent.

"That little shit Flic in on it too?" Chase asked after a minute. The set of his jaw said he already knew the answer.

Arden told them what he knew and Nic joined in to fill the blanks. By the time they got to the crossing ceremony, the atmosphere in the room had gone from bad to downright malignant.

"Any idea where we might start?" Arden asked the pair.

"I'd say the Fourth," Chase said. "But there's no way you can take her down there."

"I can handle myself," Nic said. "I'm going to get Drew, and if I have to take out a few nasty fiends on the way, so be it."

Asmo chuckled. "Well said, my dear."

"You don't understand, Nic." Chase raked a hand through his hair. "The demons down there don't live like we do. They're bred to mutilate humans like you and they're *really* good at their job."

Some of her courage deflated. She reached down to fiddle with the snap above her ammo, which sat next to her *empty* holster, and recalled how well she had handled herself thus far. "It's not like I'm going down there alone."

"I'm taking her," Arden said. "And no, Chase, you're not going with us."

"But—"

"He's right." Asmo leaned forward and put his elbows on the table. "You need to stay here in case you have to track."

"What do you mean 'track'?" Nic asked.

"Chase is a Tracker. It's his Gift," Arden said. "What you saw me do with Jimmy, that's mine."

"What, hypnotizing people?"

"I don't hypnotize them, I make them do what I want. I get them to buy whatever I'm selling. I'm a Convincer."

"So, you're like a used car salesman?"

The roar of laughter from across the table was almost deafening.

"Shut up, Chase," Arden said.

"Can't..." he said between laughs. "Too funny."

Nic laughed too. Something about the way Arden's family made his sharp edges soften set her at ease and made him infinitely more likeable. He was still an arrogant asshole in her book, but at least he had some form of humanity. Seeing him laugh with his brother made her miss Drew in a way she hadn't for a long time. It made her miss her parents too, but she couldn't think about them right now. She had bigger problems.

"You can't take her down there dressed like that," Chase said when he got himself back under control.

"Good point," Asmo said. "We'll have to see if we can find her something less conspicuous."

Her uniform? Why would it matter? "How are you going to get me down there anyway? Wouldn't it be unusual for a human to be roaming around with a demon Prince for an escort?"

"I've got that covered." Asmo didn't elaborate. He excused himself and left the dining room through the door he'd entered from.

Chase and Arden exchanged a strange glance but kept eating.

She didn't really know what to think about the demon King's exit or the silent communication between the brothers, so she let her raging appetite take over and kept her mouth too full to ask any more questions.

———

"Where are the other ones?" Nic asked him as he led her out of the dining room. They had left Chase at the big table, still shoveling food in his mouth.

"What other ones?"

"Your other brothers. Your father said there were seven of you."

"They're probably on a Call."

"Do you all do the same thing? Go to earth and trick mortals?"

He didn't look back at her to answer. "That's not what we do."

Funny, she got the impression it was. Different tactic. "Are all of you always working?"

"No, not all the time," he said.

"So what do you do when you're not busy?"

She followed him through the door into what Nic could only think of as a ballroom. The floor was golden parquet and the walls were ivory with gilt-trimmed scrollwork along the edges. She gazed up at the ceiling to see delicate pastel frescoes dancing above her.

Even though the room was not as contemporary as the others she'd seen, it fit in with the quiet sophistication of the whole house. Visions of dancers in their finery twirling across the floor while a string quartet played in the background spun in her head while she tried to keep up with Arden.

"We do have entertainment," he said, opening another set of doors.

Nic stepped through and understood what he meant. The room was decked out with plush sofas as big as pickup trucks, and chairs that could each hold six people comfortably. On one wall, a monstrous flat-screen television stretched above an even wider black marble fireplace. Along the other end of the room were five stand-up arcade games, one of which, to her amusement, was Ms. Pac-Man. Next to the games stood a dartboard and a full-length bar complete with liquor and beer taps. It reminded her of a fancy frat house minus the beer cans, porn, and juiced-up jocks lounging around while they flunked out of college.

"Do you get cable down here?"

"Yep," he said. "We hack into the systems you have upstairs. We even have Wi-Fi."

She didn't have time to ask how because he was already out the door and they were back in the foyer where they had first come in. Instead of going under the stairs, they went up. At the landing, Arden hung a right and she followed him down another long landing to another flight of stairs.

At the top was a long corridor with one side open over the atrium and the other lined with doorways. Three in all. He stopped at the first set of doors where a rotund, scale-free maid stood with a bundle of clothes in her hands.

He took the things from the servant and she scurried away down the stairs. "This is it," he said.

"Is what?"

"My chambers."

"I thought you had your own house?"

"We all do, but we keep quarters here too."

She thought about her old room at her parents' house. The lemony-yellow walls and the smell of her mother's cooking. She wondered if keeping rooms here brought him some kind of comfort, but didn't ask. His comfort wasn't her concern.

On the wall beside the door was a gorgeous painting. Nic thought she recognized the artist, but she wasn't sure. "Is that Klimt?"

"Um, yeah."

He seemed taken aback by the fact that she knew who had created the masterpiece, so she explained. "My aunt used to take us to the Smithsonian when we were kids. Drew always wanted to go see the rockets, but I liked the art."

"Do you like Klimt in particular?"

Nic glanced up from the painting to answer. "I really love his portrayal of women. He seemed to truly worship them, but I read he was a total player. Did you know he fathered, like, fourteen children?"

"It's true. When he died, he ended up down here for womanizing and blasphemy."

"Are you serious?" She found it hard to believe someone would get punished for something so trivial, but maybe all those hard-core Christians were right after all. Do the crime, do the time, she supposed.

"You'd be astonished at some of the people I've met. Dad likes to throw parties and the guest lists would blow your mind," he said. "Klimt is a regular. So is Pablo."

"Pablo?"

"Picasso."

"How can you be so nonchalant about it?"

He chuckled. "I guess I'm used to it."

"And I guess I'm still trying to adjust." She shrugged. "I'm just wondering why going to Hell is so bad. It seems like you've got it made down here."

"It's not all tea and roses," he said as he punched in some numbers on a keypad next to the door handle. "You've only seen the First level. Trust me, the other levels will make you understand why it pays to be a good person."

Chapter Six

Nic stood in the middle of Arden's room, staring as if struck dumb. Rooms like his didn't exist.

He'd set a T-shirt and some jeans on the bed and then left her to change, saying he was going to see if he could gather any intel, whatever that meant. The time alone to catch her breath helped her gather her spiraling thoughts, and it gave her a moment to marvel at the place where he slept.

The room was enormous, for starters—big enough to hold a couple of SUVs and a fire truck—but the way it was decked out took her breath away. Where the rest of the house was light and airy, Arden's private chambers were the polar opposite and...him. The walls, and everything else in the room—so black they seemed to absorb all the light coming in through the massive windows—were covered in velvet instead of paint. She ran a hand across the luxurious surface and smiled at the texture. Tall candelabra stood like stationed guards around the mammoth bed positioned right in the center of it all: a four-poster work of art draped with lush black curtains tied back with tasseled ropes. Nic had to bounce on her toes to climb up onto the mattress.

She kicked off her steel-toed work boots, unbuckled her duty belt, and shimmied out of her pants. The bedding was also black velvet—soft, like sitting on a marshmallow. But she didn't get too comfy. Sitting on Arden's bed without her pants on reminded her of the deal she had made with him.

She unbuttoned her uniform shirt and grabbed the T-shirt he'd left for her. It was a concert tee from Mötley Crüe, and on the front was a picture with the band members on Harleys and the words "Girls Girls Girls" in red at the top. The fact that the man was a fan of Gustav Klimt *and* eighties metal made her head hurt.

And her brain turned traitor, imagining him in leather pants, but Nic forced the thought out of her head and pulled on the shirt. She swam in the tee, but she was more worried about the jeans. She was only five foot five and Arden had to be two feet taller than she was. Plus, he was all lean muscle. How on earth would the jeans fit her?

When she picked them up to figure it out, she saw they didn't belong to a man—the tiny waist and curvy cut could belong only to a woman. Jealousy wiggled its way into her thoughts as she pulled them on.

"Why would he have a pair of women's jeans?" she asked the drapes.

They didn't answer.

Then someone knocked on the bedroom door.

"Just a sec," she called out as she zipped up. She bounced off the bed and rushed over to open the door.

"I assume everything fit," Arden said.

"Yep." *Especially the jeans your last visitor left.* She shut down the thought. "You have to explain the shirt." She refused to ask about the jeans.

He grinned. "I hung around with the band for most of that tour. I was supposed to be helping their manager, but it didn't work out very well. Those guys were crazy. I was lucky to get back here in one piece."

Nic wondered if that's where his rock-and-roll swagger and shaggy, jet-black hair came from. The tattoos, the jewelry...

Then she noticed her Ruger still tucked in the waistband of his pants. "Can I get my gun back now? I promise I won't use it until absolutely necessary." She tried to sound sweet and innocent and hoped he took the bait.

"No way."

So much for the sweet routine. "I want it back."

"You can't have it." The hint of exasperation in his voice was unmistakable.

"You can't keep it from me," she said.

"I can and will. You're a hothead and I can't trust you to keep yourself in check."

"Give me my goddamned gun back, Arden."

"No matter how nicely you ask, the answer will still be no." He turned his back and walked away from her.

Soft didn't work, cursing didn't work, and judging by the stubborn set of his shoulders, she wasn't going to get it back without a fight.

A plan took shape in her head and she acted on it before she could change her mind.

She still held the door open, so she pushed it closed. It snapped into place with a *thunk*, similar to the sound of a cell door closing.

He had moved across the room to stand by the windows, and the bloody light filtered through, lighting him with surreal fire. Nic crept around the bed like a cat through tall grass. Stealth was her friend. She waited until she stood right behind him to speak.

"Arden?" She adopted what she hoped was a sultry expression—lips pouted, a slight smile.

"Yes?" He didn't turn around.

"What you said when we were eating, do you still want to know?"

He spun around to face her and his eyes blazed. A shiver danced along her spine.

"You know," she said, looking up at him through her eyelashes, "about the way my mouth tastes?"

He didn't answer. Maybe she wasn't doing it right. Flirting wasn't on her list of talents. Her cheeks flamed but she stayed on task. "Wanna try it now?"

She stepped up to him, and the expression that darkened his face startled her. He looked intent, like a man ready to kill. Not exactly what she was hoping for, but at least she had his full attention.

He reached up and put his hand on the side of her neck, his thumb pressed against her jaw. His palm was on fire and heat raced through Nic's veins.

Careful, Nicolette. She didn't want to get too close.

As Arden leaned in to her lips, his grip on her neck tightened. The pressure of his hand at her throat made sparks dance over her skin. She was caught like a rabbit in the snare trap of his grasp. When he was an inch from her lips, he turned her head to the side and she felt his breath on her ear.

"Don't even think about it," he whispered.

Nic didn't hesitate. She grabbed for the gun, but he got to it first.

He palmed the nine and laid the cold steel along the other side of her jaw with her face between his hand and the gun.

She didn't want to look into his eyes, afraid he'd use his power against her like he'd done with Jimmy, but she couldn't help herself. "I want my weapon, Arden."

"And I want to taste you."

His face loomed closer and she struggled to pull away. The grip he had on her face tightened. His scent was too raw, too overwhelming up close. Her skin burned where he touched her, pulling her toward his body. The edges on the grip of her nine dug into her cheek.

"Don't fight me," he said.

The words acted like a trigger inside of her. She wedged her hands between them and shoved at his chest with all her strength. He didn't budge. "Let. Me. Go," she hissed. She tried to turn her face away but couldn't.

"Look at me."

"So you can trick me? No." She closed her eyes, but that turned out to be a very bad idea because it intensified all of her other senses—Nic heard the rustle of his shirt beneath her hands and felt the warm whisper of his breath on her lips. She tasted the remnants of tempress fruit on her tongue. He was so close, so male.

She'd kept herself reined off from physical contact with another person for so long that she'd forgotten what it felt like to want. Her deprivation had worked, but with Arden's hands on her, she ached for what she'd gone without. He inched even closer and she froze; her whole body shook with the effort of her resistance.

All she had wanted was to persuade him to give back her weapon. Her own ploy had become her enemy. She shouldn't have done it—shouldn't have gotten near him.

The first touch of his lips hit her hard, but not from the touch itself. The devastation came from the unexpected place he kissed her—her closed eyelids. Softly. First one, then the other. If she breathed any faster, she was sure she would hyperventilate. She refused to open her eyes.

Her world zoomed in to the tiny space she occupied between the cool metal on one cheek, the heat of his palm now on her neck, and the nearness of his lips to hers. The rest of the world, the whole of existence, didn't...didn't exist in that space.

Then he stroked her bottom lip with his tongue.

And she was lost.

———

Arden tasted the tempress fruit on her lips, but something else too; something so pure and delicate he had no name for it.

His cock throbbed as he inhaled the scent of her skin.

But she didn't move. He might as well have been kissing a rock. Her satiny mouth trembled. He knew she wanted more—could feel the rush of her pulse beneath his palm—but she wouldn't let herself give in.

And that made him more determined to take what he wanted.

He would show her how dangerous it was to play games with him. He slid his tongue over her lower lip again, but slower this time, more of an invitation than a demand. A tiny noise escaped her throat. He knew it would be only a minute's work to have her panting, begging for what he had to give her.

Arden pulled back but didn't release her. He stroked her jaw with his thumb. "All I want is a taste."

Her eyes flew open and she wrenched around in his grip. "Let go."

"You need this. You think I can't see how badly you need to be fucked?"

He saw pure flame in her eyes, then fury. "Let. Go."

"No." It would be nothing for him to capture her with his talent, but he'd get more amusement if she capitulated on her own. He allowed her to turn her head. If she thought looking away gave her some advantage, she was mistaken. He kept the gun pressed flat against her neck and slid his other hand down, over her arm, and around to the small of her back.

She tried to break from him then, so he moved his arm around her waist and lifted her off the ground, dragging her body up and tight against his own, until his erection met the mound of her sex. He ground his hips into her and she gasped. "I can give you what you need, Nic."

The moment her eyes moved back to his, he knew he had her. Her mouth opened and she wet her lips.

That was it.

He crushed down on her mouth so hard his teeth bit into his lips. Then her mouth was open and his tongue was inside, smoothing over every crevice and exhaling breath into her. He yanked one of her legs around his waist, forcing his erection tighter into the space between her thighs. Her hands danced over his chest, then dug into his shoulders.

Her mouth was a sanctuary. As he tasted her, she whimpered and he swallowed it down his throat. He grabbed her other leg and lifted it, pressing his hard-on against her until the friction almost made him explode in his jeans.

He'd never had a woman in his bed, here, or in his own home. It always seemed too personal, too intimate, and he didn't want any of them to think they were special. But he wanted Nic in his bed. Immediately.

He kept up with his assault as he backed them toward the bed. When they bumped into one of the candelabra, it clattered to the ground, candles scattering over the floor. But he didn't care, didn't even pause as he lifted her tight little body and tossed her back against the pillows.

She lay very still, and her cool, gray eyes darkened. He didn't want her to move, so when he knelt next to her, he gathered her wrists up into his hand and lifted them above her head. She looked amazing stretched out over the black velvet—like a sculpture, like a prize. Her back arched as he used the cold steel barrel of her gun to push up the edge of her shirt. Goosebumps spread across her bare skin. He leaned down and licked a trail from her navel up to the edge of her bra. She lifted up into his touch. The flavor of her skin—sweet, honeyed—threatened to tear away his focus.

Arden needed to put down the weapon if he was going to do this right, but he didn't want to take his hands off of her for fear she'd still be ready to bolt. He looked up—she'd closed her eyes, so he tested her acquiescence by loosening his hold on her wrists. She didn't move. He kept his gaze on her lips as he slid the weapon and his free hand down the length of her body, tucking the gun under a fold in the blanket at the foot of the bed. Not an ideal hiding spot, but it didn't matter—he'd make sure she stayed distracted enough to not notice.

She reached for the edge of her shirt but he batted her hands away. "No. I will." He wanted to be the one to reveal her skin, one piece of clothing at a time. After all, she was his prize. He would set the pace.

Her hands fell away and something about her surrender made him pause. He wanted to lick every single inch of her delectable body—wanted to make her scream before he was through. But for his plan to work he had to get her down to the Fourth. Would she agree after this? Or would she be even more combative and hard to control?

If he didn't get inside her right away, he was going to blow his load early like an adolescent. He needed to feel her wetness sucking at his cock as he tore into her. And what did a small sample matter? As long as he got her down there in the end, he could satisfy his curiosity and still get around to deceiving her later. Two birds, one stone.

Arden lifted her shirt and tossed it aside. Her skin shimmered with sweat, and the scent of it assailed him, but he forced himself to slow down—keep her off her guard and she'd be begging for him to give her what she needed. He laid one palm at the base of her throat; her heartbeat thudded against his hand. He brushed her short dark hair back from her face and bent down to kiss her again, this time slow and deliberate, milking her tongue and nipping at her lips. He sank down until he was stretched out next to her. He could feel the heat of her skin through his clothes and he knew she had to be dripping wet, because he could smell her arousal.

She writhed on the bed while he continued his assault on her mouth. He wasn't sure how much longer he could stand this. When she snaked her hands up into his hair and grabbed it by the handfuls with a throaty moan, his fragile control was obliterated.

He tore at the front of her bra—not caring if he shredded it—and yanked it down over her small but perfect breasts. Her nipples hardened under his palms. He replaced one hand with his mouth, nibbling and sucking. She gasped when he bit down.

He snatched at the front of her jeans and unfastened them, then shoved them off over her knees and feet. The spicy scent of her arousal assailed him as he yanked down her panties, desperate for access to her sex.

She moved as if to cover herself, and he grabbed her hands, pinning them to the mattress at her sides.

"Open for me." He almost didn't recognize the rasp of his own voice.

"I...I can't." Nic closed her eyes and turned her face away. "I can't do this. I have to get Drew."

It might take a softer touch than what he was used to giving, but he'd make her forget. He'd make her think of nothing except for his hands, his mouth, and the pleasure he gave her.

She tossed her head back and forth against the pillows. She breathed the word "no," but he noticed the way her thighs parted the smallest fraction. He could wait no longer. He let go of her wrists and shoved her legs apart, the soft approach—and his control—forgotten.

This is what I really wanted to taste.

Her flesh was sopping, her thighs glistening with it. He felt, more than heard, the growl that emanated from his body as he fell on her and lapped at the delicate folds of her sex, swallowing her juices like an elixir.

His cock had never been so hard. No female, human or demon, had ever made him as geared up to fuck as Nic. Females always fell at his feet. He never had to work for their cooperation. And something about Nic's bad attitude and her steel facade made him even more frenzied to get inside her—to make her submit.

She tried to back away, so Arden grabbed her thighs and glanced up at her face. Instead of the grimace of passion he expected, she looked like she was in pain. *Shit.*

He had broken her too soon. This could put all of his machinations in jeopardy. He was supposed to play her out. Fool, betray, and in the end, throw her away.

What the fuck am I doing? He'd let himself get distracted by her flesh. She was the key to him being free of weakness forever and he had lost track of the goal just to prove he could get whatever he wanted?

And what if taking what he wanted now made her even less willing to follow along later? How was he supposed to get her to the Fourth then?

———

Nic struggled to stay afloat in the world behind her closed eyelids and the wash of thoughts racing through her mind. Tears came and she fought them. Had all of it been a trick? What had she agreed to? And what would happen if she gave in? Her body ached with need, but she had responsibilities. Would he have her, crush her, and then shove her into some dark corner of his world where she'd wither away until death found her, if it ever came for her at all?

But his hands—his mouth—awoke things in her body she'd long ago abandoned, and the hunger for those things drowned out most of her arguments. Except for one...

Drew. What was she doing? She had to save—

The spin of her brain halted when she realized Arden had gone still. He withdrew from between her legs, and she opened her eyes to find him up on his knees staring down at her. His jet hair stood wild where she'd grabbed on to it and his eyes seemed clouded over. A muscle worked in his jaw.

She scrambled to sit up and move away from him. Or to move away from what she'd almost done. She grabbed at the blanket and pulled it over herself. Shame clogged her throat.

Arden looked away and didn't speak. He stepped back, off the bed, and walked toward the door. He reached for the handle, then stopped. "Get dressed. We'll leave as soon as possible."

He left the room without any further explanation. Nic clutched the covers to her chest. What the fuck had happened? She knew he wanted it too; she'd felt the press of his erection against her thigh. Why did he stop?

And why did she care? She didn't give the question any more thought. Damn it. She'd lost control. The man—no, *demon*—was arrogant, annoying, and bossy. If and when she had sex again, she didn't want it to be with someone so... so...

Her skin flushed as she landed on the right term for what Arden had been: forceful. He'd been just shy of holding her down and ramming into her.

How would she have reacted if he had?

You would have enjoyed every single sweaty second of it and you're a fucking liar if you deny it.

OK. So maybe she would have enjoyed it, and she would make the most of it when the time came for her to pay up on their bargain. But that still didn't explain why he hadn't gone through with it. She'd practically begged him for it by letting him get her on the bed and allowing him to get her naked…

That was it, wasn't it? He'd taken one look at her, gotten a good, thorough examination in, and then realized she wasn't up to his standards. He probably had gorgeous women dropping their panties at his feet everywhere he went. Why would he settle for someone like her? She was built like a teenage boy—no curves and A cups.

A sharp needle of pain stung her right below her left collarbone. If she didn't know any better, she might have thought it was heartache. But whose heart ached because some fucking guy, some *demon*, decided to get his kicks elsewhere?

She supposed she deserved it. The whole point of coming down here was to find Drew, not to get it on with a demon. She'd lost sight of her reason because there was something about Arden that turned her brain to mush.

No more.

Their arrangement was a business deal, and she'd make sure it stayed that way. Period.

And, hey, if he found her so repulsive, maybe he'd change his mind about the sex. In the meantime, she'd try to come up with something different to offer him for helping her. If all else failed, she'd pull out the "true name" card and use it. Maybe she could use some tricks of her own to get the name out of him.

Of course, there was always her soul. Didn't demons want those too?

She'd make it work, the same way she'd done every day since she and Drew had been orphaned.

Or she could get the fuck out of this house and go on alone. Perhaps, if she found the demon King, she'd offer him her soul just to be rid of Arden.

She threw off the blanket and pulled her bra back up into place. Her panties and borrowed jeans were lying half off the end of the bed. When she snatched them up to put them on, she saw a beautiful sight.

Her nine, lying among the rumpled velvet bedding.

Episode Three

Chapter Seven

Arden wanted to punch something—anything—to get rid of the disgust in his gut.

The image of Nic's body in his bed and the smoldering-stone heat in her eyes twisted like a knife in his skull. He'd gotten her through to the First. Had even managed to get his father on board without giving up any of his secret plans for the female. And then he'd almost trashed his success by giving in to what his body wanted.

Nic was human, mortal, and no matter how big the chip on her shoulder, she was still out of her element. But *fuck*, he wanted her. So much that his cock still throbbed from the denial. Why had he let it go so far?

He needed to get to the Fourth as soon as possible and be done with her. The less time he spent with her, the better off he would be.

But there was still the little matter of getting her down there in the first place, if she still wanted to go after what he'd done. He could have put everything in jeopardy by listening to his dick and not his brain. Which completely answered the question of why he'd let it go that far.

And if she did want to continue, how would he get her there undetected? Sure, he could give her other clothes to wear, but she was still a living human and vulnerable. She could be killed far too easily. Although, if another demon tried to snatch his prize...

That wouldn't end well for the demon.

She was *his* until he was done with her.

He stopped at the bottom of the stairs and took a moment to breathe. He needed to find his father and figure out what he'd meant about having Nic's presence in the lower levels covered. He turned to go back up the stairs when a raised voice reached him, coming from the study.

"That's bullshit." It was Chase, and from the sound of things, his brother was less than happy.

Arden slipped in through the open door. His father sat at the big desk with his hands covering a long, slender box. Chase stood a few feet away, staring at the box as if it might grow legs and attack him.

"Arden, I have something for you to give to Nic."

Chase spun around and blocked the path to the desk. "You're not letting her wear it. I won't let this happen."

His brother looked amped up and ready to brawl. Arden might have found an outlet for his frustration. He crossed the room and stopped a foot from Chase. "I don't know what's got you so bent, but I'm more than willing to beat you back into shape."

Chase crossed his arms over his chest. The move was slow, almost casual, but Arden knew better. His brother was trying to use his bulk to block the view of the desk. "I'm not letting this happen."

"I don't know exactly what I walked into here, and I don't particularly care. I came to talk to Dad. Move." Arden noticed Chase's jaw was clenched so tightly he could almost hear his teeth grinding together.

Asmo stood and cleared his throat. "Chase, perhaps you should go."

Chase didn't look away from Arden as he spoke to his father. "I'm not fucking leaving until you stop this."

Arden kept his focus on his brother but saw in his peripheral view his dad coming around the desk with the box in his hands.

Then, with a mental click, he knew what the attitude rolling off of Chase was about.

The necklace.

The sight of the bloodred velvet box made his insides knot up with memories—ones he refused to let surface.

The necklace was his father's plan for getting Nic through. A great idea, but it would cost a lot of pain.

"Here, Arden." Asmo held the case out toward him. His knuckles were bright white against the red. "Take it."

Chase moved to block Arden again. "You need to back off, little brother."

"Nope." Chase's hands had dropped to his sides and his stance widened. The muscles in his arms flexed.

Asmo sighed. "Boys, this isn't the time. The necklace is the only way." He set the box on the edge of the desk. "I don't want you two brawling over this. I am doing what is necessary. Put your hackles down."

Arden didn't stop to consider why his father would be willing to hand over the necklace. Truth was the old demon had been acting strange for the last twenty years at least. One night he'd even seen his father leaving the First, a thing that hadn't occurred for more than fifty years. But none of those things mattered in the current situation. He needed that necklace.

And Chase wasn't going to stop him. He stepped forward and put his finger on Chase's chest. "You don't get a say in this. Dad wants this, I need this, and that's the way it is."

Chase knocked his hand away. "Don't fucking talk to me like I'm ten, First Born."

"You need to watch your mouth." He really hated that title, hated the box it forced him into.

Chase swung, but Arden ducked out of the way. He and his brother had scrapped enough times for him to know the patterns—swing first, then a roundhouse. But the miss had Chase off balance, and Arden took advantage of the split-second weakness to land a nasty right hook to the center of his brother's face. He felt the crunch of nose under his knuckles and blissed out on the rush of adrenaline.

Chase recovered and dropped into a low crouch, ready to tackle, when Asmo stepped in between them, looking back and forth to make sure he had their attention. "Enough. This matter is settled. Nic will wear the necklace." He reached over, picked up the box, and handed it to Arden. "Take it."

Arden almost didn't want to touch it. The red velvet was too perfect—too clean—to hold what was inside. He looked up to his father's face. There was a smile on his mouth, but not in his eyes. He opened his hand, forcing it to not shake, and grasped the box. "Thank you."

"For something this important, I know your mother wouldn't have hesitated either." Asmo turned away and started across the room, his cane thumping quietly on the carpet.

Chase didn't say anything. He wiped the blood away from his mouth and nose with the back of his hand, gave Arden a hard, hollow look, and then followed his father out of the study. Arden stared down at the box, the velvet soft beneath his fingers. Maybe seeing it on Nic would remind him to stay focused. And remind him of the human half of himself he needed to get rid of.

———

Nic grinned. In his desperation to get away from her, Arden had left her weapon within her grasp, and grasp it she did; the Ruger greeted her like the cool handshake of a long-dead friend, and the weight of it snapped her mind into instant focus.

He didn't want to fuck her, fine. She had a brother to rescue and it was about time she got on with it. She didn't have the time or the inclination to "girl up" and worry about why he'd stopped when he did. Besides, dwelling on it wouldn't help anything.

Once dressed, she picked up her belt from the floor, and the routine of fastening it calmed her down. She slid her weapon back into its home at her hip.

Damn it. Why did she agree to this?

Because she needed help and she didn't have any options. And, at the time, she thought she was losing her mind.

Unfortunately, she was sane. If she were crazy, the emotions his refusal had stirred up wouldn't sting on a level that disturbed her so much.

Her mind flashed back to the look in his eyes when he'd demanded she open for him.

No. Nope.

No way would she think about what she'd seen in those icy depths.

Nic made her way to the door and flung it open, expecting to see him in the other room, but she was alone.

The antechamber looked like a cross between a gothic teen's fantasy room and the midnight dreams of a depressed poet. The same onyx velvet covered the walls, and old-fashioned chairs framed a dark marble fireplace. Instead of candles and windows for light, a smoky crystal chandelier hung above. One wall, lined with shelves, had leather-bound books and a couple of silver figurines. When she got closer to the figures, she realized they were Pan-like devils with wicked gleams in their tiny sterling eyes, and the smiles on their little faces mocked her.

Oh, that's it.

She'd had enough of smiling demons to last her a lifetime.

She stormed out of Arden's rooms with rejection burning in her gut and escape on her mind. The knowledge she was trapped almost choked her. She needed to get out of there, but calling for a servant didn't seem like a good idea. How would she explain herself?

Well, Arden almost fucked me, but then he changed his mind and left me naked in his bed and now I want out of this place.

Definitely not going to happen.

And the thought of having to seek out a servant made her even angrier. Did he think she would stay in his room and wait like an obedient dog for its master's return? Was this how he treated women in general, or just her?

As she tromped down the first set of stairs, the rejection morphed inside of her, then got swallowed whole by fury. She stood on the landing for a moment and made up her mind. She'd find someone who would get her out of this place. She didn't need Arden or his version of help.

Then she saw Chase coming up the stairs with blood smeared across his face. The frown marring his forehead couldn't have been deeper. She didn't want to be seen—wanted to run the opposite direction. But he was almost to the top and she didn't have anywhere to run. "What happened to your face?"

He seemed startled at first, and then his expression softened. "Had a little disagreement with my older brother."

"Brothers are such a pain in the ass."

He laughed and then grimaced as fresh blood dripped from his nose. "Shit."

"Let me take a look at that." She stepped over and he dropped his hand away from his face. A stream of red leaked over his lips and down his chin. "You need ice."

He used his shirt collar to block the flow and motioned for her to follow him.

She wanted to help him; it wasn't his fault his brother was an asshole. Plus, she figured if she helped him with his nose, maybe he would return the favor somehow. She followed him up to the door opposite Arden's. A painting hung beside this one too, but she didn't recognize the artist.

He punched in the code one-handed and opened the door. "Come on in." His words were nasal and muffled by fabric. "It's not the first time he's given me a bloody nose. I'm sure it won't be the last. It'll heal in a minute anyway. Let me get something to clean this up with. Have a seat."

She opted for the sofa against the wall and he disappeared through an adjoining door. Instead of the vamp, moody decor of Arden's chambers, the room looked more like an office. The space was dominated by a large wooden desk with two matching chairs in front of it. A green shaded lamp sat next to a flat-screen computer monitor. Maps were laid out over the surface, and by the looks of them she'd guess they were very old; the edges were curled up and yellowed with age.

She was grateful Chase's rooms were nothing like Arden's. It would've been an unwelcome reminder of what had happened over there.

She stood when Chase returned with a glass of ice and a towel. She pointed to one of the chairs. "Sit down and let me do it."

"I can take care of it."

"Sit. It will give me something to do." And an opportunity to feel him out.

He turned one of the chairs around and sat facing her. She scooped some ice onto the cloth and wrapped it up in a bundle. When she pressed it against the bridge of his nose he didn't budge, even though she knew it had to hurt. Dried blood marred his cheek, and she used the edge of the cloth to wipe it away.

"Thanks," he said. "I got...interrupted on my way back up here to tell you two I found Sorro."

Her heart gave a small lurch in her chest. "And my brother?"

"Him too."

The anger she'd built up vanished, along with her plan to enlist Chase's help in escaping. "Is he OK?"

"My gift doesn't account for emotional state, but he's alive."

"Well," she said, shrugging. "I guess that's helpful."

"I'm actually surprised he's lasted this long. Most times Sorro just kills the—" Chase frowned. "Sorry."

She knew the answer, but it didn't stop her from asking, "Sorro just kills the what?"

"When he gets a fresh victim he likes to play with them. But his version of playtime is a bit...different. And when his toys get too beat-up, he destroys them. It doesn't take him long to get bored."

Nic thought about Drew, and fear coupled with sadness weighed her down. The ice chilled her hand and she looked at the maps on the desk.

"I'm sorry to hit you with that. It might not be the case this time." He shifted in the chair. "I just can't figure out how he made it back through the First with no one stopping him."

"I don't understand."

"Lower demons are only allowed to cross through the First with permission. Sorro wouldn't have gotten that."

"So how did he get through with my brother?"

"No clue." Chase tucked a piece of his blond hair behind an ear. "But it's a huge breach in our security. Sorro's not allowed to leave the Fourth and wouldn't have been able to without help. But the deviation might buy you guys some time. Right now they're only in the Second."

"How do we find him?"

"You'll know where he's been, trust me. He'll leave a bloody trail."

"Lovely."

"And, regardless of my *opinion*, my father and brother have figured out how to get you there."

His "opinion" might explain the smashed nose under her hand. Why was he at odds with his brother? She didn't really care, except it could mean he'd be more inclined to help her out. "Is there a way I can go alone?"

His closed eyes flew open. "Not hardly, even with what my father has in mind. You'll need some kind of escort, but since we're upper-level demons, it would be unusual for us to be prowling around in the lower levels. I've gone over the maps, though, and I think I found a back way."

He sat up and moved out from under her hand to grab a map off the desk. He laid it out on the table in front of the sofa. "Here's where you'll go in." He pointed to a spot at the outer edge.

The map looked so ordinary. She half expected to see something like a scene from Dante's *Inferno*, complete with writhing souls, but it looked more like a scene from a road atlas—lines intersecting bigger lines with dots all over.

He pointed at a spot toward the center of the paper. "There's a passage here that's out of the way, so you should be able to get into the Second without causing a scene."

"Yeah, but what happens when we have to move on?"

"Arden's been to the Second before. He should be able to get you through."

"Is the Second beneath here, you know, like stories in an apartment building? All the levels stacked on top of each other?"

"Uh, yeah. Sort of."

"But no elevator?"

Chase laughed, and this time when he smiled, she noticed he had a dimple on his left cheek. "Yeah, our elevator is permanently out of order."

He reached for another map from the stack and stopped. "Wait a minute. Where is Arden anyway?"

"How would I know?" *Shit.* She meant for her answer to come out light and instead it came out snappy and full of pout. She bit her lip and pretended to study the map.

"Did you two have a fight or something?"

"Or something" was close enough to the truth to make her blush. "You could say that." She still didn't look up at him, sure he'd guess the answer from the pink in her cheeks.

"He can be such an asshole sometimes, but he's not all bad. He took care of the rest of us when Mom died."

Another unwelcome emotion flooded her brain—sympathy. She knew all too well what it was like to lose a parent—she'd lost both in one night. And she'd been assuming the whole time that his mother was holed up in the big house somewhere. The piercing sting started up behind her collarbone again. "What happened to her?"

Chase's green eyes got cloudy and his pain showed through in the way his jaw tightened.

Nic wanted to eat her words. He'd been kind to her. "I'm sorry."

"It's all right."

"You were just a kid?" She could see he was uncomfortable with the questions from the tension across his brow.

"I was fifteen."

"How old was Arden?"

"He was sixteen. Since he was First Born, a lot of responsibility fell on him."

Sixteen? A pang of compassion resonated in her chest. "My parents are both dead."

"I'm sorry to hear that," he said.

The mine of grief in the room was deep, and Nic didn't want to dredge up any more heartache for either of them. A red drop splashed onto the map.

"Shit," Chase said and put a hand under his nose. "He must've got me good for it not to have healed by now."

Nic helped him maneuver around the table. He sat on the sofa and she put a hand on his shoulder to get him to lean back. She knelt on the cushion and lifted the ice pack to his face.

"I see you two have gotten nice and comfortable," Arden said from the doorway.

His voice sent an unwelcome shiver up her spine. Then she remembered she was mad at him. "Somebody had to clean up your mess."

Arden's expression read danger. "My brother could have taken care of his own face."

She leaned a little farther into Chase's side and made a show of carefully wiping blood from his lip. "I thought I would help."

"I can see that." The flame in Arden's eyes could've set the sofa on fire.

Good. He deserved it. "So what's the plan?"

"Yeah," Chase said. "What's your brilliant idea?"

There was some unspoken exchange between the two of them, and Nic could feel the tension in the room ratcheting up to a threatening level. Although she sort of enjoyed making Arden squirm, she didn't want to be in the same space as the brothers if things got ugly, so she took Chase's hand and put it over the cloth on his face. She stood up and maneuvered over to lean against the desk.

Chase closed his eyes as Arden entered the room. His presence set her on edge even more when he crossed to stand too close to her. The smell of him caused her stomach to flutter. She could still feel the trace of his caresses on her skin.

"The plan is for you to be my date."

"We're down there as a couple?" She wanted to smack him in the head. "How's that going to work?"

"Quite simple really. We'll be demon lovers out for an adventure." The smile he offered her was downright sinister.

"Yeah, one problem," she reminded him. "I'm human."

"No one will know because Dad's agreed to lend you a charm." He held up a silver necklace. Diamonds sparkled along the length of the chain. A shiny pendant in the shape of a seven-pointed star hung at the end. An emerald winked from one of the points. It was beautiful in a sharp and deadly way.

"I can't believe he's giving her the necklace." Chase tossed the ice pack and it clattered when it hit the wall.

"Would you calm down? He's not *giving* it to her," Arden said. "He's letting her borrow it until we get her brother back."

Arden leaned over and started to put the necklace on her. She froze. His touch sparked memories of the other ways he'd touched her. She wished her body had an off switch. Once the chain was secured around her neck, he backed off and she let out the breath she'd been holding.

Arden looked across at Chase. "Sorry about that bit in the library."

Chase grunted. "The only reason you're not bleeding too is because Dad stopped it."

"It was a good hit, though. Made your face look better."

The two men laughed and Nic rolled her eyes. Male apologies were so sweet.

As Chase brought Arden up to speed on the map situation, she tuned them out, picking up the pendant from her neck. The star was no bigger than the center of her palm. The silver had an aged finish—not tarnished, but enhanced by time. The seven points on the star were symmetrical except for the one with the emerald, which stretched out farther than the others. She touched the end of the point with a fingertip and flinched when it pierced her skin. She wiped the small bead of blood on her jeans, strangely afraid of getting it on the stone.

The emerald itself inhabited almost the whole surface of its point on the star. The shadowy green bore an uncanny resemblance to the sculpture of Asmodeus she'd seen in the park, like it had been chipped from the heart of the statue. She'd never worn much jewelry, always thought it was too girly, but this was something she wouldn't mind having around her neck.

Nic could tell by their tone the brothers had circled back around in their conversation. Now they were staring at her. Had she missed a question while she'd been ogling the necklace? She reached for an answer that would make it seem like she'd been paying attention instead of ogling the pretty treasure. "Sounds good to me."

"It's settled then." Arden stood. "Wish us luck."

"You're going to need more than that, brother."

"I know, but it's the nice thing to do."

"Fine. Good luck." Chase grinned, but there was little warmth in it.

She gave Chase a wave, and by the time she'd turned around, Arden was already out the door. Anger surged back to the front of her brain. He could treat anyone else any way he saw fit, but not her. She refused to follow him around as if she were a trailing puppy. The hurt and fury she'd let slide to the background rushed to the surface, burning like the fuse on a stick of dynamite.

"Stop. I need answers."

"We're wasting time."

Nic pulled her gun and aimed it at his back. "Answers."

"I see you found your weapon." He didn't turn around.

"You're damn right I did."

"Try and keep it pointed at the bad guys."

"Fuck you, Arden."

Chapter Eight

Nic followed him down the stairs and into the study. She'd cussed him out and held him at gunpoint but had gotten no response. So, now she was trying a different tactic: staying silent. No point in speaking to him. He was going to do what he damn well pleased regardless.

Like he did in the bedroom. A silent growl rattled her chest.

Arden pulled books down from shelves and put them on a gigantic desk. The room, in line with what she had seen in the rest of the house, was enormous. Her local library branch could have fit inside it and, judging by the shelves, this place had more books.

A handful of black leather chairs were scattered around the room. She picked one close to the windows and sat down to peer out at the garden outside. Except for the red glow of the sky, everything looked normal; birds flitted back and forth between trees, and a butterfly wound its way among the rosebushes.

Only twenty-four hours had passed since she'd left the guard station after her shift at Shady Oaks, headed over to check on Drew, and then…

Kaboom.

Her reality had exploded into a million fiery pieces.

Now, she sat in the library of the Demon of Lust, stewing over the actions of his First Born son while waiting to descend into the lower levels of Hell to rescue her kidnapped brother. Not to mention the fact she might be trapped here—forever—because she still wasn't sure what she had agreed to in the first place. And when all those thoughts piled up, exhaustion rolled over her like a tsunami.

Arden picked one last book off the shelf and sat down behind the big desk. He flipped through the volumes and Nic watched his brow wrinkle in concentration. Her heart did a little dance. His intensity made him even more attractive, which made her want to throw the books at his head.

His black hair fell over his face, casting a shadow so she couldn't see his eyes, but she was more fascinated by the graceful motions of his hands while he turned pages. She stared at the tattoos on his arms and realized for the first time what had been made permanent on his skin.

Angels.

Each arm—starting at the wrist and vanishing under the sleeves of his T-shirt—covered with angels; not in color, only shades of black. The artist who had done them must have been exceptional because the work was outstanding. On his left arm, the wings of one angel wrapped around his thick bicep and flowed down over his elbow to blend in with the angel below; his right arm held the mirror image. His skin was a masterpiece.

Even though she didn't want to talk to him, her curiosity about the tattoos won out over silence. "Where'd you get your tattoos?" she asked. "They're really spectacular."

"I have a friend who does them for me."

"Down here?"

"Yes."

"Oh." She guessed even an artist who could render angels so perfectly could wind up on the wrong end of things when it came time for judgment. "Why angels, though?"

He glanced up from his scribbling and smiled at her. "Irony."

Nic laughed. "That's hilarious."

"Why?"

She yawned. "You're a demon with angel tattoos." He still looked confused. "I'm too tired to explain."

"You need to rest."

To her ears, it sounded like a command. "You have no idea what I need, Arden." She might be tired, but she wouldn't take orders from him. Ever.

"I know you haven't slept since yesterday and humans need to rest."

Now he was going to use her humanity as an excuse to patronize her? *Nope.* "What I need," she growled, "is to go get my brother."

"You're not going anywhere until you've gotten some sleep."

He sat behind the big desk with an expression on his face one might use to control a petulant child.

Fuck. That.

"You know what?" She stood up from her seat, hands fisted at her sides. "I don't want to be here any more than you want me to be. And before I take up more of your time, give me the directions and I'll go get Drew myself."

It was time for her to go, with or without him. Her job was to take care of her brother. It had been her job for the last ten years and she was good at it. Well, had been *sort of* good at it until the last few days.

Nic stalked over to the edge of the desk. She'd take his notes, the maps, and then she would show herself out of the beautiful house.

Entranced.

Arden couldn't think of a better word to describe what he felt.

She stood across the desk from him, her eyes downcast but full of fury and indignation. Her walnut hair stood up at rebellious angles and her delicate features belied the strength he sensed in her. This woman—steel disguised as a flower.

He wanted to march around the desk, sweep her off her feet, and have her right there on the priceless Persian rug. But he knew he had blown that chance when he had run out of the bedroom like a virgin with cold feet.

How would he make this work? His transformation—his freedom—depended on playing nice, but his appetite for her grew with every second he was near her. The hunger had become almost unbearable. He wanted to satisfy the craving but also stay on track with his plan. For him to win in the end, he'd have to give instead of take. At least for now. "I'm sorry."

Her shadowy eyes flashed, and her mouth parted to speak, but she hesitated.

Then he smelled fear on her. The scent mingled with her natural perfume, the scent of dying roses in a wishing well. His demon instincts roared within him at the smoky, coppery fragrance, and he had to grip the arms of the chair to keep from vaulting over the desk and mounting her like a stallion would a mare.

"I shouldn't order you around as if you are a child." The words came out of his mouth stilted, like he were choking on something.

As the scent of her fear lessened, he relaxed his death grip on the arms of the chair.

"You're right," she said. "I probably need some sleep."

He'd come very close to losing control. He should have felt relieved, but instead he tasted bitter disappointment on his tongue, which confused him even more. Maybe it would be best if he separated himself from her for a time. "I'll take you upstairs to rest. When I'm done I'll come get you."

She bit at her lip. "To your room?"

Her fear assaulted his senses again with its intoxicating aroma, and he forced himself to think of maggots and rotten flesh to keep his seat. "Yes," he managed to grit out between his teeth.

"I think I'll stay here, if it's all the same to you," she said, still nibbling on her lip. "That sofa looks OK."

He didn't know if he could handle having her in the room right now. If he couldn't get her to calm—

Wait a minute. She got scared when he mentioned the bedroom. He should have known. Why would he think she'd want to go sleep in his bed when he'd left her up there naked with no explanation?

"You can stay here." He hoped she would stop being afraid so he could focus for a minute. "I'll have Remy bring you a blanket and a pillow."

The delicious fragrance disappeared, giving him time to get his shit together. He picked up the desk phone and hit the six. One buzz and Remy's voice came across the line.

"How may I be of assistance, sir?"

"Could you bring a blanket and pillow to the library?" And because he couldn't resist, "Bring a plate of tempress with cream too." He glanced up at Nic when he mentioned the fruit. A spark of excitement lit her eyes and he took it as his reward. She didn't know he did it out of a selfish need to watch her eat the very same thing Eve had used to tempt

Adam. He watched the sway of her hips as she walked over to the sofa and sat down.

He remembered he was still on the phone when Remy spoke. "Anything else, sir?"

"No." He hung up and went back to his notes on Sorro, happy for the work to keep him focused; it was easier with Nic on the other side of the room.

He flipped through a demon-written classification book, hunting for details. Every class of demon had a weakness and he needed to find out Sorro's. The easiest thing would be his true name, but one demon using the trick against another was forbidden. He doubted the demon would give up his name even if his arms were being cut off, especially with Nic around. A human with the knowledge of a true name could be brutal. Sorro would never give it up. He had to find some other chink in the demon's armor.

And he needed to remember to keep his own name safe, even if his life depended on it.

He went back to studying but was interrupted when Remy came into the room carrying a large silver tray. A younger servant walked in behind him with the requested pillow and blanket.

The butler set the tray on the table in front of Nic. The boy handed the other items to Remy and then bobbed a quick bow before retreating from the room.

Arden saw the surprise on her face when she looked at the contents of the tray. As always, Remy had gone above and beyond. Not only had he brought the fruit with a dish of cream, but he'd also loaded the tray with cheeses, breads, a bottle of wine, and two glasses.

With a click of his heels, the butler turned to Arden. "Will you be requiring anything else, sir?"

"No, thank you."

Remy fell into a regal bow and left the room, closing the big double doors behind him.

Silence hung in the air. He didn't know how to tell Nic to dig in without it sounding like an order and setting her off again. She beat him to the punch when she picked up a glass and poured out a healthy dose of the wine.

He watched her take a sip. Her delectable lips curved up in a grin. She set the glass down and selected a piece of the tempress. He watched as her mouth caressed the smooth surface, and the motion made his lust scream for attention. He knew the exact way her mouth would taste if he kissed her right now—sugary and nectar sweet. The thought had him shifting in his chair to ease his growing erection.

He uttered a silent curse. Just watching her eat was tantalizing enough to get him hard. The thought of feeding her the purple fruit popped into his head and he had to reach beneath the desk to adjust himself. "Everything all right over there?"

"I'm good. The wine helps." She took another sip and licked her lips.

The sight of her soft tongue was about all he could take. The memory of it rubbing against his own sent a raw surge of lust through him.

Even though he wasn't thirsty, he had an overwhelming urge to get some wine for himself. Right away.

He shoved the chair back and almost knocked it over. He forced himself to breathe as he crossed the room. Sitting next to her didn't seem like a very good idea so he took one of the nearby chairs and scooted it over to the table. Arden picked up the other glass and filled it up with the cold wine. In hopes of relaxing the throbbing in his pants, he took a big swallow. The cool liquid went down like a dream, spreading warmth through his body.

But when she took another bite of the fruit, not even the whole bottle would have helped him.

He slid back into the recesses of the chair, gripping the glass so hard he was sure it would snap in his hand.

Nic yawned and raised her arms above her head in a stretch, her shirt clinging to the slight swell of her breasts.

She saw him staring and misjudged his interest. "Hungry?"

"Starving." He put his glass down on the table and was about to assuage his hunger by getting her naked when she yawned again and reached for the pillow.

Instead of snatching off her clothes, he surprised himself by grabbing the blanket. Once she was settled, he laid it over her.

"Um, thanks." She seemed thrown by his gesture. He was too.

He stood over her for a moment and then retreated to the chair. Her eyes drifted closed and her long, dark lashes cast tiny shadows on her cheeks. The creases in her forehead smoothed. Arden took another gulp of wine.

After several long moments, her breathing evened out. To make sure she was really asleep, he whispered her name. She didn't stir.

He was slow when he came out of the chair to kneel in front of her. The last thing he needed was for her to wake up and find him staring at her while she slept, but stare he did.

She lay on her side with her fists curled beneath her cheek. A jagged lock of her hair fell across her brow. Arden reached over to brush it back. When he got close to her, he could smell the lingering trace of her fear. He resisted the heady pull of it and snugged the blanket over her shoulder.

One minute he was raging to seduce her and the next he was tucking her in as if he actually cared? It didn't make any sense.

For now, he wasn't going to think about it. He had weaknesses to find and he wasn't going to worry about his own.

Chapter Nine

Sorro didn't know if he could stand it any longer. The pathetic male did nothing but complain.

Fucking humans.

When the man had first realized the gravity of the situation, he'd cried—disgusting little whimpers that made Sorro want to choke him. Then, he was forced to endure the man droning on and on about his dead parents. And now—the icing on the cake—he had to deal with a drug addict succumbing to the early signs of dope sickness.

They were holed up in a house in one of the grittier sections of the Second. After sneaking all the way back through the First, Sorro was exhausted. So, he'd picked the spot here because it put them closer to the gateway to the Third. It would make for an easy escape if the sister and the asshole Prince caught up with them. But the location also had the benefit of being close to where the lower demons scored their drugs. And as soon as they had gotten settled—after the delightful and violent removal of the previous tenants—Sorro had sent Flic out to score for the human. Better for him to be drugged and silent than dope sick and whiny.

He kicked the limp body of the demon who'd once called this dump home. Blood and meaty bits clung to his shoe. He hoped they wouldn't be here long enough for it to start stinking. That would really add to his current mood.

If it weren't for the reward he was going to get for a job well done, he might have taken the male straight to his lair, had his fun, and called it a day. But under the circumstances laid out by his employer, he was supposed to babysit the human, use him as bait to lure the sister down to the Fourth, and then kill the siblings in any way he saw fit. He didn't know what his employer wanted with the female, or why she was so important, but he didn't really care if it meant getting what he desired.

Despite his employer's assurances, he never expected that the sister would follow. And he didn't understand why she wouldn't simply walk away from the useless trash she called "brother" and go on with her life. He never did comprehend the human concept of family.

She did indeed follow, though. A wide grin stretched the scales on his face as he thought about the kind of joy he would find in slicing one of them open while the other watched their cherished sibling's guts slide out of the wound in a wet, slimy flow.

Now that the First Born was with her, he'd have to be a bit more careful. He'd heard the Prince was not a demon to underestimate. But the lure of taking down one of the Princes in the fray was a hard one for Sorro to resist. As long as he managed to take care of the siblings, his end of the bargain was done. He would be sitting pretty Above and wouldn't have to worry about being punished for offing the First Born. He would consider it his farewell gift to the stench and rot that had been his entire existence.

An existence that had long ago become intolerable. He had been bred and born for gore and torture. He was sick of the pain. Sick of having to be only what he was and never anything more. He wanted out, and now he had his chance.

His daydream bubble popped when someone pounded on the door.

"Sorro, it's me," Flic shouted. "Hurry up. Open the door!"

He rolled his eyes at the panic he heard in the demon's voice. One would assume, after having grown up in the Fourth, Flic wouldn't be so skittish, but he had been a nervous wreck since he'd learned the First Born would be accompanying the sister.

The stupid Princes.

Just because their births entitled them to aristocratic status didn't mean they were demons to fear. Sorro had heard some of them were little more than spoiled children with servants waiting on them hand and foot. He had never seen the sons of Asmodeus, but he doubted they were a match for him and his employer. And their alleged talents? They were half-human for fuck's sake, and he had a few tricks of his own.

He opened the door, and Flic rushed past, almost knocking him over. Once inside, the tall, lanky twit bent at the waist and threw up all over the floor.

"What the fuck?"

"Sorry, man, but I sprinted, like, two miles to get back here," Flic said, wiping his mouth off on the sleeve of his jacket.

The fact that the gangly adolescent insisted on wearing the ridiculous leather thing only furthered Sorro's annoyance. "Don't worry about it. You can clean it up after you get rid of these two." He motioned to the bodies lying in a growing pool of crimson on the floor.

"Aw, man. Why do I have to do it?" Flic whined. "You're the one who did 'em."

"Because I said so, you impertinent little shit."

"You're not the boss of me."

Sorro stalked across the room and punched him in the mouth.

"Ow!" Flic grimaced as a thick line of blood dribbled from his split lip.

"If you ever talk to me like that again, I'll give you a wound that will never heal," he said. "Clear?" When his lackey didn't answer, Sorro drew back his fist for another go. The little brat would not come between him and his goal. "I said, are we clear?"

"Yeah—I mean, yes."

"Stellar," Sorro said. "Now give me the drugs for the human and then clean up your mess."

Flic's yellow eyes flashed with hatred, but he handed Sorro the little baggie of dope and moved over to where the dead demons were exsanguinating all over the dirty shag carpet.

The human slept in the opposite corner of the place. Or what a junkie might call sleep anyway. He was flopping around on the floor, sweat matting his dark hair. Sorro could smell the sickness leaching out of the male's pores and it made him want to kick him in the back of the head.

Instead he knelt down next to him and crinkled the baggie beside his ear.

The human's eyes flew open, and he scrambled to sit up and grab at the drugs dangling in front of his face.

Sorro held the packet out of reach. He knew the human was too sick to make a move for it. "Got something here for you, Trap."

"I told you, like, a hundred times: my name is Drew, not Trapper."

"I did not call you *Trapper*," Sorro snapped. He waved the baggie back and forth, then tittered when Drew's glossy, fevered eyes tracked the movement. "I called you Trap because that's what you are."

"Whatever, just give me the dope," Drew whimpered, and lunged for the bag of crystallized escape.

Sorro was faster and kept the treasure beyond his grasp. "Not until you listen to me first."

"OK, OK. But hurry up."

"You're becoming a major pain in my ass," Sorro said. His temper was raw, but if he lost his shit and killed the human before he could do the sister too, he wouldn't be getting the cozy room Above. He would be stuck down here miring in his own waste. Or worse, his employer would go through with what he promised if Sorro failed him. That would be...unpleasant. "Listen, your sister is coming for you."

"Nic's coming?" Hope broke through the glossy stare.

"That's right, Trap. She's on her way, but we can't let her find us."

"Why not?"

"We can't," Sorro said, shaking his head and putting on a grave expression, "because she wants to keep you from going to the Well."

"But if we don't make it there, I can't get my parents back."

The tears he saw standing in the junkie's gray eyes made him want to vomit. The weakness and the love disgusted him. Hatred, his most beloved sensation, swelled inside his heart. This worthless mortal had family who loved him, yet he threw it away to chase a high that would forever elude him. He deserved to be punished. "She doesn't want them to come back."

"Maybe she doesn't know about the Wishing Well." Drew's face lit up with an idea. "If we wait for her, she can go and see it with us."

Sorro sighed for good measure. "Perhaps we will wait for her." His precise intention was to stick around long enough for the sister to get a bead on them, then he'd lead the pair farther down. "But we won't be able to stay for long. Now, be a good boy, Trap, and take your medicine." He smiled and dropped the baggie into the junkie's outstretched hands.

Drew dug out the implements of his addiction, and Sorro watched with a mixture of glee and distaste. He reminded himself he wouldn't have to do this much longer. Soon he would be free of all of it: the pain, the suffering…the humans.

Fucking humans.

Chapter Ten

"Ready to go?"

Even though she felt like puking all over the foyer, Nic agreed. "All set."

"Let's motor." Arden shrugged into his backpack and waited while she pulled on her own.

"You have the maps, right?" Chase stood by the door with a grim expression, as if he were seeing them off to war.

Arden patted his pack. "Right here."

"You sure you don't want me to come with?" The brothers exchanged a troubling glance and Nic waffled on the idea of taking backup. She didn't think they'd need it, but it might be nice to have some company other than Arden. Being alone with him wasn't on top of her list right now and the ten-minute nap had only left her feeling more ragged.

Asmodeus glided into the room. "You're staying here, Chase." The demon King's ability to move without being heard was unnerving, but there was something about his quiet grace and knowing eyes that made Nic like him despite his title.

He looked over at her and smiled. His eyes twinkled and he offered her a conspiratorial wink.

She didn't have time to wonder about the odd gesture because Remy opened the front door and scarlet light poured in, bathing the shiny marble floor in bloody daylight, and for the first time since she had met him, Arden motioned her through the door first.

When they stepped out into the hazy early evening, Nic looked up. Her breath caught in her throat. The pink cotton-candy clouds from earlier had vanished, but it wasn't the cloud-lessness that freaked her out. The sky was divided right down the center, and half of it was starless and black—like an abyss. "What's up with the sky?"

"Night is coming," Arden answered. "We should go."

"Right," she said, not taking her eyes off the unsettling, inky darkness above her until a voice broke her fixation.

"Shall we be on our way, sir?"

A plump uniformed man stood beside the open door of the most beautiful car Nic had ever seen. She recognized the make but couldn't put her finger on the name; it was one of those pre-Depression luxury affairs with a super-long body and enough chrome on it to cover her entire midpriced sedan. The car was remarkable, but Nic wasn't surprised at seeing it here. These people had wealth beyond measure. What was another rare antique car to them?

"Sir?" The chauffeur shifted from one foot to the other and kept glancing at the bad part of the sky.

The tall, yellow-eyed demon seemed uneasy so Nic did him a favor and climbed in the backseat. For some reason, she was anxious to get away from the eerie black stain too. Arden climbed in the front seat and the servant shut the door behind him.

In a smooth, graceful arc they pulled away from the mansion. She looked back and saw Chase and Asmo standing on the front steps. They seemed to be arguing about something. Asmo stared straight ahead as Chase threw up his hands and went back inside. The demon King stayed on the stair for a moment, eyes locked on Nic, and then he too retreated.

They were driven past enormous estate after enormous estate until the houses and yards began to get smaller. Affluent neighborhoods became suburbia. Suburbia became tract houses and those in turn became tiny ranch-style homes piled on top of one another. The resemblance to earth gave her the creeps; everything was too…normal. Upper class gave way to middle class and soon enough, the ghetto.

But she noticed things besides the residences changing too. The last of the crimson sky pressed into a thin line on the horizon as if the darkness were suffocating it. The light cast by the sinking sun was brutal in its glory, the landscape bloodied by its diminishing aura.

When the car slowed, she didn't want to get out. She didn't get scared too often, but right then, she was petrified. Something about the red horizon told her this was real and maybe she wasn't prepared.

Not prepared?

She was scared shitless.

Arden's head snapped around and his eyes held a fiery emerald glow. She'd seen that look from him before—in the bedroom—and the memory burned. The blazing intensity and the muscle ticking in his clenched jaw made her scoot back in the seat out of reflex to get as far away from him as possible.

He averted his eyes, but not before she caught his frown. Before the wheels even came to a complete stop, he threw open the door and jumped out.

She didn't know how to respond and the chauffeur didn't say a word. He kept eyeballing the dark sky from his window and clutching the steering wheel. His anxiousness was tangible. She took it as a hint, gathered her composure, and climbed out of the car.

Arden stood on the sidewalk a few strides ahead with his back turned. His hands were clenching and unclenching into and out of fists at his sides. Had the night sky gotten to him too? Her hand reached for the snap over her ammo and she flipped it back and forth between her fingers.

All of her senses were fired up and the smell of the dingy neighborhood assaulted her nostrils. The place reeked of melting plastic and reminded her of the time Drew had set fire to one of her dolls. She wrinkled her nose and looked around. In the distance, above the rows of ramshackle houses, she spied a line of tall smokestacks belching out plumes of white smoke.

Well, that explains the stench. The pollution couldn't be safe, but she guessed it didn't matter when all of the local residents were already damned.

Arden hadn't moved. She approached with caution. "So, where to now?"

He didn't respond.

"Hello? Earth to Arden." Still no response. She reached out to tap him on the shoulder. "Shouldn't we be go—"

He dodged away from her hand and trudged off down the cracked, uneven sidewalk.

"What's your problem?" She was getting used to trailing along in his wake, but she wanted a clue as to their next move and why he was acting so bizarre. He was almost out of hearing range, and a small bud of fear opened in her chest. In about thirty seconds, she would be standing alone on the sidewalk. She should've jogged to catch up but instead she halted. "I'm not taking another step until you tell me what's going on."

He paused and turned back. She could see the cold fire still blazing in his eyes as he crossed the space separating them. Without a word, he walked over to her, grabbed hold of her arm, and dragged her down the sidewalk. She tried to shake loose of his grip but had no luck. She figured this was the moment when the naive heroine gets raped and left for dead like in some crappy teen-filled horror flick.

He pulled her into a dingy alcove marking the entrance to an abandoned building. No light made its way into the cramped space, so Nic couldn't see him clearly, but he was close; his breath brushed her cheek and she could smell the smoldering spice of him.

"I need you to do something for me," he whispered.

The sound of his voice so close to her ear sent shivers of a different kind racing through her. "Yeah?" Given his proximity, she couldn't manage to say anything else.

He took a deep breath and, if she wasn't mistaken, smelled her. *What the hell?*

"You have to control your fear," he said. His lips brushed against her jaw as he inhaled. "The scent is...delicious, but it will put us in danger."

"Are you smelling me?"

Arden pulled back a little. "Fear is like a drug for us. When we scent it on a human, it triggers...things."

"Me being scared turns you on?"

"I'm not sure why, but yes," he said. "Other demons might have a different response."

"Like what?"

"Like disgust, or blinding anger, or homicidal rage."

She grasped the pendant hanging around her neck. "What about the necklace?"

"The Charm only covers physical appearance. It won't be able to mask your fear."

"So, to them, I will look like one of you, but if I get freaked out, I'm screwed."

"Pretty much," he said. "But you've got me."

Nic was not consoled. "Yes, but you have an interesting habit of running off when things are getting good." The barb tasted good on her tongue.

His sharp exhale told her she'd touched a nerve. It served him right, though. She hadn't mentioned a word about what had happened in the bedroom before now and he had *that* one coming.

"Do you think I'm a coward?" His breath shivered down her neck and beneath the collar of her shirt.

She never doubted his fearlessness for an instant, but her bruised ego couldn't let it go. "Maybe...I—"

His mouth came down on her so hard she tasted blood. He pushed her back against the grimy concrete and pinned her arms above her head with one hand while the other stole around her waist and forced her hips to meet his own. She tried to wriggle out of his grasp, but he had her trapped. Her efforts only created friction. Good friction. His hardness dug into her hip.

He moved from her lips to her neck and she shivered when he crossed over her collarbone with his tongue. The hand around her waist snaked up her shirt. He dipped his fingers down inside the cup of her bra and a whimper escaped her lips when he squeezed her hardened nipple.

She felt his teeth nip her earlobe as he pressed her into the wall.

"How about now," he hissed in her ear. "Do you think I'm a coward now?"

She drew in a ragged breath to answer him, but a noise out on the street froze the words in her throat.

Episode Four

Chapter Eleven

Singing. Then laughter.

Nic peeked around Arden. Two very intoxicated males were headed in their direction. She could tell they were wasted from the loud and slurred way they talked.

Arden dragged her farther into the darkest part of the doorway and put himself between her and the approaching duo. The rough concrete bit into her shoulder. If the two were only a couple of drunks, why did he suddenly act so alert and ready for a fight?

Of course, she had plenty of adrenaline flooding her blood too. Not from whatever threat lay beyond the edge of the doorway, but from the sudden, mind-numbing arousal his touch had elicited in her. A touch, a glance, a stroke, and she lost control over her own body. Fucking ridiculous and unacceptable and the whole package made worse by her surroundings—a shady, low-end suburbia on the First Level of Hell.

The first drunk stumbled past the alcove. He looked like any other wino she had seen staggering down the sidewalk in Baltimore. Baggy, unkempt clothes hung loose on his frame and the stench of booze on him reached all the way back to her.

The second man appeared in the opening and tripped over his own feet. He lurched and went sprawling, half in the doorway and half on the sidewalk. The first drunk cackled and let out a belch.

"'Snot funny," Mr. Graceful spat out. When he pulled himself up into a sitting position, she was sure he'd see them. He leaned against the wall for a minute and his head lolled onto his shoulder in their direction. She held her breath.

Arden backed up into her and his wide shoulders blocked her view, but the sour smell of an alcoholic filled the tight space.

"Hel' me up, asshole."

She heard a grunt and some shuffling. Arden twisted his arm around behind him to cage her further. She could feel the tension in his muscles where his arm touched her side.

Then the two drunks started singing in a horrendous off-key chorus. It echoed in the alcove for a second and then dipped in volume. She heard some more shuffling and then nothing but the blessed sound of their uneven footsteps as they staggered out onto the sidewalk.

Arden's arm relaxed and dropped away. She let out her breath. He stepped out to the entrance. While they'd been stuck in the alcove, night had fallen completely and it was... dark. Darker than dark. She blinked a couple of times, trying to adjust to the lack of light. Her eyes caught up and she saw him motion for her to come out.

The street was even blacker than their hiding spot. "It's pitch-black out here. How can you see anything?"

"Another one of our gifts is night vision."

Geez, what's so bad about being a demon? "You guys have special talents, night vision, and can smell fear like an animal. Anything else I should know about?"

He glanced at her, and if she could've seen him better in the darkness she would've said he looked worried. "When you're afraid, you are ravishing."

His words caused a bizarre fluttering in her stomach. Heat crept up her neck and she hoped his night vision wouldn't let him see the blush on her cheeks.

He reached out and ran the backs of his fingers along her jaw. "Let's go."

Instead of walking ahead this time, he let her keep up with him. She couldn't think of anything clever or snarky to say. But after the scorching kiss he'd laid on her and the twisted, intimate compliment, she thought maybe she should keep her mouth shut.

Arden's silence, combined with the too-quiet night, made her edgy. She stole glances over her shoulder, worried she might see goblins darting around just out of sight. Back home, at this time of night in a neighborhood this crappy, the hoodlums and thugs would be lurking about. There might even be a hooker or two wandering around. Here, there was nothing but silence, and that disturbed her even more.

"Do you guys have crime down here?" Would it be possible to police a population of damned souls and demons with supernatural powers?

"There are no laws like the ones you have," he said.

"So everybody does whatever they want?"

"For the most part, it's a free-for-all. But there are things which are forbidden and punishable by death in the Lake of Fire."

The street seemed even quieter after he'd said those last three words. She got the gist but couldn't help asking about it. "Lake of Fire?"

"The lake was created by Lucifer to ensure there wouldn't be an uprising down here like the one he started Above," he said. "It's his insurance policy. Because we have regenerative powers, we would heal and burn over and over again…forever. When a demon commits a grave enough crime, they get tossed in."

"What kind of crime is bad enough for that?"

"The worst ones. Disobeying a direct order from Lucifer, threatening the life of a Fallen or one of their children, loving a human—" He stopped short, but didn't miss a step in his march down the sidewalk.

"Has that…ever happened before?" Some alien emotion in her gut had pushed the words out of her mouth before she thought better of her question.

"Yes," he said. "To my father."

That stopped her. "But he…"

"Because he's Lucifer's closest friend, he was spared."

She didn't want to ask about his mother. "How long were your parents together?"

"About fifty years before…they were together for almost fifty years."

Before she died, Nic filled in for him. She wondered how it went, wondered what kind of punishment his mother had received. And what happened to the lover of a demon? Paradise above? Not likely.

She'd always believed her parents were just…dead. Hadn't even believed in Heaven *or* Hell until she'd met Arden. So, where did her new reality leave Charlotte and Nathan Wright in the afterlife? They were good people. Didn't good people get to go to Heaven? What if there was something they'd hidden from her and Drew all this time and they'd been sent down here?

No. One thing at a time. She was only now getting used to the idea of Hell being real. She wasn't quite ready for the other stuff yet.

And if the conversation was causing her own internal theological debate, she was a total asshole for asking him so many questions. "I'm sorry."

"The necklace you're wearing," he said, pointing to the star at her neck, "was how they managed to keep their affair a secret for so long."

She caressed the pendant lying on her chest. The fact she'd been entrusted with something so intimate and dear to his family was inconceivable. Why would Asmo have given it so freely? It must have hurt him—hurt all of them—to see her wearing it.

She reached up to unfasten the chain. It wasn't right for her to use something so precious for her own stupid problems. And even though she didn't want to admit it, this endeavor might be a suicide mission.

Arden noticed what she was doing. "No." He crossed the sidewalk and put his hands over hers. "My father told me it was the only way."

She looked into the green depths of his eyes, dropped her hands, and stood still while he fastened the necklace back in place. There were a million things she wanted to say all at once. How she wished he hadn't gotten dragged into this. How, if she could have, she would have done this alone. She knew sex was on the table as part of their arrangement, but it almost didn't seem like enough anymore.

He laid his palm over the star and she felt the heat of his hand on her skin. She stared at him until the silence hung in the air like humidity. Too many things floated in the close space between them, and she really didn't want to talk about anything other than the way his hand warmed her. "I guess we should get a move on."

Chapter Twelve

The only sound came from their footfalls. Nic didn't know how much more quiet she could stand. She kept checking behind her to see if they were followed. They weren't. But she couldn't shake the feeling that in every dark corner, behind every boarded window they passed, someone watched their progress, and at any second a monster would jump out to swallow her whole.

When Arden grabbed her arm she almost shot out of her boots. "We're here."

"Here" was a convenience store called Big Jackie's One Stop Shop, according to the tattered awning. It appeared like every other corner market she knew back home, but this one looked more like the kind found on the bad end of town—dirty, trashy, and with thick bars inside the glass. A neon sign hung in the filmy window, and every few seconds it flashed the word "Open" in blue and red.

The similarities between things down here and the real world gave her a weird flash of disorientation or déjà vu. For a moment, she almost grabbed on to Arden to steady herself, but then thought better of it. She couldn't really trust him to console her, could she? If she got too close, he'd try to kiss her senseless again. Sure, he'd given her his mother's priceless heirloom necklace, but nothing would change the fact that he was a demon. And his species wasn't known for its empathy.

But he had let her rest, given her food, and stood between her and those drunks. She got the sense he would have fought to protect her if one of the boozy demons had made a move. Maybe that was his way of apologizing for his behavior? More likely he was buttering her up for another surprise.

He gave her a crooked grin and she lost her train of thought. The puzzle of him was like walking on a newly frozen river; the hard surface belied stability, but a raging torrent of frigid water waited below to drown the unwary.

Arden slid his backpack off his shoulder and dug around inside. He pulled out a pair of red patent-leather women's high heels. "Put these on."

She took one look at the shoes and laughed. "You can't be serious."

"Trust me," he said. "And put your belt in your pack. You won't need your weapon."

She didn't want to get rid of her nine but knew it might attract extra attention. With a sigh, she took off the duty belt and tucked it away. She eyed the heels. The jealousy she'd felt earlier over her borrowed clothes resurfaced. "These belong to your girlfriend too?"

"What?" He looked genuinely puzzled.

She pointed down at her jeans. "These clearly don't belong to one of your brothers."

He had the nerve to laugh. "You're right, but it would be hilarious to see one of them wearing those."

"Whose pants did you give me?"

"You sound a little jealous."

Damn. She did. Better bitch it up a little. "I just want to make sure I don't catch some venereal disease from the crotch."

"Careful. I don't think my cousin Valry would take kindly to that comment."

Shit. Her cheeks flamed.

"She left them in one of the guest rooms on her last stay. Remy figured you two were about the same size."

"Oh."

"But your jealousy *is* flattering."

She ground her teeth together and waggled the shoes in front of him. "Does Valry have really huge feet?" Damn it. That sounded jealous too.

"Those belong to one of the maids."

Zero points for Nic. "Well, they aren't going to fit."

"Doesn't matter. You won't be wearing them long. It's our bribe, so put them on."

He crossed his arms and stared at her with the impatient, impervious glint in his eyes she was becoming all too familiar with. She did not like someone else being in charge of her actions. And what gave him the right to order her around in the first place?

As she inhaled to give him a piece of her mind, the star at her neck shifted and the cool metal against her skin stopped her. It was a clear reminder that she was out of her element. And also being a big baby. She might not want to listen to him. She might want to tell him he'd been nothing but a complete shit to her. But the necklace and what it meant kept her from saying any of that.

She sat down on the concrete and pulled off her boots and socks. The heels were about two sizes too big and she didn't know if she would be able to walk in them without making a total fool of herself, but she slid them on and used the wall of the store for balance as she stood.

Arden shoved her stuff into his pack, zipped it up, and slung it over his shoulder. "Follow my lead," he said, offering her his hand. "Remember, we're a couple."

The first thing she noticed when she followed him through the door was the merchandise. Shelves packed with nothing but liquor, coolers along the wall with nothing but beer, and a huge display rack full of porno mags.

Arden pulled her toward a long counter where a large bearded man was, as far as she could tell, fast asleep, perched on top of a stool. His chin hung down over his considerable chest and a fine line of drool fell from his open mouth. The name tag pinned to his chest said "Big Jackie."

Arden squeezed her hand and marched up to the counter. She had to shuffle along to keep from falling face-first into the sticky linoleum because of the huge heels. When the sleeping clerk made no sign of rousing, Arden rapped his knuckles on the side of the register.

In one fluid motion, the man jolted awake and produced a baseball bat from under the counter, raising it above his head to strike.

Since fear was not an option, she bit the inside of her lip and stood perfectly still.

Big Jackie smiled and lowered the bat. "Sorry about that. Sleeping dogs and all. What can I getcha?"

"We'd like to start off with a bottle of vodka," Arden said. "Then we want to get down, right, darling?"

He turned to her, a goofy grin plastered to his face. *Remember we're a couple.* She picked up the hint, put on her sweetest smile, and snuggled up to Arden's side with a giggle.

"Out for a bit of fun, huh? Well, Big Jackie's One Stop Shop's got ya covered."

He hopped down off his stool and came around the open end of the counter. When she could see all of him, she was amazed the stool had been able to handle all that weight. Big Jackie cleared five hundred pounds easy, and he had to run about seven foot seven, at least. He made his way over to a shelf displaying an astounding array of vodkas.

After giving her and Arden a very thorough once-over, Big Jackie reached up to the top shelf and pulled down a tall, sapphire-colored bottle with an elaborate script *M* etched on the surface. Jackie wheezed just from walking ten feet.

"Mammon's finest," Arden said to Nic. "My darling deserves nothing less."

"I 'spected as much," Jackie said. He wobbled back around the counter and stepped up to the register. "That it for ya?"

"Well, since you asked, Jackie, there is something else." Arden leaned over the counter and whispered, "I promised this little piece I could get her down to the Second. I'm thinking she might part with the panties a bit easier, if you catch my drift."

She pretended not to hear and feigned interest in a non-existent speck on her shirt. Her teeth hurt from grinding them, but it helped her keep her mouth shut.

Big Jackie's eyes went round and he chuckled. The chuckle turned into a coughing fit that lasted for about two and a half minutes. When he finally got himself under control, he eyeballed the two of them, paying special attention to Nic.

His scrutiny made her fidgety, but the necklace's illusion seemed to be working. She batted her eyelashes and smiled wider.

Jackie motioned for Arden to lean closer. "That's a nice piece ya got there. I know fancy types like her need some finessin', but it's gonna cost ya."

"Oh, I have plenty of money," Arden said.

"I don't want your money," Jackie whispered. "I want her shoes."

Nic put on an Oscar-worthy performance. "Did he say he wanted my shoes?" she screeched. "He can't have them. They're my favorites!" She stuck out her bottom lip in a pout and crossed her arms. "I won't do it."

"Come on, baby," Arden said. "I promise I'll buy you twelve new pairs."

"No, they're mi-ine." There was so much whine in the words it nauseated her.

Arden winked at Jackie and then gathered Nic up in his arms. Even though they were pretending, she still felt a rush of heat when he embraced her.

"What if I get you fifteen new pairs?" he asked, loud enough for Big Jackie to hear. He snugged his arms around her tighter and added in a husky whisper, "You said you wanted to be naughty tonight."

The comment and his breath on her neck forced her pulse into hyperdrive. Her cheeks burned. He trailed his fingers up the center of her back and she fought to hide the shiver his touch caused. Was he still pretending?

"I tell ya what," Jackie said. "I'll throw in the vodka. But if ya want to get to the Second, I'm gonna need the shoes."

It took a second for Nic to remember how to act. She huffed and then stomped her foot like a four-year-old for good measure. "Fine." She gave Arden a mean look and hoped she wasn't overplaying it. "But I want twenty new pairs. Promise?"

"Twenty, darling, I promise."

She used Arden's arm for balance as she slipped the heels off and tossed them onto the counter.

Big Jackie's eyes glazed over as he reached out and caressed the shiny red surface. He licked his lips and she almost gagged when she noticed his tongue was covered with seeping gray sores.

She *so* didn't want to know what kind of thoughts were running through his head as he led them to the back of the store with one pump pressed against his heart. She also didn't want to think about her bare feet and what kinds of things she might be picking up from the repulsive floor.

They passed the rows of liquor and the array of porn and stopped at a large door with a handwritten "Employees Only!" sign nailed to it.

Big Jackie's wheezing muffled the jingle of the set of keys in his hand. He found the correct one, unlocked the door, and led them down a hallway cramped with boxes, empty crates, and a stench that had Nic breathing through her mouth.

Arden hadn't let go of her hand. She knew it was just a cover to keep up appearances, but she was soothed by the feel of his palm against hers, regardless.

When they got to the end of the hall, they made a right turn and halted in front of a door marked "Men's."

She choked back a laugh. The secret gateway to the Second Level of Hell was a men's bathroom in the back of a convenience store? No forbidding iron gate complete with scary guards? Maybe the huge, slobbering proprietor would turn into some terrifying creature if threatened.

Jackie produced another set of keys, but these were much older—they looked like hand-forged iron with rough edges and dagger-sharp points. One of them was as long as her forearm. He took the biggest key and slid it home into the giant padlock fastened to the door. She heard a small click, and Big Jackie removed the lock and stepped back, clutching the red shoe to his chest.

Arden pushed open the door. "Thanks, Jackie, I owe you one."

Jackie snorted. "You don't owe me nothin'. I got all I need right here."

Nic watched as he fisted the heel of the shoe and stroked up and down. *Ew.* "Um, thanks."

Jackie grunted and continued his loving caresses. Arden stepped through the door and pulled her into the room. The bathroom door slammed shut and she heard a clank as the lock was snapped back into place behind them.

The dirty toilet and scum-filled sink she expected were absent; it was just an empty white room with a blinking fluorescent light and black tiled floor. Set into the opposite wall was a chipped wooden door with a number two carved into its surface. She took a deep breath as Arden opened the door and led her out onto a rickety fire escape like the one outside of Drew's apartment. Goosebumps rose on her arms and her stomach did a tiny somersault.

When they got to the bottom, Arden handed over her boots and she took a seat on the last stair to put them on. The atmosphere had shifted almost as if the air itself were thicker, heavier. Did the change in levels mean more evil? She dug into her pack for her nine.

Arden laid his hand over hers. "Don't get that back out," he said.

"Why not?"

"Because it will look suspicious."

"So what? We're in Hell. Isn't everything suspicious down here?"

"Yeah, but toting a gun will give you away." He knelt down in front of her and she knew she would not like what he had to say.

"How?"

He paused. "Since we regenerate, your bullets are kind of pointless."

What the fuck? Had he left that fact out intentionally? "Why didn't you tell me this when we got here?"

"Because this is the attitude I figured I'd get. I know you don't feel secure without it."

"How do you know that?" How *did* he know that? His statement was too close to the truth for her comfort. Nic had been carrying a weapon, legal or not, since the night her parents...

Didn't matter. Without her Ruger, she was vulnerable. Unprotected.

"When you get nervous or edgy, you play with that snap on your belt."

Way to show your cards, Nic. She changed the subject. "Why exactly won't my bullets work?"

"It depends on what kind of demon you're shooting, but for the most part, they will only piss us off."

"What if I shoot one in the head?"

"If you shot me in the head, I would be down for a few days at most."

"What about the others?"

"Lower demons are tricky. You could blast their brains all over the floor and they might just keep going. They can't always regenerate like my siblings and me, but some of them are immortal as well. Most have weaknesses but the results are unpredictable."

"Do they have genitals?"

His sudden burst of laughter was rich and throaty. "Where did that question come from?"

"Well, I was just thinking that if I can't shoot them, at least I could kick them in the balls for stealing my brother."

"Good thinking, Trickster."

"What's a Trickster?"

"They're tiny lower demons. Very mischievous and—" He stopped midsentence and stood.

"And what?" She wanted to know why he called her that and why his eyes changed shades when he said it, but something in his stance read trouble.

She stood up behind him and reached for her Ruger in spite of his revelation about it being pointless. Her hand felt empty without it, and even if it didn't kill whoever was threatening her, at least she might have a chance to get away.

Arden cocked his head to the side, listening. "We need to move," he said. "Now."

Chapter Thirteen

Something was wrong. Arden could feel it.

It was full night in the Second. There should be demons wandering around, carousing, boozing it up, and drugging themselves into a frenzy. Down here, the revelers didn't take nights off. He didn't know what to make of the silence, but he *did* know they needed to get off the steps, out of the light, and gone.

He also knew he needed to stop getting distracted by Nic. Distraction meant trouble in more ways than one. "Let's go."

As soon as he started to move, Nic was on him like wallpaper, matching his long strides with her own. Her courage was astounding, given the situation. Here she was, gallivanting through the Second without a hint of fear.

Thank the Dark One for that. He wasn't sure he could make it through another one of those "episodes" without ripping her clothes off. And it would be a shame to ruin his favorite T-shirt.

He led them along the edge of the building to the corner. Shadows were their friends. When they got to the end of the wall, he peeked out and saw an empty street in the front of the building. It too lacked partiers.

Then it dawned on him why. They must be close to the Third. He'd learned the area around a gateway tended to stay quiet—nobody wanted to catch the attention of something coming up from below. If Chase were standing next to him, he would have hugged him. The little shortcut his brother had sent them through put them at the farthest end of the Second. The doorway must be close. Now he just needed to find it.

He reached behind him to give Nic's hand a quick squeeze, and then jerked his own back. What the fuck was he doing?

She was the means to an end, his currency for what the Incubai King had for sale. And nothing more. Sure, she was the single most interesting female he had ever encountered and had enough steel within her to make a lion tuck tail and cry like a kitten, but she was human.

And his meal ticket to a more interesting future.

But first, he had to deal with the brother situation and one of the most vicious, bloodthirsty, unpredictable demons in all of Hell.

Piece of cake.

Arden felt a tug on his shirt and his thoughts zoomed back in to their present situation. "I'm going to take a peek out front and make sure the coast is clear," he said. "Then we need to find somewhere safe so I can check the map and see where the next gate is."

"Copy that," she said.

He crouched down and peered around the edge of the building again. No one was in sight in either direction. He scanned the perimeter. A few rusty, broken-down cars dotted the street out front. Their shelter was neighbored by other brick buildings in various states of decay and corruption. Across the street were more of the same dilapidated structures and an empty lot. The place reeked of garbage.

They didn't have a lot of options, but they had to move. The quiet was unsettling, and the longer they stayed, the more positive he was that they would run into trouble.

His plan was simple. Follow this street to the next intersection. They could use the buildings as cover and maybe one of them would be a good spot to huddle in until he got his bearings.

He motioned for her to crouch down next to him. "I go first. Wait until I'm in place. If nothing moves, you follow. Got it?"

"I'll be on your ass, don't you worry," she said. "Just stop bossing me around like I'm an idiot."

"I hear you," he said. "But remember, if we get separated, I know my way home, and I won't hesitate to leave you down here."

His night vision helped him to see he'd gotten his point across. Her eyes blazed and her full lips pressed into a thin line, but he knew she would follow anyway. Not like she had much choice.

He took one more look left and right and then hot-footed it across the pavement to the shadow of one of the cars. In half a heartbeat she was next to him. They were still clear, so he made a dash for the brick two story next to the vacant lot. There was a mangled awning drooping down over a side door with enough shadow to cover them both. Just as before, Nic was next to him in a split second.

Paranoia weighed on him. He couldn't risk being spotted. She had the necklace, but if they ran into some trouble and she panicked, it wouldn't matter.

There was no light, but he could see the white gleam of silver against her chest. The sight of his mother's necklace on Nic kindled a streak of protectiveness in him he hadn't realized he possessed. It gave him one more reason to worry but also helped keep him moving. The less time he spent dicking around, the better.

They moved from one secluded spot to the next, all the way to the end of the block. He heard before he saw that the street out in front of their cover was littered with demons. So much for it staying quiet around a gateway.

He squatted down and peered around the edge of the building. There were about thirty of them. Some sat on cracked, cobbled stairways leading into buildings. Others loitered in groups and he spied drugs being passed back and forth between them. They were all dressed in dirty clothes, and he could smell their filth from the small alley in which he and Nic crouched, not ten feet away.

"What do we do now?" she said. "They're all over the place."

Shit. He couldn't just waltz through the crowd with her in tow. Necklace or not, the situation was way too sketchy. "We go around."

Arden grabbed her hand and beelined for the other end of the alley. He stopped when three scraggly figures appeared, blocking their exit.

"Whatever you do, stay calm," he said to her under his breath. "Remember fear is a weakness."

She straightened up and squared her shoulders. Steely determination radiated from her gray eyes.

Damn she was sexy.

"We're just going to walk right by them."

They made it about six feet before one of the figures spoke up.

"Hey now, what's this?" The speaker was in front of the other two. Arden thought he looked like a cross between a python, a troll, and a pig; he was squat and round with uneven scales marring his face and tiny yellow eyes. Arden guessed him for the leader and the other two for muscle. They were brutish, hulking things with raggedy clothes and dead eyes.

"By the looks of 'em, I'd say they don't belong 'round here, Ritter." This came from the one on the left. His eyes were glossy with insanity and as dark as the stygian night around them. He smiled and showed crooked, canine teeth.

"You got that right, but I'm more interested in the little one," Ritter said.

Nic stiffened behind him and he hoped she had enough sense to keep her mouth shut.

No such luck.

"Hey, you guys know where we can score?" She stepped around Arden but kept hold of his hand. "I'm in the mood to party."

Her tenacity knew no bounds. He couldn't help but admire her cleverness. If these three thought they were just looking for drugs, they might get through this.

"She's pretty, Ritter," Dog Teeth said. A dribble of drool ran over his bottom lip. "Can I touch her?"

"I wanna touch her too," the other one said. His red eyes gleamed. He grinned and revealed a row of blackened fangs, long and curled back like a viper's.

The pair turned on each other, snarling as if they were feral dogs.

"Boys." Ritter's tone was firm and the growling was reduced to a low sound in the back of his toadies' throats. "Don't be rude. Besides, if anyone is getting a taste, it's me."

Arden stepped in front of Nic and slid his backpack off of his shoulders. Her plan had fizzled before it even got off the ground. "She's with me."

"Not for long."

The toadies rushed forward. Arden clocked the first one in the jaw and he went careening off into a wall. The second comer took a wide swing. Nic was there with the assist, putting out her foot and tripping him. He went sprawling onto the grimy cement.

Ritter came next. But when Arden took a swing for his gut, Ritter faked left and came up with an uppercut. The punch hit Arden right beneath his chin. His neck snapped back and he felt his teeth knock together with a painful crack.

Nic kicked the demon in the knee dead-on, and there was a popping noise when he staggered back clutching his leg.

The other two had recovered and came at them again. Arden pushed Nic out of the way, and she landed on the ground with a thump; her pack dropped from her shoulders and fell beside her. He threw a hard jab to Dog Teeth and it connected with his mouth. Arden felt the lower demon's canines bite into his knuckles. The demon fell to the ground with dark blood rushing down over his lips.

Viper's turn was next. He must have realized he wouldn't get a punch in and instead lunged for Arden's throat. His mouth was stretched wide and his long, corrupt fangs oozed with yellow liquid.

Venom.

Arden heard Nic yell, and he glanced over to see that Ritter had her pinned against the slimy brick wall. The second's distraction was all Viper needed—he sank his teeth into Arden's shoulder. Searing pain surged up his neck and down his arm as the demon's fangs sank into his flesh. He shoved at Viper's face to push him off, but the fangs were in too deep and the range was too close to land a fist. He brought his knee up between their bodies and snatched hold of the demon's sagging jacket. Using his knee for leverage, he wrenched the jacket around until the demon's hold weakened. The moment it did, he tossed Viper to the ground and pinned him there. He put his hands on either side of Viper's face and snapped his neck too far to the left. Bones crunched inside the demon's head and his eyes filmed over. Done.

Nicolette.

He spun around and saw Ritter ram his hands between her legs.

Then he smelled it. The sweet scent of copper and dying roses reached his nose.

Fear.

Arden reached down and pulled the shining blade out of his boot.

Dog Teeth was still down, jellied blood smeared over his face, but he must have smelled it too. His black eyes gleamed with hunger. The demon's head tilted back, and a ravenous howl poured from his broken, bleeding lips. He tried to stumble to his feet, but Arden and his blade got there first. He swung the knife down in a violent arc and sliced through the skin of the demon's neck all the way to his spine. Blood splattered over the ground and Dog Teeth crumpled.

Arden moved toward Nic. The demon had her face crushed into the wall. She kicked at her assailant, but Ritter outweighed her by at least a hundred pounds and he had her hands pinned behind her back. Laughter rippled from the demon as he ground his hips against her backside.

"I'm going to fuck you until you bleed, human," he said.

Chapter Fourteen

Nic tried to wrestle away, but he had her arms gripped like a straitjacket.

Her thoughts scrambled and she panicked. Fear coursed through her muscles and she hoped the adrenaline would give her the boost she needed.

Then suddenly her arms were free and she spun to attack.

Arden had yanked the demon off of her. He stood a few feet away with a knife clenched in his fist. She saw the bodies of the other two lying on the concrete in a mess of spreading black fluid.

Ritter tottered on his bad leg and lurched toward her, his yellow eyes lit with lunacy.

Arden threw the blade. It spun through the air and then stopped, lodged to the hilt in the demon's chest. Ritter stared down at it; confusion muddled his piggy features. His arms pinwheeled as he fell face-first onto the cement.

Her heart hammered in her chest and she struggled to get her breathing back under control. She leaned back against the wall and sagged to the ground.

Arden dropped to his knees in front of her. She looked up and saw that the color had left his eyes. Now they were white, as if frozen solid, with no sign of pupils. Was that what happened when he fought? It was disturbing—no, *terrifying*—to look at, so she averted her eyes.

The shoulder of his shirt was ripped wide, jagged teeth marks trailed down his skin, and the wounds lay open showing the muscle beneath. He winced when she tried to pull a piece of the shirt out of one of the openings.

"Are you all right?" he asked.

"Me? I'm more worried about you. That looks nasty."

"Motherfucker had venom."

"Will it heal?"

"Yeah, but it will need to be flushed out," he said. "Right now it feels like someone's digging around in there with a welding torch."

"We need to get somewhere," she said. She eyed the buildings on either side of the alley. One of them had to have a back door. And maybe, if they were lucky, running water. "Stay here. I'm going to see if—"

"No way. I'm not going to let you out of my sight." He rose and reached for her hand. His eyes were normal again. Weird...

She took hold of his outstretched palm and they started down the alley. Ritter lay motionless, his blood making a puddle beneath him. When she went to step over him, his hand flew out and grabbed her ankle. She stumbled and fell. The sharp concrete shredded the knees of her jeans and bit into her skin.

Then she saw the demon spring up from the ground. The blade that had been in his chest was at his hip as he ran at Arden.

The demon's movement was a blur. She shot to her feet and made a dash for Ritter, her hands curled into fists.

He knocked Arden to the ground with his momentum. Ritter twisted the knife in his grip, and before she could leap the remaining distance to tackle him, he plunged it into Arden's abdomen. He rammed the blade in and sliced forward until he stopped at the breastbone. Ritter drew the knife up and continued his cut all the way to Arden's throat.

Her feet left the ground as she sailed through the air. Ritter's breath whooshed from his lungs when she smashed into him. He toppled to the side and she landed across Arden's legs. She snatched the knife from his bleeding chest and rolled into a crouch.

Ritter was rocking back and forth, trying to get to his feet, but she was faster. She pounced on him and knocked him back to the pavement.

Her fingers curled around the handle of the knife. She drew her arm back. The demon's mouth opened as if to scream and she shoved the blade down his gullet. She stopped when she felt the tip of it hit the concrete underneath his skull.

Noises still gurgled from Ritter's throat, so to make sure her job was complete, she drew the knife out and slammed it into his temple, piercing his eyeball. A spurt of blood leaked from the ruptured socket and ran black over the hit of the blade. His other eye went glassy. The demon's head lolled to the side.

Nic climbed off of him and rushed over to where Arden lay on the ground. He wasn't moving. She felt fear rise in her throat but she shoved a lid over it. Now wasn't the time to panic.

His eyes were closed and the corners of his mouth were tilted down. In the dimness she saw he was pale, and sweat beaded on his forehead in tiny droplets.

Now it was time to panic.

"Arden?"

His T-shirt was split open and the wound gaped like a canyon; it stretched from the hollow of his neck and ran in a stuttering line all the way to the top of his jeans.

She knelt over him and smoothed a hand over his cheek. His eyelids fluttered, but he didn't speak.

"Fuck," she said to the alley full of dead or dying demons…

Arden's words came back at her: *You could shoot them and they just keep on going.* Any second the alley could turn into zombie central.

OK. She needed to get Arden *and* herself inside one of these buildings, but that meant she was going to have to go around the back to look for a door. Alone. Panic pushed at the lid she'd slid over it and she mentally mashed it down again.

OK, Nic. Put on your big-girl panties and get your shit together.

"Here's the deal, Arden. I'm going to leave you for a minute and go check out these buildings."

He mumbled and a frown creased his brow.

"No choice," she said. Leaving him alone, bleeding, with a chasm carved down the center of his torso wasn't her first pick, but beggars didn't get to choose. "I gotta get you inside. I'll be careful."

His hand snaked up and reached for the edge of her shirt. She grasped it and laid it down over his chest. "I'll be back before you can say motherfucker."

Nic stuck close to the wall as she made her way to the back end of the alley. When she came to the end, she crouched down and peered around the corner. Nothing stirred. She leaned back against the warm brick and closed her eyes, listening. A tiny waft of sound carried to her from the revelers down the street, but other than that, all was still.

She took a deep breath and edged around the building. Garbage cans overflowing with refuse sat in a crooked row on the ground; it smelled like week-old roadkill. Above the cans, hanging at a dangerous angle, was a fire escape leading up to the third floor, but some of the rungs were bent out of place or missing. She scanned the lower level and didn't see a door.

One more deep breath and she sprinted to the other building. This one looked to be in a bit better shape than its neighbor. No reeking garbage in sight, but no stairs either. Then she spotted wooden steps and at the top of them, a windowless steel door.

Bingo.

Before she went back for Arden she had to make sure it was unlocked. The wooden stairs held her weight, and when she went to try the knob, she realized the door was ajar. She planted a finger against its surface and pushed it inward. The hinges screeched and she flinched away from the entry.

But nothing reached out and grabbed her. If she could get Arden inside, she'd be able to search the rest of the building for a better hiding place.

She ducked back into the alley and sped to where Arden lay. He was too still. She reached her hand to the side of his neck. *Do demons even have a pulse?* Beneath her fingers, the uneven thrum of his pulse—weak but there.

With sudden viciousness, an awful thought stabbed into her head—what if he couldn't heal from this? What if he died and she was left alone here?

Like a swig of strong liquor, fear spread out from her stomach to the tips of her toes. The fine hairs on the back of her neck stood on end and sweat sprang to life on her upper lip.

"Stop...Nic," he groaned.

Her hands shook as she pulled back the torn edges of his shirt. His tattooed torso was cut down the middle. The wound gaped; the skin filleted and lifted up like an envelope flap. Blood trickled from the opening and pooled on either side of him.

"Oh shit. Shit." The sight of his blood did something vile to her, like all the red was a rape. "Shit."

He was in bad shape—very bad shape. Her thoughts immediately plummeted to worst-case scenario: she would have to either go on alone or try to find her way back to round up reinforcements. Both of those options had her heart hammering against her ribs. And the *very* worst possibility? Arden could die.

That last thought was the clincher. Panic rose to clog her throat. Her pulse raced, and she balled the edges of his shirt up into her fists.

His eyes flew open and his hand shot out. He grabbed her by the back of her neck and pulled her face down to his. "Calm down." His breath stuttered against her cheek. "Help me up."

Up? He was delirious. She pulled away. "You're gutted like a fish."

He rolled his eyes and started to sit up on his own, but his wound spread apart when he leaned forward. He sucked air in between clenched teeth and sank back to the pavement.

No way would he be able to get upright without having something around him to hold his organs in. A quick dig in their packs didn't show anything of use, and she fought through the panic for a solution.

A lightbulb flared in her head. She untied her boots, stood up, and kicked them off. Then she unfastened her jeans and shimmied out of them. They were long enough to reach around his middle, and she could tie the legs together at the ends.

Either from panic or insanity she snickered. Arden might not be completely awake, but he had *still* managed to get her pants off.

"What in Hell…could possibly…be funny about this?"

He had to be in a lot of pain, but he barely reacted when she maneuvered the pants around his waist. She tied a loose knot in the front and helped him stand. With his arm draped over her shoulders, she managed to get him around the back of the building, up the steps, and through the door.

She left him leaning against the wall and went to do some recon, her pack slung over one shoulder. The inside of the building smelled fleshy and acrid with a hint of rotting corpse, but there was no noise.

The first couple of doors she tried were locked. Did people live here? The building did seem a bit nicer than the others. What if someone heard them? But Arden couldn't very well hobble around in his current shape. *Damn.* One of them had to be un—yes. Unlocked.

She pressed herself to the wall next to the hinges and flung it open. Nobody came barreling out so she switched sides to peek inside. A rickety set of stairs led downward. She spun the backpack around and found her nine. Regardless of what she'd learned about its effectiveness, with the gun and its comfort in her hand, she squared her shoulders and stepped onto the landing.

She kept the barrel aimed for a head shot should anyone decide to rush up at her. Each step creaked. At the last stair, she paused and counted to ten. Still no movement.

Her eyes had adjusted enough to the darkness for her to see a bare bulb hanging from the ceiling. She pulled on the chain, and the light made her squint as it swung back and forth, casting menacing, flashing shadows over the walls.

It was almost identical to the basement in her rental house back in Baltimore. The cracked, dirty concrete floor had puddles on the surface in random spots. Cobwebs hung from the low ceiling, draping over the tops of shelves and along the walls. A few paint cans, a stack of boxes, and a filthy box spring propped up against the wall cemented the similarity to her home. Two windows high up on one wall looked filthy and impenetrable. She spied a utility sink against one wall, the faucet dripping in time with her heartbeat.

She heard footsteps approaching the door above her and her breath caught in her throat. She swung around underneath the stairs. Whoever it was, she would be waiting to put a bullet in his Achilles as soon as his ankles came into view.

If the stranger had come in the back, what if he'd already killed Arden? Would he have been able to defend himself with that crazy gash up his middle? How long did it really take for him to regenerate? And what if those filthy bastards out in the alley could regenerate too and now all three of them were coming to get revenge on her? Or worse. She hadn't heard a struggle from upstairs. Maybe they'd killed him before he'd even had a chance to yell.

Shit. But if this was how she was going to go out, she'd at least take as many of them with her as possible.

The barrel of her pistol shook, and she tried to steady her hands around the grip as the first shoe clomped down onto the step right in front of her. Because of the position of the light, she couldn't see more than a silhouette. She held her breath.

Two more steps and this guy is toast.

The stranger swayed and she heard him scrabbling for a hold on the wall. As soon as he came within better range, she'd take her shot. Once he went down, she could stomp a hole in his head with her boot while he was busy screaming. When his buddies ran down to see what happened, she'd shoot them too.

A smile pulled at her mouth. She steadied her weapon, but she couldn't get a clear shot because the figure swayed and stumbled down another stair. This time he couldn't get a hold on the wall and his feet went out from under him. He came down on the last four stairs and she heard him moan.

Then his face came into view and the breath whooshed out of her.

Episode Five

Chapter Fifteen

Nic rushed around the stairs. Arden sprawled across the steps and the light illuminated his face: ashen skin and pale lips. "What the hell? I almost put a bullet in you. Why didn't you wait for me?"

"Thanks for not shooting me." He smiled. "Don't know if I would've been able to get over a gunshot wound on top of all this."

She'd left him lying in the alley where they'd fought and killed three demons. He'd been almost gutted, and from the look of him, things weren't getting any better. The jeans she'd tied around him to keep the wound closed were still wrapped around his middle, but above and below them she saw the ragged ends of the huge gash in his torso. Blood covered the makeshift bandage and dripped steadily from the bottom onto the cement floor.

"Not really the time to try being funny." She lifted his arm around her shoulder. "We need you closer to that sink." How fast did his ability to heal kick in? Should he still be pale? And not even pale—his skin was gray, mottled with splatters of blood.

Together, they hobbled across the room. She eased him down into a sitting position and he braced a hand against the floor.

"Lie down and let me see what's doing under there," she said.

He actually listened and lay down on the concrete—which she took as a sign of how injured he truly was. She set her weapon on the floor next to him. He winced when she started untying the jeans, and when she got a glimpse of his wound she couldn't believe he wasn't screaming.

The raw edges were laid open and when she pulled back the pseudobandage, fresh blood streamed over his skin.

Fuck. "OK, first we gotta stop this bleeding." Why wasn't he healing like before?

She tied the jeans back up and went to the shelves to find something to use as a dressing. This wasn't a skinned knee—flushing it with water and putting a cartoon-covered bandage over it was not going to make it better. She needed thick gauze and about eight more years of schooling with a focus in surgical medicine if she was going to get him back to normal. But, seeing as she was a security guard with no more than basic first aid in her repertoire, she would have to make the best of what she could find.

When she glanced back at him, she could see he'd gone pale. If he was too quiet, she knew fear would creep up on her again, and it was the last thing either of them needed at the moment.

She needed to keep him talking. "You all right over there?"

"Still here," he said. "Not up for dancing yet, but still here."

How could he joke around at a time like this? "I'm going to find something to wrap you up with."

The first set of shelves was full of rusty, half-full paint cans and some rattraps. The next was the same except on the bottom shelf, under a thick coat of dust and rodent droppings, there were cardboard boxes. She pulled one off and onto the floor.

When she lifted the flaps, she couldn't believe her own luck. Clothing. Nothing new, but after she picked off the top layer, the stuff looked mostly clean. She dragged the box over to where he lay.

"Found something useful," she said, holding up a pink floral blouse for him to see.

"I'm not wearing that."

She laughed; it sounded about as real as faux fur. "But I think it would be perfect for your complexion."

He tried to laugh too, but all humor vanished as lines of pain arced across his face.

His features tightened and she frowned. He'd lost so much blood—was still losing it—and the wound wasn't closing up in some miraculous regenerative way. Maybe it was too deep. Maybe if she didn't go get help, he would die in this shitty, damp basement.

Right. Get moving.

She went to the sink and cranked on the hot. The pipes groaned and a flow of brownish, stinking water stuttered out of the faucet. For a moment she felt like she had the same chance down here in Hell as the famous snowball, but when she turned on the cold handle, the water cleared.

After soaking the blouse, she knelt down beside him and ran the cloth over his face. She wasn't sure why she did it— his stomach was the main issue—but the gesture soothed her somehow. Beads of sweat had gathered on his forehead and she patted the perspiration away.

A flash of memory shot through her mind of her mom dabbing a wet washcloth on her fevered forehead. The cool, cottony fabric and the worry in her mother's eyes were so clear in her head. The suddenness of the recollection stung as if someone slid a dagger between her ribs.

"What is it?" he asked.

The vision of her mom had stopped her ministrations in midstroke. "Sorry." She avoided his gaze—and any questions he might be thinking of asking—by focusing on her task.

She wiped the blood off of his chest, above the jeans. Some of it had run over his collarbones and up his neck. When the flowery shirt began to leave red streaks across his skin, she picked another out of the box, ran it under the water, and laid it over the top of his wound. She shrugged the remnants of his T-shirt off of his shoulders and untied the jeans. The legs hit the concrete with a wet smack.

The gaping slash running up his middle was violent but looked much better after she wiped away the blood. She was gentle with the edges of it even though Arden didn't so much as gasp in pain. He lay still as stone, but she saw the muscles of his jaw clenching and unclenching each time she touched the ruptured skin.

The next thing she pulled from the box was a towel. Maybe her luck was improving. After getting it wet, she folded it over the worst part of the injury. The magic box rewarded her again when she found two pairs of polyester pants at the bottom. She tied one pair around his waist and the other around his chest to hold the towel in place.

She checked the bite on his shoulder. It was nasty—red, oozy—but seemed to be starting to heal. The broken, tattooed skin was sealing up like a crack in dry dirt after rain. She wiped it off as best she could and folded a shirt over it.

"There." She relaxed back onto her heels and gave him a smile. "All done."

The warmth in his eyes made her want to stroke his jaw with her fingertips. She reached out to do it but pulled her hand back and reached for the edge of the sink instead, pulling herself up to her feet.

There was something so fundamental and instinctive about cleaning his wounds, as if she were responsible for him or something. If there was another reason, she couldn't name it without asking herself some seriously hard questions, and she didn't have the answers—didn't want to answer at all.

Who am I kidding? Caring for him didn't just make her feel responsible; it made her feel like he meant something— like his well-being mattered to her—and not just because he was escorting her through Hell to rescue Drew.

She peered down into the sink and watched as droplets of water, tinted by Arden's blood, made their way to the drain and disappeared into the empty void.

She had to get to her brother.

Soon.

Chapter Sixteen

The pain was mind-numbing. Arden could feel each of his nerves restructure and grow, reaching out to meet the outstretched hands of the other nerves to reknit their web and be whole again. His entire chest ached as if it were being burned, healed, and then scorched anew.

Nic stood at the sink above him. She was too quiet, but the excruciating sensation of his flesh mending across his abs wouldn't let him break the silence.

If she had been one of his usual female companions, he might be dead now.

But she had fought, stood strong, and dispatched that pig Ritter as if she did stuff like that every day.

Her sudden and violent action had impressed him, but the way she had cared for his wounds afterward shocked him.

So did the fact that she seemed to have forgotten she wasn't wearing any pants.

He looked over his shoulder and saw the backs of her boots. The tops stopped at the slimmest part of her calf. Her legs were lean, but he could see the muscle dancing below the surface. The smooth skin behind her knee called to him and he eyed the line of her leg up to her thigh. When she shifted, he glimpsed the dark recess of her inner thigh, and the memory of the taste of her flooded over him.

The stiffness in his pants confirmed he was well on his way to being back to normal.

In an effort to distract from his growing erection, he thought about the way she had wiped the cloth over his face; it was such a simple thing, but an intimate one. A cloud had crossed over her face when she did it, and the grayness spoke of pain. "Can I ask you something?"

His question must have startled her because she flinched. "Um...sure."

"Why are you so gung ho about going after your brother?"

She didn't turn around, but he saw her grip the edge of the sink. "He's my brother. My responsibility."

So she probably had to clean up a lot of his messes. "You've saved him before?"

"I had to. I'm all he's got. After our parents...I had to hold us together."

"What happened to your parents?"

Her fingers flexed on the lip of the sink. Her voice was almost too soft for him to hear when she answered. "They were murdered."

He knew the topic was dicey, but he couldn't just let it go. He was risking his life, chasing after some junkie. Sure he'd get the big payoff in the end, but the yawning cut up the center of his gut and the incredible pain of his regeneration made the danger of their situation all too real. And he wanted to know, why all the fucking trouble?

Then it hit him. "It was because of Drew."

She knelt down and started rummaging through the box of old clothes she'd used as bandages. He knew she was trying to avoid answering. She also avoided looking him in the eye.

"I swear I saw a pair of jeans in here." She shuffled the things around in the box over and over.

"Nic?"

She looked up and the shadow of hurt on her face made him wince. Her stony eyes had gone from ash to the gray of a rain-soaked highway. "It wasn't Drew's fault."

"What happened?"

The box commanded her full attention again. She pulled out a jacket and a pair of faded jeans. The jacket she folded and handed to him. "Here, use this for a pillow." She looked away again. She kicked off her boots and pulled on the pants. They weren't like the designer number he'd given her before, but even though she had to cuff them four times at the bottom, they still showed off her high, tight ass.

Focus, damn it. Focus. He wanted to know what had led her to being the sole caretaker of her wayward sibling. "How old were you when they died?"

Her fingers moved slowly as she fastened her belt. "Eighteen."

"How old was Drew?"

"Sixteen."

The same age when his own mother had been stolen from him. He remembered the pain, and it still tasted bitter on his tongue no matter how many decades had passed. "How did it happen?"

"I don't want to get into it right now, OK?"

"Look, I know you don't want to answer. But as you can see, I'm putting myself in harm's way. I want all the information I can get." He also wanted to know what made her toughen up into the person she'd become.

She sighed and sat down on the floor, staring at the toes of her boots. "I was away at college. Drew was selling pot out of the house to his friends, but then I guess he decided to get more hard-core and move a little coke and meth. He was an idiot and bragged to everyone about how much cash he was making. One night, a couple of his tweaker clients decided to break in and take Drew's stash and his money. My parents came home and interrupted them." She rubbed her palms on her knees. "They slit my dad's throat while my mom watched. Then they strangled her with a lamp cord."

Her face was as still as a marble sculpture and just as coldly beautiful. The sight of her vulnerability triggered something powerful inside of him. He would kill to have the names of the ones who had wronged her, because he would find them and show them what Hell was *really* about.

"As it turns out, Drew had been shooting meth for at least six months. So, I left school and took over guardianship of my brother with my aunt's help," she said. "I was going to be a cop, but the closest tech school only offered a security guard program."

"Didn't he stop?"

"After my parents..." She shook her head. "He got clean for a while. Even finished high school. But then something just kind of snapped in his head and it was all downhill from there."

"And you've always taken care of him."

"I had to. I was his big sister. It was my responsibility." She glanced up at him and tears stood in her eyes.

Arden didn't hesitate—couldn't stop. He sat up and gathered her into his arms.

———

Nic didn't know if it was the stress that had been building inside her or the sting of the memories that made his arms feel so good, but she didn't care. She pressed her cheek against his bare shoulder and let the tears fall while she inhaled the fiery scent of his skin.

He held her without words, but soon enough she started to get uncomfortable with the closeness. She didn't want his sympathy. She'd had enough of that from all the people who came to her parents' funeral and then disappeared off the face of the earth. She pressed her hands against his chest to push away and he cringed. In her hurry to get away, she'd forgotten his wound. "Shit. I'm sorry."

Arden tucked a finger under her chin and lifted her face. "It's all right. I'm mostly better."

When she looked into his eyes she expected to see the pity she hated. Instead, the frigid fire was back and blazing; it made heat spread across her skin. Her hands lingered on his chest. The muscle under her palms flexed when he leaned toward her.

Nothing about it was right, and it didn't make a bit of sense, but she wanted him to kiss her. If only to push away reality for a little while.

The moment his lips touched hers, thoughts of consequences and responsibilities disappeared. It was the softest kiss, like an impossible whisper, and she wanted more.

He was gentle, and so warm, but the hammering demand of her body could only respond with ferocity. She snaked her hands over his shoulders and dug into the flesh of his back, forcing their lips together. Her teeth ground against the inside of her lips. It hurt, but she welcomed the pain.

She heard a moan and didn't know if it came from him, or her, or both. He thrust his hands into the long part of her hair and forced her head back. His tongue parted her lips and slid inside her mouth.

The sight of the bloody, angry gash on him was fresh in her mind and she wanted to be cautious, but with one smooth motion her worries were obliterated. He pushed her back onto the floor and loomed above her. He broke away from the kiss and went for her neck, biting into the tender skin and weaving a trail of fire down to her collarbone.

She yanked at the hem of her shirt, needing to bare herself, to feel his skin on her own. "Off. I need it off."

He smiled. "Yes."

Slow—so slow—he lifted the bottom of her shirt. He ran his fingertips over every inch of skin he uncovered with feather strokes. The powerful mix of her urgency and his delicate handling intoxicated her, and she shivered.

She reached for him—needed to feel his skin under her fingers—but he dodged away.

"Not so fast," he said. "I want to see all of you."

He lifted the shirt over her head and tossed it aside. His hands traced the curves of her shoulders and followed the line of her bra down her sides and across her stomach. His palms spread over each of her hips, and his thumbs dug into the hollows beside her pelvic bones, dipping down inside her secondhand jeans. Her hips lifted and she bit into her lip until she tasted the salty tang of blood.

He wasn't fast enough. She wanted him inside her, ramming into her, and bruising her flesh on the concrete floor.

What the fuck am I doing? The thought struck her skull, an ax thrust right into the middle of her need. *I can't do this.*

She tried to scramble out from under him, but he straddled her knees. "I said I wanted to see all of you." He grinned, crooked and sexier than anything she'd ever seen. "Don't make me tie you up."

The thought of being bound by him sent a fresh flood of wetness between her legs. She wanted this.

No, she wanted to get away.

She closed her eyes when he took hold of her hands and brought them up to his lips. He kissed her palms and then licked the length of one forefinger before pulling it into his mouth.

When he released her arms, she opened her eyes and shoved at him. He didn't move. She tried to buck him off by rocking her hips, but the friction almost made her come right then and there.

He grinned. It was a smile the devil himself would have envied.

There wasn't any point in resisting. He wanted this. She wanted—no, *needed*—this. And the sooner she accepted it, the faster he would be inside her.

He slid the jeans down over her hips and then she watched his slow, deliberate motions become frantic, like he was just as desperate as she. Her underwear and socks got yanked off with the jeans and thrown across the room. He kept his stare locked with hers as he ran his hands up the insides of her legs and spread her thighs apart. If it had been anyone else staring at her the way he was now, she might have been frightened. But her need burned too hot and the desire she saw in his gaze erased all fear.

He moved up and over her, reached around her back, and undid the clasp of her bra. He dragged the straps down her arms and flung the garment off into a darkened corner.

Once again she was naked and at his mercy. Her traitorous brain flashed to the last time she'd been like this with him. The rejection she'd felt when he had walked out of the bedroom zoomed to the forefront of her mind and she knew this had to stop.

But before she had the chance to do anything about it, his mouth found hers again. This time she felt the frantic intensity in his kiss as his lips crashed over hers. His tongue was merciless. There would be no stopping. Not for her and, she hoped, not for him either.

He broke off the kiss and made quick work of undoing the makeshift bandages. His flesh had mended, leaving nothing but a thin line of scarred skin down the center of him. He bent down and kissed her. The feel of his skin against her own was a revelation, and when his fingers traced the delicate flesh of her nipple, she shuddered. She felt the hard thickness of his erection through his jeans when he ground it into her hips.

She wrenched her mouth free and fumbled for his zipper. He shoved her hands to the side and undid it himself. With one hand braced on the floor beside her, he kicked off his boots and tore the pants down his legs.

She sucked in a breath at the sight of him. His body was broad, hard muscle, and every inch of him glistened with a sheen of sweat. The angels covering his skin framed every muscle, defined every inch of him, and moved with him in a perfect blessed rhythm.

When she traced the winged edge of his ribs and ran a finger along the edge of the fading bite mark on his shoulder, he groaned. "Does it still hurt?"

"Nothing hurts when you touch me."

A flush stole through her. If she was in this all the way, then she wasn't going to hold back. "Then you won't mind if I touch you more."

She slid her palm across his chest and then lower. He hissed when she touched the head of his erection. His hips surged forward and she clutched the hard shaft in her hand, stroking up and down.

Not letting go, she used her other hand to pull his face down to hers. When she felt the brush of his lips, it made her brave. She squeezed him and whispered at the same time. "I want to feel this inside me."

He strained against her hand. She dared to steal a glance at his face. His eyes had changed again—the pupils were wide, darker than a night sky in winter, and the rich emerald green had spread until there was almost no white around them.

But suddenly he stopped moving and looked away. A muscle twitched in his jaw. Then he moved from over the top of her and knelt on the floor, not speaking and not meeting her eyes.

It hit her then. The same thing as before. "You don't want me." How could she have been so stupid?

She had thrown caution to the wind. Maybe even risked her chance at saving Drew. All because he had taken her in his arms and comforted her. *You fucking idiot, Nic.*

And just when she didn't care anymore, he had stopped everything.

The answer was simple; he just couldn't lower himself to having sex with a human. She had been an idiot to think otherwise.

But their agreement. Why would he offer his help only for sex in return if it was so unappealing to him? He must have something else riding on this, but what?

She needed to know. "What's in this for you?"

He tensed. "I don't know what you mean."

"Don't give me that shit." She propped herself up on an elbow so she could see his face better. "You know exactly what I'm asking."

"No, I don't."

"Why did you agree to help me in return for sex when you so obviously don't want me?"

In a flash he was on top of her, crushing her into the concrete. "You think I don't want you?"

His mouth was like fire when he latched on to her breast. She could feel his hot tongue flick against her nipple and she arched into his lips.

He dipped lower, licked a path down her ribs to her hip, and nipped her flesh. Goosebumps broke out over her skin. All her nerves awakened to his mouth.

He pushed her thighs apart and ran his palm over her sex. The heat of his hand incinerated any barrier she had left.

She watched as he slid his forefinger along her, dragging it through the soaked crevice. His touch roared through her—a fire without end. He met her eyes as he licked the moisture from his fingertip before sliding it deep inside. A moan escaped from her mouth when he pressed his lips against her wetness. She arched into him when he smoothed his lips across her skin. He nibbled at her, sucked her, and slid his hot tongue inside her, stroking and plunging over and over.

He moved back up above her. She mourned the loss of his tongue from between her legs until he stroked the tip of his cock over her hardened clit. When he kissed her, she mouthed his name against his lips and he growled.

The world fell away. Nothing mattered. Nothing existed except for his body and hers, and the way they moved together.

His hand slipped around her back and he pulled her up by her hips. The impossibly hard tip of his erection pressed into her, slow...so slow. Her sex clenched, clinging to him, desperate to have him deeper.

She raked her nails down his back and he drove into her. She could feel the muscles beneath his hot skin twitch. Fire bloomed in her as he pumped in and out with fierce, deliberate strokes. The flames grew to a firestorm, twisting and tightening, singeing her from the inside.

He grabbed her hips and rolled onto his back so she straddled him, her hands braced on his chest. The new position forced him even deeper. Her thighs burned as she rocked up and back, riding him, relishing the feel of him.

All the tension within her tightened, a knot pulled ever more firm. Her vision zoomed into a sharp, blinding pinpoint. She squeezed her eyes shut, and with another thrust her universe exploded. Ripples rode through her. She cried out and shuddered as pulses of pleasure racked her body.

Arden didn't stop. He grabbed her hips, lifted her up, and then shoved her back down. She arched her back—her orgasm hadn't stopped either. His fingertips dug into her skin as he moved her back and forth.

The skin of his chest was slick with sweat and she lost her hold. She slipped into his arms as he sat up, clutching her to him. He palmed the small of her back with one hand and the other gripped her shoulder, pushing her down.

Without warning, another climax flooded over her. He thrust harder, faster, as she throbbed around his cock.

Then, with a final push, all his muscles seized up at once. A rough, animalistic noise erupted from him as he spilled inside her. He shuddered hard and pressed her head against his chest. The breath came from his lungs in great heaves and stirred the hair on top of her head.

She inhaled the scent of him—she dared to hope it would stay on her skin like a mark; a perfumed tattoo reminder of this moment, of the way he held her clutched in his arms. Afraid to move or speak for fear of reality returning, Nic hovered somewhere between pleasure and pain. What had she done?

"The sun will rise soon," he said. Just like that, the moment was over.

She hadn't noticed the change in the room; the darkness had begun its retreat already. Wan morning light filtered through the muck-covered windows, but she didn't want to move, didn't want it to be over. But just like the relentless dawn, reality had returned.

Her voice sounded like that of a stranger when she spoke. "I guess we should get dressed."

———

Arden grabbed a black, long-sleeved dress shirt from the stack of clothes left in the box and shrugged into it. As he did up the buttons, he realized he could still smell the soft saltiness of her sweat on his skin. When she turned her back, he pressed his palms to his nose.

She was the scent of things lost to him and things he didn't dare wish for.

Nic reeked of salvation.

"Which way do we go from here?" she asked.

Now, that's a good question. But he didn't know the real answer. "I'll take a look at the maps and see. Chase left a mark to show us the next gate."

"Good, because…" Her voice trailed off.

He could tell by the look on her face, and the way her hand flew to where her weapon was supposed to be on her hip, that something was wrong. "What?"

Then he heard it too. Voices. Shouting from the floor above them. He rushed over to stand between her and the stairs. If someone came down, they would have to face him first.

Even though he had told her it might be pointless, she bent down and picked up her weapon. If it kept her calm, that was fine with him. One whiff of her fear, he had no doubt, would bring every demon within a block crashing down the stairs.

He scanned the basement for another exit but there was none. They were cornered.

A shower of dust from the ceiling rained down on their heads as something above thumped to the floor. There was more shouting and another thump followed by a curse.

He glanced over his shoulder at Nic and pressed a finger to his mouth. She nodded and tightened her grip on the gun.

Chapter Seventeen

Sorro tasted the closeness of the human who sought his captive. On his tongue, it had the flavor of a steak left out in the sun for a week, then cooked for six seconds—maggots included—and served with rotten mayonnaise.

Time to get the junkie moving. It wouldn't do for the female to get *too* close. His orders were to keep the brother just out of her reach until they got down to the Fourth.

His employer had given him a priceless bit of info about the Princes—the farther they got from the First, the weaker their Gifts became. And not even the great Asmodeus knew of his sons' weakness. By the time he lured the pair down to the Fourth, the First Born would be practically mortal himself. It would be a piece of cake to make them all disappear.

Then he would be free, but he had every intention of playing with them first. The thought made him smile and his heart ached for the promise of what was to come.

If only he could have more bearable companions, this might be the easiest job he'd ever done.

"Hey, Sorro, is this guy OK?"

Flic was over in the corner, watching Drew as he paced back and forth. The human had injected himself with the poison and then proceeded to go completely off-the-charts berserk. He mumbled to himself and then headed back across the room, running his hands through his hair over and over. He stopped, glanced at Flic, backed all the way to the other end of the apartment, and paced some more.

"He's fine," Sorro said. "That's what happens to them when the drug gets in their system."

Flic stood and ran over to stand in Drew's path. The human didn't even respond—just changed his course and kept going. "Whoa, it's like he doesn't even see me. And he's talking to himself like we're not even here. Freaky."

Sorro resisted the urge to waltz over and kick the adolescent's teeth in. He'd chosen Flic because of his stupidity but was now coming to realize how much extra work it took to train a lackey.

He took a deep breath and reminded himself again of the reward he was going to get for this job. As much as he hated having the kid around, he needed him. "You have to go back out."

"No way, man. It's still kinda dark out there."

"You're going back out," he said. *Or I'm going to reach down your throat and rip out your vocal cords so I don't have to listen to your fucking voice for another second.* "You have to make sure our route is unblocked."

"But—"

"No." The anger awoke inside Sorro like an ancient serpent uncoiling from a disturbed slumber; it snaked through his muscles and sank its fangs into his mind. "You are going."

Flic must have sensed the change in his boss's demeanor because he didn't say another word. He got up and slinked toward the door. If he had been a dog, his tail would have been tucked up underneath him.

Sorro waited until he heard the boy's footsteps retreat down the stairs and the door at the bottom open and close. Then, he went over to where the human stood, staring at a wall and picking at a scab on his cheek. "Time to go. Your sister is close. Can't let her get us, can we?"

"Nope." A trickle of blood trailed down Drew's cheek. "She won't stop me."

"Good boy."

Sorro stepped away as the male started pacing again. He had never understood addiction. All that chasing and chasing for something—some high—just out of reach had always seemed so pointless and stupid to him. But now that he had the chance to break free, to spend eternity in bliss, he understood the chase very well.

He figured that made him a junkie too.

———

Nic wanted to say something—anything. She had to know if she'd just compromised her chances of getting to Drew, but there wasn't time. They had to get out of the basement. And since the room still carried the scent of arousal, she was inclined to vacate it ASAP. Her questions could wait.

After listening to footsteps across the ceiling above, and more muffled conversation, the unmistakable sound of a door slamming had been followed by silence.

Arden stood halfway up the stairs. He turned back and held up his hand, palm flat, parallel with the ground. Was he telling her to keep quiet? She rolled her eyes and waggled the Ruger at him. His response was to do the *be quiet* motion again.

In a blink, it was back to him giving orders and her following them. Oh, she would give him a reprieve for now, but she would get answers. The rollercoaster game was getting old. Ancient, even. One minute he's holding her as if she were something precious and the next he's ordering her around like she's an idiot. She refused to be toyed with.

Oh yeah? Then why did you have sex with him?

Nic wanted, more than anything, to figure out how to turn off the voice of her conscience. She didn't have time for those questions and she really didn't want to examine the situation any further at the moment.

You need to.

Just shut up.

While she was busy arguing with herself, Arden had crept up another three steps. She couldn't help but appreciate his catlike grace; he could move his tall, hard-muscled frame without sound. She considered herself agile, but in comparison it made her feel clumsy and awkward.

It also made memories of the way he had moved inside her flood her mind. At least he was turned the other way. She didn't want him to see the blush that stained her cheeks as he paused at the door, listening.

She had never had problems with claustrophobia, but the basement suddenly shrank until she swore she could feel the ceiling grazing her hair. The dampness and the telltale scent of sex in the air made it hard to breathe. She needed to get out—away. The adrenaline rushing in her system added to the mix. And there were too many thoughts running through her head. She needed action. She needed conflict. Anything to distract from the urge to push him aside and throw open the door on whoever or whatever stood beyond it.

She took a deep breath and held it until she thought she would burst. Her fingertip stroked the trigger of the nine, letting its cool, satiny touch give her focus.

He must have been satisfied they were alone because he opened the door and stepped out into the hallway. She was on his ass without a pause. Red daylight streamed into the building from the front windows and she sucked down a huge lungful of un-sex-scented air.

Her regret was immediate, though. The stench of death filled the hallway.

A bundle of dirty carpeting stood propped up by the front door, and sticking out of the end, a bloody hand. Two of the fingers were missing, and by the looks of things they had been either bitten or ripped off.

"Well," Arden said, "that explains the smell." He walked over and peeked into the end of the carpet. His mouth pulled down into a tight line and he backed away. "Someone had a bad night...or a really good one."

"I'm gonna go with bad. Think that explains all the commotion upstairs?"

He didn't answer before he opened the front door and stepped out into the day, leaving her to trail after him. Again.

The aloof treatment had been tolerable before. This morning it had new bite. The incredible sex might have been just that—sex—but she couldn't help thinking somehow it would've changed the dynamic between them.

Nope.

And he wasn't even looking back to make sure she followed.

"Hey." She grabbed his arm. "Aren't you even going to tell me where we're going?"

He looked down at her hand on his sleeve and then back at her face, his expression unreadable. "First of all, you need to put your weapon back into your pack before someone sees it." He shook off her hold. "And you need to keep quiet. This end of the Second is rough even during the day. We can't afford to be spotted."

Oh boy. *Stay calm, Nic.* "Look, you need to get something through your thick skull. Whether you like it or not, we're in this together." So much for keeping her cool. Her face heated in pace with her temper. "And I'm not going to put up with any more of your orders until you tell me the plan."

"The 'plan,'" he sneered her word back at her, "is to get to the gate as soon as possible without getting in another brawl."

"I have the necklace, remember."

"Yeah, and we saw how well that worked the last time."

The sting to her pride over how she'd let fear get the better of her and almost gotten them both killed, coupled with leftover emotions from the basement, made for an acid brew in her stomach.

Pick your battles. Her mom's words and some of the greatest relationship advice she'd ever heard. Not that she and Arden were in a relationship or anything, but still.

Drew needed her. "OK, I'll follow. I'll even be quiet, but I at least want a clue as to where we're going."

"The Third is where we're going. Follow my orders and we'll get along just fine, Trickster."

To keep from smacking the smile off his face, she crossed her arms. "Stop calling me that."

"It suits you."

"I don't even want to know." Even though she sort of liked the way he smiled when he said it. She put her frustration away. "Let's get moving."

He didn't respond, just walked down the sidewalk away from the building.

In the light of day, the area looked worse than she thought it would. *Way* ghetto seemed the best way she could think of to describe it. Dilapidated structures that had *never* been nice once upon a time lined the narrow street. Garbage was piled everywhere and she'd even seen some crack vials and a couple of discarded hypodermics. Lewd but colorful graffiti decorated the boarded-up buildings. Twice she had to dart around the feet of a sleeping derelict.

Arden kept quiet. She didn't feel very talkative either. And as the silence lengthened, she got uncomfortable. Was she supposed to make small talk? Didn't regular people do that after they had incredible sex together?

Thanks for the good time? Here's my number, but don't call me?

Not that she had a lot of experience to compare it with. She hadn't been in a relationship in a while. She refused to count the idiot she'd dated when she was away at school. What a disaster that had turned out to be.

She had seen him one last time before she left U of M for good. Right after her parents were in the ground. After screwing in his tiny dorm room bed, Mike had dumped her. He said she was too controlling and her life was nothing but drama.

She'd wanted to knock him over the head with his Baltimore Orioles signed game bat.

Since then she had suffered the occasional flirtation, a few coffee dates, and a few instances of disappointing sex. She went out of her way to avoid the advances of male co-workers, or even the eighteen-year-old kid who made her morning latte and insisted it was on the house every day. Her life was complicated enough dealing with Drew. The last thing she needed was a relationship. The only male who had managed to find a place in her heart in the last ten years was William, her goldfish. Of course, she didn't even know if he was indeed a male.

William.

"Oh no." A vision of him belly-up in his aquarium filled her head. "No."

Arden spun around. He eyed the buildings on either side of the road, searching for attackers. "What is it?"

The words clogged up her throat. "It's William."

"Who's William?" He scanned the street. "Where?"

"He's not here, damn it."

"Who the fuck is William?"

She blinked and swallowed. "My goldfish."

If she hadn't been so upset she would have laughed at the look on Arden's face; he looked like a man about to either have a stroke or die from asphyxiation. His shaggy black hair hung down, shading his eyes, but his jaw was clenched and his face started to turn red. He was going to start laughing any minute, and when he did she was going to clock him.

"Don't you dare laugh at me."

A sputtering noise bubbled out of his mouth. "I wouldn't dream of laughing at you for worrying about a fish."

"Go ahead." She crossed her arms. "I know it's killing you."

He let out a bark of laughter and she smiled despite herself. The sound of his laughter eased the tension in her neck.

When he regained control she gave him a mean look. "It's really not that funny."

"Consider it from my perspective," he said. "The woman who literally went to Hell to save her brother from demons is about to cry over a disposable pet."

"William is not 'disposable.'" She couldn't avoid the pout she heard in her voice. Her fish, like her Ruger, was one of the few things that made her happy.

Arden closed the distance between them and, with his finger under her chin, lifted her face to meet his stare. "I'm sure he will be just fine."

His light touch and the softness in his eyes sent a chill over her skin and a thrill...lower. How was it possible that something so simple could send her hormones into freakout mode?

"But if he doesn't get fed..."

"William will be fine." He cupped her face in his hand, and his thumb rubbed over her cheek.

She leaned into his warm palm. If she didn't watch her step, she would end up kissing him again, and that would get them exactly nowhere. Fast.

Damn it, damn it, damn it. What am I doing here?

His fingers flexed on her neck and his head bent down.

Tires screamed on pavement down the street. She turned to the noise. The car fishtailed around the corner and spun out into the intersection, pointed back the way it had come. The driver braked, reversed, and plowed up onto the sidewalk half a block down from where they stood.

Then the driver floored it.

Nic shouted, but the car kept coming. It ran headlong into a huge pile of trash, and litter burst into the air over the hood. The roar of the engine filled her head. She held her hands out in front of her as if that would do anything to stop the inevitable. The driver sped up and the grill of the car sped closer, larger. Twenty feet. Ten.

Then, a jerk on her arm, and Arden yanked her out of its path. They fell back against the hard brick building with a thud. He smashed her between himself and the wall, the air whooshing out of her lungs.

The unmistakable groan of crumpling metal signaled the end of the car's journey. When she peeked out of the protective circle of his arms she saw the smashed remnants sticking out of the building across the street. As she watched, the female driver crawled out of the mess, kicked some debris out of her way, and staggered onto the pavement.

It might have come from training, or from the way she was raised, but Nic's Samaritan instinct kicked in. "We should go check on her."

"No, we most certainly will *not*."

She planted her hands on his chest and shoved him off. He grabbed for her arm but she dodged him and sprinted over to the woman. "Are you OK?"

The driver looked up at her from beneath a waterfall of frizzy blonde bangs and gave her a lopsided grin, revealing three missing teeth and a lack of lipstick application skill; the red of it was smeared all over the edges of her mouth and onto her chin. Long streaks of smudged eyeliner trailed down her pockmarked cheeks.

Those aren't acne scars; those are scales.

Nic pushed the thought away and stared at the woman. Her dark eyes never really focused on anything and her pupils were the size of nickels even though the red sun proclaimed daylight.

She was wasted. And judging from the outfit, a prostitute. Or just a really bad dresser. She had on a black miniskirt that didn't cover much, snagged red stockings, and a pair of sparkly platform heels, all topped with a stained purple bustier.

Her hands shook as she tried to light the wrong end of her cigarette. "Stupid fucking lighter." A thick line of blood crawled down her forehead and over one eyebrow.

The woman—demon—didn't react to the blood even when it trailed down into her eye. "Are you OK?" Nic asked again.

The hooker came around a bit and glared. "What's it to you?"

"Nothing," Arden said. Nic hadn't heard him come up behind her. He tugged on her sleeve. "We just saw the crash and wanted to see some blood."

The hooker demon smeared her hand across her brow and held it out to them, her fingers dripping. "Here ya go."

Nic cringed away and the female's nostrils flared. She threw the unlit cigarette to the ground and her eyes focused in on Nic's face.

"Somethin' ain't right about you..."

Arden grabbed Nic's arm and dragged her away. "The necklace, damn it. Your shirt's covering it up."

The woman followed them. "Hey, man, don't I know you? And who's that with you? She looks...weird."

"Shit." Nic reached up and pulled the necklace out.

As soon as the charm was visible, the hooker stopped, blinked a couple of times, and staggered back over to the smashed-up car.

When they got farther away down the street, Nic puffed out a relieved breath. "Well, that was interesting."

Arden stopped midstride and took hold of her wrist. "Next time you decide to get all Little Miss Do-Gooder, ask me first."

"I can't help it. It's part of what I do."

"You mean it's part of who you *are*. You see someone hurt, you want to help them. It's a human response."

"And what's wrong with that?"

"Things don't work that way here. If you show interest in someone's pain, it better be because you're enjoying it."

Just because they were demons, they didn't help each other out? "That's dumb."

"No, it's not dumb. It's fact."

"Whatever," she said.

He threw his hands up in the air and began to walk away. "This is exactly why I asked my father for the necklace. I knew you wouldn't be able to get through this without showing your humanity."

That was the very last straw. Hurt feelings she could handle. She'd had plenty of those. Most recently because of him. But discrediting her whole species just because she had some personality quirks, including the desire to help others in need? She stomped across the concrete and stopped in front of him. "What is your problem?"

"My 'problem' is you never listen." He glared at her and crossed his arms. "This is not your home. You don't understand the game down here. The only kind of human who belongs in Hell is a dead one."

Wow. "Oh, I see. It's not just *me* in particular, it's my species? At least we have the capacity for compassion and sympathy and love."

Fuck. She hadn't meant to say that last thing, but it was out now. Nothing to be done about it.

His eyes flashed darker green. "Yep. You're also weak and have more evil in you than we do."

"It was a *human* who saved your ass in that alley last night," she said, poking a finger into his chest.

"Yeah, and it was one of *you* that killed my mother."

Episode Six

Chapter Eighteen

Shock hit Nic like a slap in the face. She stepped back. "I thought it was a demon who killed her." The info dropped a huge wrench in her perception of things. Before she'd agreed to his offer of help to get her brother back, she'd had a clear understanding of the basics—good and evil. No crossovers. No deviations. Sure, humans were capable of evil too, but she thought demons were all bad, all the time. And now, besides traipsing through the *real* Hell, having all of her preconceptions about the place blown into oblivion, she had to accept more horrors.

On top of that, she had to resist the urge to comfort Arden while every cell in her body longed to reach out to him, pull him to her chest, and wrap her arms around him to ease his pain.

"No, she was betrayed while on earth." He started walking again, and she matched him step for step, refusing to miss one word. "My mother's twin was dying and she was desperate to see her. She ignored my father's warnings and went up to say good-bye. That's when she was taken."

"But why...who?"

"A religious zealot. My aunt had confessed my mother's perceived sin to her priest and the man was insane. He waited for her, counting on her connection to her sister. Then he stabbed her in the heart." He paused and shook his head. "The wife of a demon, yes, but an innocent, slaughtered by a man of the cloth."

"Not all of us are believers."

"I know that. But if it weren't for my mother's humanity, her human need to see her sister, she would still be alive. Her human heart made her weak."

"Not all humans are weak."

His eyes glinted. "If my mother were a demon, she would still be alive."

A retort hovered on her lips. All creatures—human, demon, and any other kind she'd yet to learn of—had the capacity for vileness. But nothing she could say would undo all that had been done. He believed humans weak, brutal, betrayers.

And that meant any closeness she had felt while wrapped in his embrace was nothing more than good old-fashioned physical attraction on his end. Lust, plain and simple.

She might be *only* human, but she wasn't stupid. Although if she'd been lucky enough to be anything other than human, the knowledge that he'd just been getting his rocks off wouldn't hurt as much.

The weight of his stare lingered, but she refused to look at him. Without a word, he turned and headed down another alley. She followed, unspoken words clogging up her throat. He had to know there was more to humans than what he'd experienced, right? Did he think there was more to *her* than that? She doubted he'd ever be able to see beyond the past.

And she *didn't* care, she reminded herself. His opinions didn't matter...did they?

While she'd been busy inside her head, he'd led them down another alley—a dead end. In the center of a brick wall, a black door stood between two overflowing Dumpsters. On its surface, a sloppy spray-painted *3* appeared pink in the glow from the ever-red sky. She didn't know what she had really been expecting, but a plain, unguarded door in the back of an alley was a little anticlimactic. Especially after her experience with Big Jackie.

"That's it?"

"Yep." He slung off his backpack and unzipped the top. After pulling out a map and stuffing it into the front of his shirt, he slid the pack behind the closest Dumpster. "There won't be any place safe for our stuff down there and it will probably be too hot to lug these around. Take out whatever you need and stash your pack."

More good news. "What will I need?"

"I think Remy put a sandwich in there for you. I'd bring that and a bottle of water."

"And my weapon?"

He rolled his eyes. "If you have to, stick it in the back of your pants, but leave the belt."

Since he let her hold on to the nine, she complied. The old jeans she'd found were a little loose and the extra room allowed for space in her pockets, but not enough for her second magazine after she tucked away the other items. She held the extra clip in her hand a moment, fingers clenching around the metal.

"All set?"

"I guess."

Arden gave her a hard look. "It's going to be different than it was here."

"OK."

"The Third is…worse. I've never been, but as the levels rise in number, so does the chaos."

"Gotcha. Lovely." Should she sacrifice food for ammo and leave the sandwich behind? What would be the point? The extra rounds wouldn't work anyway.

"And this door isn't like the last one either," he said. "This one will be like the crossing ceremony."

She hoped he wasn't talking about the weird sucking feeling. That hadn't felt good at all. "No stairs this time. Check."

He chuckled, but there was no laughter in his eyes. "Don't let go of me."

"What happens if I do?"

"You explode into a million tiny fragments of yourself and live out eternity swirling in the Abyss."

Her heart sped up inside of her chest. She struggled to rein herself back in.

"And the fear thing?" A ghost danced behind his eyes. "You're going to have to watch it. Closely."

She nodded and tried to shove the trusty internal lid back over her emotions as he took hold of her arm and leaned down until their eyes were level. She could see flecks of white in the frosty green of his gaze, and having him that close sent a ripple over her skin. "I need more than a nod. I need you to remember to control your fear."

When you look at me like that, Arden, I'm not afraid at all. "I will remember."

Arden nodded, locked hands with her, and then opened the door.

She didn't even have time to adjust to the new space because as soon as he closed the door, everything dropped away.

It was like someone had turned on a giant vacuum and she was nothing more than dust snatched up into its mechanical guts. Her knees turned to jelly along with her ankles; her heart bottomed out to meet her stomach. She gulped for air, fighting to catch her breath.

It was a thousand times worse than before. The air around them had become like an entity: a crazed, malicious animal tearing at her flesh and sinking its fangs into her consciousness. Angry, nebulous streaks of color blurred her vision, and her eyes filled with tears. She squeezed them shut against the assault but could still feel it pressing down on her, squashing her into herself as if it wanted her to disappear or become one with the madness.

A scream burst from her mouth but was lost to the chaos. The first fine strings of panic threaded through her blood and somehow the air knew. It spun into a tornado of hatred and started sucking her into its cyclonic embrace.

Arden's hand began to slip from her own. Nic scrambled to hold on. Then she felt thick arms around her and she mashed her face into his chest to keep out the thing—whatever it was in the air—threatening to rip out her mind and tear her soul to pieces. She screamed again and again.

At the last moment, when hopelessness descended over her like a thick woolen blanket and she knew all was lost, they hit the ground.

Arden hit first. She landed on top of him, still locked inside the protective guard of his arms. Panic raced through her and she wrestled to free herself from his clutches, flailing her arms and pounding her fists against his chest.

She could still feel the swirling aberration clinging to her skin, sucking at her pores as if to drink the sweat of her fear.

———

Arden grabbed her arms. He shook her as her eyes darted back and forth, not focusing on anything. Her mouth opened and closed with screams but no sound broke from her lips.

"Look at me, damn it." He let go of one wrist and grabbed her jaw, forcing her eyes to meet his. "Come back."

Her gaze danced one more time and then settled on his face. "Arden?"

"I'm here. It's all right."

"Fuck. Fuck that was bad." She leaned forward and sucked in air.

He let out the breath he'd been holding and pushed her hair out of her face. "Take some deep breaths." What if he'd lost her?

He had figured the crossings would be hard on her, but he'd never expected something like this. And what would happen if they had to do it again? Would the next crossing break her mind? The thought sat in his gut like a boulder.

Nic didn't protest when he pulled her into his arms; a sure sign that she was shaken up. He stroked her hair, soothed by the softness of it on his palm. Scenting her fear was one thing. Feeling her slip into all-out panic was a different monster altogether. It threatened to awaken something inside of him, something he refused to let live, and yet it was here, with her cradled in his arms. His response—tender, careful—was unnatural and, he realized, human. He should have been disgusted by it, revolted, but with Nic, it seemed...right.

No. He had to stop making her safe. She was a pawn. Why did he need to keep reminding himself of the facts?

She stirred and looked up at him through her dark lashes. "I don't think I want to do that again."

"Let's hope we don't have to," he lied.

"Help me up."

Good. If he had her that close to him for another second, he would be tempted to…to what? Fuck her again or comfort her? He pulled her to her feet and took two steps away from her. "Better now?"

She dusted off her jeans and checked her weapon. "I think so."

"Crossing can be a bit rough."

"That's putting it mildly, don't you think? Does it feel as bad for you?"

"Like your brain is getting sucked out of your nostrils?"

"Pretty much, but there was something else." She bit her lip and shook her head. "It wanted me."

"Wanted you?"

"Yeah, like it was trying to swallow me."

Strange. In the crossing they traveled along the edge of the Abyss, but no cognizant thing existed there. "You were scared and understandably so, but there's nothing out there."

"I'm telling you," she said, "there was something in that place and it was trying to eat me."

"You're so sweet they would love to have you, so hold on tight."

His mother's words. Back when it was safer for her to do so, she would take him to earth. She'd called the adventures their "field trips." During his very first crossing, she told him creatures from Above, ones that hated demons, swirled in the Abyss. They sifted through the particles, searching for souls to reclaim. If they found him, they might snatch him up too.

But if that's what Nic had sensed, it didn't add up. Angels didn't frighten humans.

"It felt vengeful, angry. Like it would tear me apart."

"I'm sure it was nothing," he said. He almost believed his own words.

Chapter Nineteen

They had walked about a mile before Arden realized he was holding her hand. He didn't even remember reaching for it. Why would he have done that?

He corrected his loss of reason and dropped her hand to pull the map out from inside of his shirt. The only landmarks were the few haggard shacks alongside the road, huddled together under the brutal red sun. More dust-blown paths veered off in every direction. There was no way he would have been able to navigate without the maps. He had to remember to thank Chase.

Well, if and when he saw him again. He drove the thought from his mind as fast as he could, but the feel of it lingered. Once he was full demon, how would his brothers react? Pissed off and out for blood—his blood—most likely.

Maybe they'd all be glad to be done with him. Maybe they'd even forget he was their brother.

The sparse surroundings didn't help his turn in thoughts. The place looked like one of earth's third-world slums...on a good day. Not a cloud crossed the stretch of the crimson sky and the heat intensified with every step. It only looked to be about noon and he could feel sweat dampening his clothes.

Nic pulled the bottle of water out of her pocket and took a careful sip before handing it to him. As he drank, he looked over the map and marveled at his brother's ability.

Chase had never been here himself, but he used his Gift to render an accurate model of the landscape. It was brilliant in detail down to the number of shanties on the road that led to...not a town. On the map, it looked more like a pile of random pieces of rock stacked up all together and surrounded by a wall, and then a scattering of more shacks on the outskirts. He and Nic stood on what seemed like the main road, but there were no viable options for shelter or rest. No hiding either, which bothered him because it meant no hiding Nic to keep her safe.

The sun's reflection off of the necklace around her neck blinded him for a moment, and he hoped it would do the same to anyone who crossed their path—blind them to her humanity.

"We've got about another mile of walking before we get to the center of things," he said. "It looks like we should be able to skirt around the edges to check the place out."

"What, you don't think we should just saunter in through the front gates?" She grinned as she took another drink of water.

Her ability to find humor in the situation amazed him. He grinned back at her. "I know, let's just waltz in there screaming Sorro's name and see what happens."

She laughed and the sound was like a cool breeze against his skin. But as fast as it had come, it was gone. "Make sure the necklace is out at all times."

"Of course." Nic reached up and ran her fingers over the star. She pulled on the chain and arranged it so the pendant was lying right over her heart. "Good?"

It would look better if you were naked. "Yes." He stuffed the map back inside his shirt and resisted the urge to hold out his hand to her.

Arden headed down the road with Nic next to him. When they made it to the outskirts of town, he wove them a path in and out of alleys, always keeping to the shadows on the edges of the dirt streets. Windowless shanties lined the narrow alleyways and the place stank like a public toilet. Trash lay in heaps in doorways. The place was as still as a ghost town. Or a morgue.

Wait a minute. The place was as quiet, if not more so, than the Second when they'd first arrived there. Why?

The route they'd taken through the Second and the path they were currently on had only one thing in common—Sorro.

It didn't make sense. The demon had almost a full two days' head start. What had taken him so long? Plus, Sorro could've confronted them at any time. So why was he running?

And Drew...what did Sorro want from Nic's brother that would make him go through all this trouble?

Where was Sorro leading them?

Nic interrupted his thoughts with a whispered question. "Where is everybody?"

He shrugged and lied. "Maybe it only gets crazy at night."

"Maybe," she said, "but this quiet is giving me the creeps."

"Just keep your eyes open."

She nodded but didn't say anything else as they crept along.

They rounded a corner and saw the gate indicated on the map—two matching slabs of iron, open just enough for one person to slide through. No guards in sight.

She started to go on through but he pulled her back. "I'm going first," he whispered. If it was an ambush, he wanted her behind him.

A mean glare was all she offered in response. The angry pout on her lips made him want to kiss her then and there.

He didn't understand how it was possible to want someone the way he wanted her, and at the most impossible moments. She was a prize. His prize for accepting nothing less than victory over his human half.

And he was going to get what he fucking wanted. Period.

Arden had to turn sideways to squeeze through the opening. He glanced back to make sure Nic followed him, and stumbled over something. He recovered in time to keep from landing on top of the torso lying right inside the gate. A puddle of blood and intestines soaked the ground beneath his feet. "I think I figured out why there are no guards."

Nic stepped through and jumped over the body. "Yep." She swallowed hard and stepped around a leg lying adjacent to the torso. "So, where's everybody else?"

"From the look of these two, I'd say they're hiding."

He knew exactly who had done the guards. The signs were in the level of brutality—from the dismemberment to the disembowelment—it had Sorro's name all over it, and his signature left a bloody mess. But still, why? Why was he clearing the path for them?

"My brother was here."

He walked over to where she knelt down next to the remains of the second guard. Something metallic glinted in the sunlight. She picked it up and held it out to him. A silver spoon. "What about a piece of silverware makes you so sure?"

"It's Drew's spoon," she said. "A junkie never leaves home without it. It's from my grandmother's silver. Rose pattern with a *W*."

She ran her finger along the widest part of the stem. He could tell she was trying to keep her emotions in check, but the sheen of unshed tears in her eyes revealed enough. And made him want to find Drew. And beat his ass. "We're on the right track then," he said.

"The blood trail leads across this courtyard and into that building," she said, standing. He watched as she started to pocket the spoon, then paused and let it drop to the dirt. Arden guessed she'd probably seen enough of her brother's drug paraphernalia.

The two-story building across the way looked like something from an ancient earthen ruin. Rough cut stone cobbled together and chinked with gray mud. Windowless holes in the upper floor of the facade resembled empty eyes, and the arched entrance, with its jagged stones, a mouth.

A couple of smaller buildings and the gate wall enclosed the courtyard, but the space was wide-open. Besides the guards' body parts, it was empty. Anyone could watch their approach from inside the building. Including Sorro.

He pulled his blade from his ankle sheath. If someone were watching, he wanted them to know he was armed. Nic eyed his knife and reached for her own weapon.

When they got to the archway, he motioned for Nic to get behind him as he hugged the wall and peered inside. It was dark, but his demon eyes saw no movement. He didn't want to leave her alone in the courtyard, but he didn't want her going inside either. Especially if it was a trap. "Stay here." She started to mouth a protest, but he cut her off. "I can see better than you. I'll whistle when I know it's clear."

She didn't like the idea—he saw the way her eyes narrowed—but she gave him a quick nod.

He ducked inside and pressed himself against the inner wall. Signs of a struggle were evident. Furniture had been knocked over and the ripe smell of death and blood filled the air. Arden took a few more steps inside and stood, listening. Nothing moved as he crept farther into the room. Silence. So far, the place was full of only the dead. He whistled for her to come in, but she didn't appear. He pressed his lips together to call again and then heard grunting sounds coming from outside.

No.

He sped back through the doorway, and instinct drove him to run his blade through the first object he encountered. The edge met no resistance as he drew it up and through the demon's chest, ripping the flesh wide and apart. He didn't pause as the body crumpled beneath his feet.

Twenty feet across the courtyard, the hulking body of a demon hid Nic from Arden's sight. All he could see was that she still had her weapon and wrestled to free her arms for a clean shot. But she was no match for the thick gray arms wrapped around her.

"Hey," Arden shouted. He didn't stop his forward momentum as he spoke. He flipped the handle of his dagger over and caught it midair, the dripping edge of it pointed at the dirt.

The monster paused and turned to face him. Its head was misshapen and bald, but keen intelligence shone in its radiant orange eyes. A Colossai. From between its crusty, ashen lips came a hiss. It focused on Arden and the hiss turned into a growl, showing a mouthful of serrated, uneven teeth.

"Love the smile, pinhead, but I'm afraid you've got something that belongs to me."

Nic's eyes were cold when they met his, but Arden could see the veiled terror in them. At least she understood that keeping her cool was vital. If she freaked, it would be over in a split second.

With a grunt, the behemoth squeezed Nic to his chest. "Mine."

The demon's words toggled a switch in Arden's head— some internal mechanism clicked over to full-on rage. Nobody got his prize but him.

His grip on the hilt of his blade tightened. The world lost focus as if everything but the monster in front of him were melting. He could feel ice pulsing through his blood, like a glacial blanket descending over his whole body. It had happened once before—when he'd seen that foul fuck, Ritter, put his hands on Nic—and it made every movement, every heartbeat an agony, but made his enemy shine like a crystal beacon in the darkest night. There was no courtyard, no ramshackle buildings, no sun. All was dark except for the pulsing white light of the one who held his prize in its crushing grip.

He became one with his dagger as his feet left the ground. It was an impossible distance, but he soared through the air, a cry of utter rage pouring from his mouth. The beast had no time to react before Arden's blade met flesh and tore through to bone.

The demon shrieked. Blood sprayed from the place where the monster's arm used to meet its shoulder.

Arden clung to its back, and his knife came down again and again into the meat of the brute's massive chest. The white glow of its life force dimmed with each stroke, but he kept on.

Nothing mattered, nothing existed but his need to kill the light.

The demon fell to the ground but he kept on stabbing until he saw the glow flicker. There was no movement beneath him, but he didn't stop his slaughter, didn't cease his killing strokes.

He felt a hand on his shoulder and spun, the frigid fury still racing in his veins, his knife thrust out before him like a fist.

"Arden?"

The voice stilled him, thawed the frozen place inside of him enough that he could see the blurry outline of a human standing in front of him.

Then the world snapped back into focus and he saw Nic staring at him. Her fear scented the air and tainted the cool gray of her eyes.

He breathed in the soft, coppery aroma, and calm crept over him like a shadow. He reached out for her but she backed out of range.

"Your eyes," she said, edging away. "What's wrong with your eyes?"

"What?"

She ran across the courtyard, picked up the spoon she'd dropped, and then dashed back to hold it up in front of him.

The grainy, tarnished reflection he saw made Arden understand why she had backed away. His eyes were solid white.

"They did the same thing when you went after Ritter."

What the fuck? He'd never seen the phenomenon before in one of his kind. Other demons changed, sometimes into another creature entirely, but not Asmodai or any other children of the Fallen. What would have caused it and why? Rage? "Did I say anything before I killed that...thing?"

"Yeah, you said it had something that belonged to you, and then you went ballistic."

The memory zoomed to the forefront of his brain.

"Mine" was what the beast had claimed. Everything after that was a blank except for the rage. He could still feel the remnants of it coursing through his blood. It would be a total lie for him to not admit liking—no, loving—the ice of it in his veins.

"They're turning back," she said.

He didn't need to look again to know she spoke true—he could tell; his pulse slowed and his breath evened out.

One more thing he needed to talk to his father about when they got back...

They? If he went back to his father's house at all, Nic wouldn't be with him. She'd be long gone and he would be transformed. She would be forgotten and so would his half-human parentage.

The sooner the better if he was thinking of the two of them as *they*. "We need to find Sorro."

The confusion was plain on her face. "The eye thing?"

"Never mind that. Let's move before we have any more visitors." He waved an arm at the bloody mess lying in the dirt. "I'm thinking your large, dead friend over there was a distraction to buy our quarry some time."

"How would he know we're here?"

"If he didn't before, he does now."

"Good point," she said. "Let's go."

He wouldn't risk his pawn again, so he insisted they go in together, him in the lead.

Past the entryway, it became very clear why the place was so quiet.

Bodies were stacked knee-deep along the walls of the dim hall. The liquids pooled on the stone floor made it sound as if they were walking through mud.

He could tell Nic was having trouble seeing in the low light so he reached out to her. Although the contact calmed him, he was still firm in his opinions about her being a means to an end. If he helped her it was only to help himself in return. Holding her hand and leading her to Drew was simply the best way for him to get what he wanted and he refused to think of it any other way. End of story.

The corridor ended in a large, round room with a dirt floor and not a stitch of furniture. Instead of chairs or tables, there were more bodies. Instead of paintings or calendars, or any normal paraphernalia, viscera decorated the walls.

She squeezed his hand, and when he turned to look at her, she was greenish gray in color. "What the fuck?"

It was gory, but Arden saw the room in a completely different way than her human eyes could.

This was no ordinary bloodbath; it was a trail of crumbs. Sorro wanted them here—wanted them to follow him. Arden knew, in the pit of his gut, Sorro was trying to get them down to the...

Fourth.

Now wait a minute.

Sorro wanted them to go to the Fourth, which was exactly where he needed to take Nic?

Way too much of a coincidence. Did Sorro somehow know what Arden had been up to? He hadn't told anyone of his desire except for the King of the Incubai. And if this whole foray was some kind of test for Arden, what the fuck did Nic and Drew have to do with it?

Maybe he could get his father to petition the Dark One to intervene. That would solve this mess altogether. But the truth was he needed to see this thing out until the end if he had any chance of escaping the endless boredom, and his father would only try to keep him from leaving. He could not continue his mundane existence and face his humanity for another century. He was one step closer by just being here, and not his father nor the infamous Sorro would stop him.

Heaps of dead or no heaps of dead, he would get what he wanted.

"Come on." He led her through the room and up a narrow staircase to the top floor. The carnage wasn't as bad, but the rotting flesh smell persisted; sweet like overripe fruit left in a Dumpster. He had to breathe through his mouth a little before he adjusted. He couldn't imagine how Nic was able to keep from gagging.

Then he saw a piece of paper lying on the floor right in their path. He knew better than to think it was accidentally dropped.

"What's it say?" she asked as he picked it up.

"Bring her farther and I'll have them both," he read. The lacy, sprawled handwriting had to be Sorro's, but why would he bother being so obvious?

"He must be crazy if he thinks I'm not coming after him."

Why did these two humans mean so much to the demon? What was so important about a mortal woman and her no-good junkie brother, and what did Sorro have riding on it?

And if he threatened me in any way, he has to know the punishment for it. "You're right. He is crazy." It was the only thing he could come up with to answer the nagging questions in his brain. But he couldn't shake the feeling that there was something more to all of this.

Then a thought careened to the front of his skull. Nic couldn't go. If Sorro was willing to risk the Lake of Fire, he would be willing to do anything. Arden couldn't get his head around why it was this particular pair of siblings, but the demon wanted them dead.

If he took her down to the Fourth now, she would get annihilated. Then his prize would be lost. He couldn't risk taking her to the Emissary until Sorro was dead.

"You have to stay here," he said. He didn't even have to glance at her to know the expression on her face.

"The fuck I will."

"He *wants* you to come after him." Arden needed time to figure it out, but he couldn't risk losing his ticket to freedom. Nic couldn't go.

"So? You think that just because I'm human I would lie down and let him kill me?"

Why did he ever let her in on the way he felt about humans? Why did he care if she knew what had happened to his mother? He should have just kept his mouth shut.

"You're out of your damn mind if you think I'm not going." She crossed her arms. The tendons in her smooth neck stood out and he knew she was probably thinking of pulling her nine on him. Her flashing eyes and full mouth were rife with rebellion.

This wouldn't turn out to be another roadblock. Sorro had put enough of those in his way and he wouldn't allow Nic's stubbornness to be another one. All he needed to do was make her see that his way was the best option. "It's too risky. I'll go by myself."

"No. Nope. Drew is my brother and why the fuck would I trust you?"

If this went any further, she'd be even less inclined to agree with him. Why couldn't she just…cooperate—

Damn.

The perfect solution lay within him and he hadn't even thought of it.

His talent.

He was a Convincer, a salesman. His special Gift, passed through the demon blood of his father, would allow him to make her believe whatever he wanted her to believe.

Arden had used it on her only once before. Back when they had been standing in Drew's dirty apartment. That time, it was only to show her what he was capable of. But now, he would use it to betray her and get what he wanted.

He'd find Sorro, kill him, and use Drew to lure her down to the Fourth for his own ends.

There was a tiny flicker of doubt in his mind, but he pushed it down to the deepest part of himself where the remainder of his mother's blood pulsed in his heart.

Chapter Twenty

Nic was angry.

No.

Fucking furious.

The scorching sun added to her mood, its crimson glare casting long shadows across the dirt street.

She held her arm over her forehead and glanced at the sky. It seemed to be late afternoon. A chill ran up her back when she thought about the black stain of night returning and what kind of creatures she would encounter in the darkness. If they weren't all dead.

That thing back in the courtyard had been weird enough. She could still feel its gray, mottled skin against her own; soft but cold, and hatred seeping from its pores like sweat.

But then Arden was there, throwing himself at the creature and slicing through the arm that had been wrapped around her like a vise. If he hadn't come back out, she would've been the monster's meal for sure.

How kind of him to save her and then leave her here.

She stomped down the road until she was back outside of the main cluster of shacks and shanties, trying to walk out her anger.

"That arrogant asshole," she said aloud. Then she ducked under the roof of a rough lean-to, remembering where she was and regretting her outburst. It wasn't really a good idea to go spouting off at the mouth when anybody or any*thing* could be lurking just around the corner. So she whispered instead. "Left me here in the middle of Hell because he wasn't getting his way. Well, he's just a spoiled brat who thinks he knows everything."

A flush stole over her skin and his words came dancing back to her.

"I'm a spoiled brat who knows everything."

Weird, she didn't remember that being part of their argument. They had disagreed about something...about which way would be best...

The thought trailed off and her memory of the words grew hazy in her mind. Something about him not wanting her to go down to the Fourth. She had refused and then...

Nothing except her fury and the cloudy, intense feeling of his eyes meeting her own.

And the worst part? She had slept with him—no, not just slept with him—she'd had *sex* with him, which was what he had wanted from her in the first place.

"Guess that means the deal's off," she said to the shadows.

Now that he'd gotten his rocks off, his obligation was over. And he'd left her down here, alone, to rot.

How could she have been so fucking stupid?

Lesson learned. She wouldn't give up. She'd find her brother. But how on earth was she supposed to find him if she had no clue where to start?

But she *did* know where to start.

To find a rat, you followed the trail of crumbs. To find a murderer, follow the blood.

Nic went the opposite direction from the gate they'd gone through, counting on there being a different way in. She didn't want to have another run-in with a boulder demon. Besides, the outer wall made good cover since most of it was bathed in shadow. When she'd walked halfway around the stone wall, she spotted a small wooden door embedded into the stone. The rusty handle came apart in her hand when she tried it, so she kicked at the wood until some of it broke away.

Hooray for steel toes.

The hole she made wasn't big enough for her to crawl through, but she did get a good view of the tiny, empty room inside. She used the grip of her pistol to shatter another board as quietly as she could and managed to shimmy underneath what was left of the door. As she pulled herself through on her belly, one of the loose boards caught her shirt and dug into her skin.

She stood, brushed the grit and dirt from her front, and rolled her stinging shoulders. The room was no bigger than a closet. Dust floated in a ray of light coming from a slit in the wall near the door. The gap in the stone reminded her of the ones in castle walls for archers. Maybe it was a guard post?

She doubted Sorro had come through this way. By the look of things out front, he'd waltzed in and slaughtered everyone in his path. But why would he bother? He was killing either for fun or for a purpose, but what would be the point if he could go wherever he wanted?

Maybe Arden—

Her thoughts stopped at the name. She made a silent vow to never think it again. From here on out, she would call him Prick and nothing else.

The anger rushed over her anew. It had been nothing but a tug-of-war between them the whole time.

Take the gun; give me the gun. You should be scared, but don't be scared. As if it mattered to him one way or the other what happened to her. *Don't look at me; look at me.*

"*Look at me.*"

Like a lightning bolt connecting with a tree, her synapses flared and events fell into place.

They were standing in that blood-spattered room not fifty yards from where she now stood and he had taken her face in his palms and forced her gaze to meet his...

And he had used his fucking talent on her.

The whispered words came back at her. "*Go back to the place where we crossed over and wait. We argued. I abandoned you because I'm a spoiled—*"

"Brat who knows everything," she told the empty room. "Motherfucker."

Why? She couldn't wrap her brain around his reasoning. If he wanted to go after Sorro alone, he could've run his little game on her before now. He could have done it back at his father's house and she could be sitting in the luxurious library eating tempress fruit, none the wiser. He could have done it when she had been naked, stretched out on his bed. It would've been easy for him to make her stay there, wanting him, until he'd returned.

She shook a bit more of the fog from her mind, and when the dust settled, only one question remained.

What was in it for him? Why did he need her to come along if he could have done it by himself?

There was a reason he wanted to bring her down here, get her farther and farther into the labyrinth he called home. It was a lot of trouble to go to for a piece of ass. By the look of his hard body and gorgeous face, she didn't imagine him having any trouble in that area. So what was he really after?

What he did or didn't want wasn't a factor. Besides, whatever it was, he wasn't going to get it from her. Not in a million years would she sit around idle while he went off alone.

She needed to get Drew. Once he was safe, the rest would sort itself out.

First, she had to find Sorro.

And if the Prick formerly known as Arden tried to get in her way, she would put a bullet right between his glittering eyes.

———

She crept through the rest of the building and decided the blood, brains, and bodily fluids had to be a step in the right direction, so she picked her way around through the mess, following the trail down the narrow stairs and into the basement.

Sorro had to be close. She hadn't come across any other living thing. If anyone in the area was still alive, they were probably hiding, which suited her just fine—fewer obstacles.

At the bottom of the stairs more corpses littered a long, gloomy corridor. It stretched out in two directions, neither of which she thought looked appealing. The dead she could deal with, but it was the unnerving silence hanging thick in the air that set her teeth on edge.

A small amount of light came from windows high up on the wall. The red glow of the fading sunlight illuminated the right-hand passage more, but the left looked like it had less gore to trudge through. Her much-abused lower lip took another beating as she chewed over her options.

If I had a fucking map, this would be simple.

She opted for the brighter path and headed down the hall, away from the darker, bloodier half of the corridor.

The floor under her feet was gritty and made her footsteps sound like sandpaper sighs on the stone. She moved slowly and kept her back against the wall. Every few feet was a doorway. The first one was open to a scene of bloodshed that paled in comparison to what she'd seen so far. She inched closer to check inside.

One body—or just the remnants of one—lay right inside the door. The skin had the same splotchy gray tone as the beast from outside, but this demon was smaller, thinner. Its neck had been twisted all the way around and its angular face had rough, jagged tears in the flesh of its cheeks, revealing the bones beneath.

The worm that slithered from one of its lifeless apricot eyes did her in. She backed out of the doorway and retched up the remains of her last meal, heaving until there was nothing left in her stomach. She wiped her mouth with the edge of her shirt and moved on.

Two more open doorways displayed similar scenes, but she didn't go in for a closer look. Her stomach lurched at the thought of what she might find.

She paused to take a deep breath in the space between doors. Fear began to crawl into her blood and she knew what would happen if she let it take over. If anybody was still alive down here, she might end up in the same position as the unfortunate fuck three doors back.

A couple of deep breaths in through her nose and out through her mouth settled her quivering stomach. Inching along the corridor, she saw that the last door was closed to her, but it didn't take a genius to figure out there would be more of the same in that room too. She flexed her hand around the grip on her gun and stepped toward the door.

The wood was shattered around the handle; splinters stuck out from the frame in cactus points. No light came from inside the room, so the hole in the wood looked like a blackened mouth with wooden teeth left to pierce the flesh of anyone who dared try the knob.

She was torn. Opening the door didn't seem like a good idea, but maybe the crossing place was inside. What if Sorro had already taken Drew to the Fourth? If she didn't go in the room, she'd never know.

For a moment, she wished Arden were with her. No. He was the last person on earth—or in Hell for that matter—who she wanted around right now. It would only complicate things and cloud her mind with his sharp jaw and piercing eyes, his soft lips—

Then she heard something—no, someone—weeping on the other side of the door.

It had been a very long time since she'd heard the sound of his tears, but her heart knew who was inside that room.

Drew.

And he wasn't alone.

Nic heard two other voices: one agitated, whiny like a teenager, and the other hard and smooth.

Sunlight from the window at the end of the hall slanted across the door in slashes like a pink police-tape warning, but she didn't care.

All the frustration and hurt inside from Arden's betrayal centered her. Her internal reserve of calm focus—there since her parents' murders—spread through her blood and became a warm blanket of resolve, and her Ruger became the linchpin reminder of duty.

She backed up against the opposite wall to give herself room to maneuver. The doorknob was smashed. Had they braced the door? If so, she'd need a running start if she planned on breaking through.

Drew's raised voice was her cue, and she lunged across the space. Pain lanced down her arm as she rammed the door with her shoulder. It didn't budge. She'd have to make another run.

"What the fuck?" The shout came from inside. She was out of time.

On her second run she put all of her weight and determination into the blow, and when she connected, the door shattered and buckled inward. Long, thin splinters of wood pierced her arm as she tumbled into the room. Her chin connected with the floor and the impact knocked her teeth together. Pain pulsed inside of her skull.

She hopped up onto one knee and leveled her pistol at the demons standing before her.

The tall, waifish one was closest, but she couldn't see enough to get a clear shot. A single candle flickered in a wall sconce, but the room had no window. What seemed like an eternity passed before her eyes could adjust to the gloom, and when they did, her heart sank.

Teen demon didn't compare in girth to the gray thing she'd met outside, but his long, skinny limbs moved in a detached, spiderlike way. He was dancing in place as if he'd gotten his first glimpse of a shiny new toy, and his arms bent back and forth at lean, odd angles. The way his leather jacket hung on him made him look like a dancing skeleton...with a short, dark Mohawk running down the center of his pointy skull.

He smiled wide, and she saw a neat row of tiny, sharp teeth. "Oh, man, Sorro, she's so pretty."

Her eyes caught up to the darkness at last and she got her first glimpse of the other demon in the room.

Sorro.

Chapter Twenty-One

Nic knew it was him. Without doubt. Just looking at him made her want to grieve. His gaze crawled over her, and when he met her stare a feeling of intense despair overcame her, causing her heart to clench in agony.

His were the eyes of one who brings death—the very absence of life shone in their poisonous sapphire depths—and if she stared too long, she could see herself drowning in the ocean of violence there. His skin was porcelain pale and his features sharp like an albino raven. Scales covered his face in a crocodilian pattern, wide down the center and smaller near his hairline. The length of his crystalline hair fell over his shoulders, making him look as if he'd just broken free from a black widow's web. The translucent strands reached down to his waist. His scarlet suit was the crowning jewel; its lines hugged his wide shoulders, and Nic could see the fabric strain when he crossed his arms over his chest.

He laughed and his mouth lacked the predatory teeth she expected. Instead, his smile revealed a row of perfect white teeth. "You are indeed very fetching. Maybe I'll keep you for a pet."

A lump of fabric at Sorro's feet moved and turned. Drew. He was alive.

But she knew without question he was high—his eyes were wide and glossy and darted from side to side, focusing on nothing and everything. He didn't even glance at her.

How'd he get the meth? As soon as the question formed in her mind, she knew the answer. If someone wanted a junkie's cooperation, they fed him drugs.

Her anger flared until the words came out as little more than a growl. "Get away from my brother."

Sorro's plastic smile faded and the cobalt seas that were his eyes shone. "Where is the Prince?"

"You've got ten seconds to get out of here or I'm going to put a hole between those big blue eyes."

"The Prince, I said. Where the fuck is he?"

"I don't know what *Prince* you're talking about, you creepy piece of shit." She raised the gun up and her vision of his face was divided in two by the barrel. "You have seven seconds left."

His laughter sounded like glass breaking. "Oh, poor thing. You really don't know what he's up to, do you?"

She didn't want to take the bait, but she needed to know what Arden had riding on this. However, it wouldn't do to show all her cards to the enemy. "You're wrong. I know everything."

"Stupid human. You think you can outwit me," he said. "How quaint."

Can he read my thoughts? Why didn't Arden prepare her for this? How was she supposed to get the advantage in the room if the demon could pluck her actions from her head before she made a move?

"There is your problem. You will not get the advantage over me. Ever."

He *had* pulled the thoughts from her mind, but she wouldn't let him do it again. She called an image into her brain of a vast, unending desert; it was her only defense besides the steel in her hand.

"And now you think to shut me out entirely with visions of a wasteland? Clever girl." He smiled, showing off his too-white teeth. "Allow me to explain some things to you."

It was difficult for her to not meet his gaze when he knelt before her. She locked on to the endless sands in her head and focused her stare on a point just to the left of his face. The lanky young one made no move. She figured he wouldn't do so without a direct order.

"Ah, yes, you're right. Flic here would never disobey me. He's a good lad." Sorro looked over for a moment at the teen and a shadow darkened his grin. "It would be nice if I could take him with me." He sighed. "Enough of that, though. Let's get back to you, lovely girl, and your Prince."

Drew made a whimpering sound from behind him, and Sorro reached out a long-fingered hand to his shoulder, stroking the back of his shirt. "You came all this way for your drug-addicted brother *and* relied on the First Born's help? Maybe you're not so clever after all."

"Stop touching him."

"He likes it, Nic, can't you tell?" Sorro ran his hand down Drew's arm. "Time to sleep."

At the words, Drew's muttering ceased and he drooped to the floor, curled into a ball around Sorro's ankles.

"Back to the matter at hand," he said. "Why do you think your Prince brought you down here?" When she didn't answer, he went on. "Oh, let me guess. You think he cares for you, but not just that, you care for him."

"No." Nic held her breath. She knew if she said anything else, it would feed into his game.

"And now he's abandoned you. Don't you want to know why?"

"No."

"You lie to me, but I will tell *you* the truth."

Sorro settled himself into a sitting position on the dusty floor, mindless of the fine red suit. He placed his pale, long-fingered hands on his knees. "The Prince is using you."

She clung to her poker face and her scorching mind-desert with all she was worth.

"Don't you see the truth of it?" His face danced in front of her, seeking eye contact. "No? Then let me make it clearer for you. He is using you—your desperation—as his catalyst. He gained your trust, he played on your fear and your humanity, and now he has his final triumph."

Sorro smiled wide. "You fell right into his plan. And all because he wants to become something new. I bet he toyed with you too. Made you believe he wanted you. Maybe even seduced you."

Her teeth reopened the bite on the inside of her lip, and the gun gained ten pounds in her grip.

"He did. I can see it on your face. Stings a bit, doesn't it?" His face became the picture of compassion. "You poor thing. To think of how far you've come only to have it all blow away like so much dust." He lifted one palm and blew over it, releasing motes into the stale air. "I'm sure you must be wondering what your options are now."

"No, I don't."

"Pretty lies from a pretty girl." He rose from the floor and stepped back to loom over Drew. His slender fingers fluttered over her brother's neck. "Wake up," he said, running his hand through Drew's hair. "You have a visitor."

Her brother stirred to consciousness again; slow and sluggish, as if he'd been asleep for days instead of minutes.

"Hey, Sorro," Drew said. The words stretched out of his mouth in a slur. "Wha'd-you s-say?"

Sorro pointed at Nic. "There's someone here to see you."

Drew sat up and turned around to follow the direction of Sorro's outstretched finger. He blinked a couple of times and rubbed at his eyes. "Who is it?"

"Your sister, dear boy."

She saw her brother's light-gray eyes clear and snap into focus on her face. "No, no. You can't be here." His voice grew panicked and shrill. "No—you have to go away."

"Drew, it's OK," she said. "I'm going to get you out of here."

"No!" He skittered back into the corner away from her. "You'll ruin it, you'll ruin everything. Go away. Go away!" He gathered his knees up to his chest and rocked back and forth into the wall, his head thudding into the stone.

It's the drugs. She'd have to come up with something to get him calmed down or things were going to go bad in a hurry. Then it came to her. It had worked on him before when he was a mess, so she'd try it now, even if it broke her heart to say it. "Come on, Squirrel."

The rocking stopped and when he looked at her, she could see pain break through his high. It mirrored the ache in her chest.

Their dad used to call him that. He'd say, *Come on, Squirrel*, then ruffle Drew's hair, always after some bit of innocent mischief like taking one of her dolls and beheading it in the backyard. Way back before the trouble started, he'd been her constant companion, her one true friend. Then came the "bad crowd," then the drugs, and then the night of violence when their parents' lives had been cut short. Nothing was ever the same again, including her relationship with her little brother. Although it hurt them both, she had no choice but to use the nickname.

"Come on, Squirrel," she said again, a shaky smile plastered to her face.

Drew stood up and she sucked in a relieved breath. He staggered toward her and brought his arm up to point at her. "Don't you call me that."

"Squirrel, we have to—"

"Don't fucking say it again. Don't fucking say another word." His eyes were open so wide that she could see the whites all the way around. "I won't let you ruin this."

He had no idea what was happening. Probably didn't even understand where he was. Nic stood up but didn't lower the Ruger. "Drew, just step away from him and we'll figure this all out." As soon as he was clear, she'd let her bullets fly.

She watched, stunned, as her little brother reached for Sorro's hand and clasped it in his own. A pretty smile broke over the demon's features, and the wide scales across his chin drew taut.

Drew's voice was clear and crisp when he spoke. "Go away."

"But Drew, don't you wa—"

"Go. Away." He turned to Sorro and nodded his head. There must have been some kind of silent communication between them because as one, they backed up to the wall behind them. The one called Flic sidled up to his master, his eyes locked on the barrel of Nic's weapon.

The stones of the wall were scored with a rough cut in the shape of a door. High up in the left corner were four deep grooves cut into the rock. She hadn't even seen it.

The Fourth. The gate. They were going to go through.

After all she'd done. After fighting and running and being betrayed. Her brother had turned against her too. And she was alone. All alone.

A sudden blast of fear arced through her like the curved blade of a scythe.

Flic's nostrils flared wide and his ochre eyes bugged out of his head. A raw, guttural moan broke from his lips. The room filled with a sound like someone ripping a wet towel in half, and his skeletal body made an impossible shift—in a blink, he'd grown a foot taller. His limbs stretched out until she saw his bony forearms sticking out of the sleeves of his jacket. Nic tasted the coppery sting of fear on her tongue as it pumped faster through her veins.

She knew Sorro struggled to contain himself from attacking her; she could see it in the tight lines of his face and the way his lips pressed into a thin, white line.

But the real problem wasn't Sorro—it was Flic. His body continued to change, stretching and elongating into something only a nightmare could create. She saw lust and panic etched in the lines of his face. His lips peeled back and the tiny points of his teeth grew, the neat little row replaced with inch-long daggers. Drool dripped from the shiny fangs and ran over his chin, soaking the front of his shirt. His clothes began to tear at the seams—not from bulk of muscle, but from the sheer stretch of bone. The leather jacket struggled to maintain its integrity and then, with a rending sound, the sleeves broke loose and fell from his arms onto the floor.

She had been frozen to her spot on the floor until she saw what his arms had turned into. She scrambled back until she felt the door frame dig into her shoulder blades. The leftover splinters there sliced deeper into her skin, but she didn't—couldn't—feel them because of the gruesome metamorphosis across the room.

Even Sorro seemed taken aback by what his lackey was becoming. He pulled Drew off to the side and stared with open admiration at the abomination coming to life no more than three feet away from where he stood.

The rest of Flic's clothing dropped to the floor in tatters, and he was naked, his penis rock hard and pointed like a stinger. She struggled to keep her fear from overwhelming her, but every pop of changing bone, every wet tear of flesh from the creature in front of her, threatened to send her over the edge into sheer panic. Or madness. Or both. She didn't dare take her eyes off the thing and kept her Ruger aimed for the face even though the nine-millimeter rounds would probably be no good against the...monster. She was transfixed and repulsed by the sight but couldn't move, afraid to draw the atrocity's attention.

Skin and muscle fell from his body in thick clumps, and the bone underneath was no longer smooth; the shiny white surface was now blanketed in fine black hair. The lengths of his arms and legs had grown extra joints. He cried out, and the sound was a deafening, desperate screech like the slow, painful whistle of an out-of-control train.

The flesh of his ribs broke open, spewing sticky green bile, and new limbs burst forth on either side, shooting outward.

He—the spider—gave a final wrenching cry before his head turned in an unnatural circle to face the wall behind him. The back of his scalp split up the center and a new head emerged, fur covered with three rows of yellow eyes. The fangs dripped with saliva, which had become milky and thick. When the drops landed on the floor, they popped and sizzled and dug craters into the rock.

She spared a glance for her brother. He cowered behind Sorro's shoulder, and she hoped he hadn't seen the show she'd just witnessed. Sorro pressed him farther away from Flic, almost as if he were protecting him. But why—?

The creature's legs ticked against the stone wall, and with uncanny, perverse grace, it flipped its body over and scrabbled up the wall to perch in a corner. Its frame shook and the rest of what remained of Flic fell away.

The teen demon was no more.

Sorro made his move for the gate, Drew leeched to his side.

She couldn't let them get out of the room. "Drew!"

The thing in the corner spun and focused its citrine eyes on her. The body drew up into itself and it sprang from the wall.

The blast of her Ruger wasn't loud enough to drown out the sounds of her screams.

Episode Seven

Chapter Twenty-Two

As Arden stepped onto the landing, the dead stillness of the stairwell was shattered by a piercing scream.

Nic.

Then gunfire.

He vaulted down the stairs into the guts of the basement. He had no thoughts, only actions, and his blood iced. At the bottom of the flight his feet left the ground, launching him over the rest of the steps.

If anything happened to her, he could blame only himself. Fuck. He'd thought using his Gift on her, convincing her to forget about going after her brother, had been the best option. He needed her in one piece to use her for his own ends—he thought he'd been taking the safest course to see his plan to fruition. She was *his*, damn it, his key to being rid of his human half. And again he'd put his scheme in jeopardy. This time, by trying to keep her safe for his own use. But it seemed his trickery hadn't been any kind of assurance.

Which way? He froze at the bottom of the stairs, listening, waiting for some audible clue as to where she was, but there was nothing.

Then he heard a ticking sound like the drum of fingernails on a coffin. It came from the hallway on his right.

He bolted down to the end and leaped through the shattered door. It took a moment for his brain to comprehend the scene in the room.

The scraping he'd heard came from the twitching legs of a giant black spider. The sharp tips scratched against the stone floor. He could see the beast's body convulse and shudder. Two of its six eyes were gone and the hollows where they used to be oozed orange, gelatinous filth.

And beneath the pulsing mass lay Nic.

Ice flooded his veins and, as before, the world dimmed until only the light of his enemy remained. The spider's life force was no more than sputtering candlelight, a dim and fading illumination.

Then a new light engulfed his vision. This one was strong and shone with a brilliance so vivid he had to shield his eyes. At the center of the glow was an onyx void, a great hollowness—the purest embodiment of threat.

He would eat the black heart from its body.

As he crouched to leap at the glowing form, someone laughed. It cut through his frozen mind.

The world zoomed back into focus. A room. Walls. A stone floor.

A huge, eight-legged monstrosity.

Nic, her body too still, too quiet, beneath the arachnid.

The laughter continued and he focused on the source.

Sorro.

A passage behind the demon slid open and, with a wave of Sorro's pale fingers, his human hostage followed him through the gate. They disappeared into the darkness and the door slid back into place with a thud.

His heart hammered inside his chest as he lifted the heavy carcass off Nic's body and threw it back against the wall. The small table it landed on collapsed beneath the weight and a long, jagged splinter pierced its belly with a pop. A trail of orange slime leaked from the wound.

Nic lay on her back, her limbs sprawled out, with the gun still clutched in her delicate hand. He fell to his knees beside her and reached for her neck, his fingers seeking a sign that her heart still beat in her chest.

No. She would not be dead. Not dead. Not dead. *Please not that.*

His hand felt a slow, rhythmic pulse underneath the smooth skin, and he released the breath he'd been holding. He ran his knuckles over her jaw, but she didn't stir. She was unconscious but alive.

Alive.

His pulse quickened and he checked for damages. Her shirt sleeve was torn and he could see several long splinters sticking out of her arm at odd angles. Blood seeped from the punctures as he removed them one by one. He figured it was better that she was out; otherwise she would have felt everything. But it bothered him that she didn't even whimper in pain.

His heart thumped against his ribs. There was something else wrong with her. Had to be, or else she would've flinched, if only in reflex.

The rest of her seemed to be intact, but the itch of fear on the back of his neck told him to keep looking. *Keep looking.*

He ran his hands down her arms. There were no breaks. He repeated the motion with her legs and got the same result. When he got to the waist of her secondhand jeans, he saw it.

No more than a darkening of fabric with a few holes in it. He hadn't spotted it before because it was just a dark spot on a black T-shirt, but now he saw the cloth was wet with blood and it was no mere trickle; it was a growing, sickening stain.

With numb fingers he lifted the edge of the shirt. Her flat stomach was untouched, but the skin of her chest, just above her breasts, had been torn open—a chunk of her flesh removed. The edge of the wound was a fleshy zigzag. Only one thing could leave a mark like that...

Teeth.

The spider. It must have gotten the bite in before she'd removed its eyes with bullets.

And Arden knew—with a knowledge from that deep place inside him rich in human blood, and the other place in him that ran with the purest blood of the Fallen—that monster lying on the other side of the room had fangs.

And those fangs had venom.

He pulled the shirt up the rest of the way to reveal the lower edge of the gash. The fangs had left long, ragged lines on their way out, and the marks were dripping a trail of foul, ichorous slime.

No. Unacceptable. She would *not* die from this. If she died, he would never gain his freedom. He would continue on the vicious cycle that was his life, forever trapped by the boredom of his station—trapped by the very thing racing through his veins and forcing his heart to pound like a violent drum in his chest. He was bound by his parentage to live out his infinite existence in torture. Until Nic, there had been no end in sight.

But now, his last chance was dying in front of his eyes in some shithole room in the basement of a shithole castle on the Third Level of Hell.

No.

Not going to happen. He wouldn't let her go.

His mind spun with possibilities. The venom would drain the life from her if he didn't act. A web of poison grew around the wound and turned her beautiful, pale flesh a shocking shade of gray.

Brain, Arden, brain. Use it.

She would die because her human blood was no match for the—

The solution jumped forth in his mind as if spring-loaded.

She was human, all human, but he wasn't and his own body would kill the toxin. He needed to get it out of her and there was only one way to do it.

He would have to suck it from the wound.

If she were awake, he could only imagine what Nic would have to say about the idea. The thought of anger flashing in her stony eyes brought a grim smile to his lips.

He lifted her body enough to pull the shirt over her head. Her petal-soft skin was pale, but the sheen of sweat he saw there spurred him on. He would think about touching her later. For now, he needed to save her life.

The fabric of her bra was sticky with blood and more of the spider's killing saliva. The bleeding hole in the middle of her chest was like a corpse lying in an untouched field of snow, and he laid his cheek over her heart, his mouth next to the gap in her flesh.

Beneath his ear he heard the staccato throb of her heart, but he knew it struggled. The pace was slow, and with every breath it grew slower still.

Time to make like a vampire.

At first, he only licked at the edges, but tasting the vileness, feeling the sharp sting of it against his tongue, he realized he needed to move faster. And the slow beat of her heart beneath his ear called to him. *Hur-ry...hur-ry.*

He drew himself up and pressed his mouth down into the wound. The poison needled his lips and chin but he nuzzled into the flesh, sucking and swallowing the threat to her. He drank it down and felt his own body responding to its presence. His demon blood would conquer it without question.

After several long draughts on the wound, he pressed his ear again to her chest. Her heart sped up. He moved back over the injury, and as he suckled he began to taste less and less venom mixed into her blood.

And then it was only blood he drew into his mouth. There was something remarkable about tasting her in this way. More intimate than when he had lapped at the soft folds between her legs.

This was the very essence of what made her; the life that coursed through her veins and made her into a being.

Made her a puzzle, a pleasure, a thrill.

He literally drank her humanity into himself, and it made him hungry—for all that she was and all the marvel of her very existence. He drank of her life and found himself filled by it. Her heart pumped something into him, something foreign and frightening, and he couldn't get enough.

As his body quelled the remaining drops·of venom, a stunning realization came to him.

If he helped her rescue Drew, if he led her into the Fourth and slaughtered Sorro for her, he would have to let her go. Keeping her had only been wishful thinking.

She was *human.* No matter how beautiful or how delicious she tasted, he had no business keeping her around. Nic made him weak. She made him want things he could never have.

So, when the time came, he would do what had to be done. He would hurt her—destroy her—and then he would have what he'd always wanted.

He licked the sweet blood from his lips and laid his head on the rise of her breast. The victory he thought he should be feeling was nothing more than a hollow space in his chest.

———

The sharp throb in her chest woke Nic up. She had a moment of utter confusion and panic until her mind arranged itself and her surroundings came back into clear focus. She started to sit up and then looked down at the weight on her chest keeping her from doing so.

Arden's jet hair tickled her collarbone and she could feel his breath flowing over her exposed nipple.

What. The. Fuck?

Then, like the breaking of dawn, events flooded over her.

Sorro's sapphire eyes had threatened to steal her soul.

Flic had turned into that...thing. Out of the corner of her eye she saw the giant spider on his back, a long, thin splinter stuck through his abdomen.

And her brother had chosen the hand of the enemy over her own.

Tears stung her eyes and she blinked them away. How long had she been out?

She wrapped her arms around the demon lying against her and held him there. It was her only comfort in the room besides the seeping body of the spider that had tried to kill her. Arden had come back for her, and for one brief moment she would allow herself to feel consoled by his presence. In another minute, she would hate him again for what he had done, but for now she wanted to feel him in her arms.

But just as fast as the comfort had come, it fled as Sorro's words came dancing back at her.

"He's using you."

She shoved the demon off of her. How dare he lie there? She wanted him to face her so she could see the look in his icy eyes when she told him she knew everything.

Right before she kicked his teeth in.

He leaped to his feet, his dagger appearing from nowhere. The blade shone golden in the diminishing candlelight.

She stood and staggered. He reached out to steady her and she flung her arm out of his reach. She wouldn't let him touch her ever again. Her bra and T-shirt were lying on the ground and she wrestled back into them.

Without a word she went to the wall where she'd seen the mark of the gate. The four slashes on the wall were still there, but the lines marking the door were gone. She felt along the stones, searching for the place they had been. The rock was rough under her fingers and cold; it matched the feeling behind her aching sternum.

She could feel Arden's stare boring into her back, but no way would she speak to him. His illusion of help had ended and she refused to need him any longer. She would follow Sorro down into his home and save Drew herself.

The *Prince* standing behind her could go fuck himself.

What she needed was something to scrape the surface off the wall. Maybe if she got down into the rock, the door would reappear; it had to, because she wasn't going to ask for Arden's help. Ever. Again.

She went to the shattered door she'd broken through and picked up one of the larger splinters. The wood wouldn't hold up long against the hard stone wall, but it was her only option.

Not true. The dagger he held in his hand would be the perfect thing. Maybe she would try it *after* she knocked him out.

She gave herself a little mental shake and continued to ignore his stare as she dug into the stone. The piece of wood crumbled in her hand after a few passes and she tossed it to the ground.

He didn't say a word when he stepped up to her, but she knew he was there just the same. Her body temperature rose and she could smell the raw spice of him, smoky and dangerous. She saw the flash of his blade pass over her shoulder and watched in awe as the stone split where the metal made contact; lines cracked across the surface of the rock, and clear as daylight the edges of the door reappeared.

"It's the blade," he said. "Forged by demon hands so it has power."

She watched the muscles in his forearm flex and the wings tattooed on his skin flutter as he dragged the knife over the wall. With each stroke, the edges grew deeper and the door was once again right in front of her.

Arden took hold of her shoulder, turned her around, then used his knife to cut the front of her shirt open down to her bra.

"Back the fuck off." She shoved his hands away.

His eyes met hers for a second but she didn't look long enough to see if there was any trace of emotion in them. "I have to check your wound."

At his reminder, her chest started throbbing again. But she couldn't have been injured too badly or she wouldn't be up and moving around. He leaned in to get a look and his fragrance filled her nostrils.

She hated him, wished to see him bleed for what he'd done to her, but her body didn't take the hint. Her skin lit up like a firecracker under his gaze. He ran his fingers over her skin, soft and slow. Every few inches she could feel a spike of pain from his touch. It was agony and pleasure and she felt her nipples stiffen and ache for his hands.

How was it possible that she could want him so much when she despised him?

Then she felt his warm lips on her throat and her need swept the anger away. He wove a trail of heat up her neck with his mouth. When he reached her jaw he stopped and held her face between his hands.

There was nowhere else she could look now but into his eyes, and when he spoke she could feel the whisper of his breath on her lips. "I don't know what I would've done if I had lost you."

She almost believed the sincerity in his voice. Almost.

But he'd made it crystal clear for the second time how much he wanted her. First, he'd left her lying naked in his bed. Second, he'd used his little talent to trick her into walking away from what she'd come down here to do in the beginning.

And then there was that bit about his transformation. Whatever that meant.

"He's using you."

She could still hear Sorro's laughter in her head and see the bottomless depths of his oceanic eyes.

No. Arden didn't want her, didn't care about her—he *needed* her. The part of it that messed with her the most was the fact that she needed him too, if only to get her brother back.

And *nothing* more.

Chapter Twenty-Three

Sorro knew the sight of his employer would have shoved the male right over the edge into full-blown insanity, so it was a good thing he'd knocked Drew out.

He had a moment of envy for the human's ignorance; the small space of the cave seemed to shrink with the presence of his employer, and just being the object of the creature's gaze made him feel suffocated, closed in, like the red, thirsty rock of the Fourth would collapse and crush him.

Something about the eyes. Yes, that was it. Had to be. The clear irises made a great example of the way their sight worked—they saw everything as plain as looking through glass and no one, not even a demon, was exempt from their view.

His employer turned back to him and shone his gaze on Sorro like a spotlight. "I am afraid you do not realize the importance of your mission."

"They will follow. I still have the brother."

"Yes, they will follow for the man," he said, "but you failed to keep an eye on that sycophantic teenager and he almost slaughtered the sister before she lured the First Born far enough."

Sorro wished Flic were still around so he could have ripped each of his legs off one by one. Stupid kid picked *that* moment to hit puberty and almost ruined everything.

He needed to smooth this over. "Your abilities are astounding, Your Highness. The way you made her bullets effective at the last minute? Pure genius."

"Your flattery is disgusting to me, demon, and because of your incompetence I had to intervene. You do remember what will happen if you fail me."

"I won't fail," Sorro said. He felt the tiny hairs on the back of his neck prickle and he rushed to correct his statement. "I won't fail, *Your Highness.*"

The creature moved closer. His translucent gaze did not waver and he moved with the grace allotted him by birth. Sorro didn't dare turn away, but his employer stepped even closer. He had to crane his neck upward to maintain eye contact.

"In order to assure me that you will indeed be successful, I think I will give you a taste of what failure will feel like."

The sensation started in Sorro's fingers; at first, just a minor irritation—an itch he couldn't scratch. He couldn't move because, at the moment, his body wasn't under his command. The itching in his hands turned to a dull burn, and then the burning morphed into pure scald. He closed his eyes. Any show of fear would be very, very bad.

The flesh of his fingers began to melt. He felt the skin slough off to reveal the bones beneath. He felt the tug as those bones were wrenched from their sockets. And although the pieces were gone, he could still feel the nerves there; his digits were separate from him, but their sense of touch remained connected to his mind. Every exposed nerve, every tendon screamed in unison to be reunited with his flesh. The pain was as clear and divine as the eyes of his employer.

"Now you see what awaits should you fail. One such as yourself can see the purity in it, the beauty."

As his molecules spread farther and farther apart from their home, the agony overcame him, and Sorro cried out. He hated himself for showing weakness, hated hearing the whimper. As a child, during his training, he had whimpered enough to last all of eternity. The sound was too close to fear, too close to the sound of his own name.

And then it was over.

He exhaled in quick bursts. He didn't want to open his eyes, afraid to look down at his hands and see the mutilation.

"Look at them," his employer said.

"I can't."

"Look."

Sorro knew that any further disobedience on his part would result in only more pain. He looked down.

His hands were unmarked. The agony had been an illusion. He cursed his pathetic weakness and the long-ago child who'd been so afraid.

"The First Born must die. Do what you wish with the humans, but do not leave Arden alive. All of the Asmodai *must* be killed."

"Yes," Sorro said. He wanted to ask more, wanted to know why the death of Asmodeus's sons was so important, but he knew not to.

"Yes what?"

"Yes, Your Highness."

Sorro flinched as a burst of light filled the room. And then his employer was gone.

But those too-seeing eyes remained in his mind as he glanced around the room.

A new resolve raced through his veins, further fueled by the simple example of what would happen if he failed. He would not fail. That child, that part of himself he'd closed off and hidden away, would be free and he would have all that he wanted.

The brother would die.

The sister would die.

And the Prince?

Before the First Born drew his final breath he would come to understand just how powerful a lower demon could be.

Those children of the Fallen. Arrogant. Spoiled. They never knew pain. They never knew want. None of them knew torture from their first breath, like he had. They sat in those palaces on the First as if that were the only world that existed. Nothing below them. No one below them.

Sorro gave the human a quick kick to get him moving. The closer they got to his nest, the more his powers would return. The First Born would be no match for him then.

As he pushed the human out of the cave and down the craggy slope toward his lair, he smiled.

But the smile didn't feel very real; he could still see those eyes in his mind and hear the rustle of wings in his ears.

———

Arden didn't like the look of her skin—too pale. Maybe he hadn't gotten all the poison out of her. If she didn't get some rest, he didn't know if she would be able to keep moving, and the small alcove seemed hidden enough. "We'll stop here for now."

For once Nic didn't disagree—another indication of how much damage had been done.

And another reminder of the fragility of humans. She was weak and breakable; frail and naive to true evil regardless of her hard-assed attitude. He stole a glance at her as she slid down the rough cave wall to sit cross-legged on the ground. She might have all of those too-human attributes, but she was beautiful and still here. With him.

For a moment he let himself imagine keeping her. Not as a pet or an amusement, but as a mistress. Her face with its petite features and the cool rock of her gray eyes would rival the greatest of demonesses. She would shine like a jewel in the eyes of all who beheld her. He would give her any object she desired and she would want for nothing. And she would be his for as long as she lived.

The sound of her cough stopped his daydreaming. He went to her and sat down. Her color hadn't gotten worse, but the wheezing that followed each cough troubled him. "Is it the bite?"

"No, my chest feels fine. I just can't seem to catch my breath." She managed to pull in another couple of deep breaths before coughing again. "I don't think the air down here is doing me any good. It's too hot." Right on cue, small beads of sweat broke out on her forehead.

At least he'd remembered to grab the water before they'd gone through the gate. He dug out the last bottle and held it up so she could take a drink. Only after she'd gotten her fill did he take some for himself. He used his knife to cut away a section from the bottom of his shirt and poured water over the fabric until it was damp, then pressed it to the back of her neck.

The tension eased out of her face for a minute and she closed her eyes. He cut away a little more of his shirt and used it to wipe her brow.

She needed to rest and he figured this was as good a place as any. The cave was small and hidden by an outcrop of rock; anyone who passed by wouldn't even notice them. Besides, defending her didn't seem to be a problem.

When anything threatened Nic, it seemed he went on autopilot, becoming something fierce and violent. She awakened the raw demon within him, and the thought of having that weapon only added fuel to his daydream of having her for himself. Forever.

The water must have helped some because she closed her eyes and drifted off without another word. He slid up against the wall next to her and put himself between her and the entrance.

His first trip to the Fourth and what did he have to show for it? A wounded mortal woman, a cut-up secondhand shirt, and an enemy that had eluded them. He would kill Sorro more slowly just for the inconvenience.

If he had any hopes of staying on track with the plan, he had a lot of juggling to do. The real trick would be the moment when he had to abandon her. It was still the only way he was going to get rid of the lesser half of himself.

Maybe he could let her go and, once he became full demon, rescue her from…whatever was done to her. Then she would be grateful to him.

She nestled into his shoulder and a lock of her mahogany hair fell across her face as if her tresses knew his thoughts and offered her a shield against his evil.

The Emissary from the Incubai had said he would receive sign of where to abandon the human. But would it be before or after they'd reached Sorro's nest?

The other obstacle was her brother. He knew she would fight to the death to protect him, no matter how pointless.

Perhaps Sorro would do him a favor and dispatch Drew before they could catch up. Then, with the true cold heart of an Incubus, he would leave her where she stood, lost, alone, and helpless.

He just had to get his traitorous mind to stop presenting him with images of Nic naked in his bed. He also needed to quit fucking thinking about what might happen to her before he could return to claim her for his own.

If he could reclaim her at all.

———

Arden woke up as soon as the sweet scent of her fear filled the cave.

She had the front of his shirt clenched in her fists and tears streamed from her still-closed eyes.

He wrapped his arms around her. "It's all right, Nic," he said. "You're safe."

"He was there. Right there in the room with me and I wasn't supposed to see him."

"Wake up, it's just a dream." He needed her awake and lucid before her fear brought the whole population of the Fourth headed in their direction. He kept his voice quiet, calm. "There's no one here but us."

She fully woke then and, as if his touch burned her, pushed away from him. "Not here. Back there, in that room. Right before that *thing* jumped on me." At the mention of the spider she shuddered. "He was glorious and he hated me."

Glorious? "Sorro?"

"Not him." She had backed all the way across the ground and leaned against the opposite wall of the cave, rubbing her arms.

"Flic?"

"No. Not that…thing. This was more like a man, but taller and stronger. He looked at me like he wanted me to die."

"Are you sure it wasn't just part of your dream?"

She gave him a scathing look. "Don't patronize me. I know what I saw."

"There was someone else in the room?"

"Yes, and he hated me."

"What exactly did this person look like?"

"He wasn't a person, but he wasn't one of you either."

That didn't make any sense. There were only three kinds of beings who would be down here: humans, demons, and…

Nope. He wouldn't even *think* of the third kind. What would bring one of them down here and why in the fuck would one of *them* bother with Nic? Stress must have caused her subconscious to add a phantom to her dream. He needed to be sure, though. The presence of a creature like that would really change the game, especially if she had caught its attention. "Did you happen to notice anything weird about his eyes?"

Shock and recognition broke over her features. "Yes."

"What was it?"

"They were transparent, and when he looked at me, so was I."

He plastered a look of boredom on his face so she wouldn't see what that bit of information had done to him. If she saw the apprehension in his eyes, her fear would only escalate again. "Have you ever seen this person before?"

"I already told you. He wasn't a person."

"Have you seen him before?"

"No, but I felt him."

"When?"

"When we were crossing over into the Third," she said. "It felt like someone was trying to pull me into the Abyss. I told you about it then. He was the one trying to get me. I don't know how I know, but it was the same guy—crea-ture—whatever you want to call him." Then, almost as an afterthought, she added, "He wants me dead."

Arden could see from the tense set of her shoulders that she spoke the truth, or at least was truthful about the way it made her feel. He wouldn't put it past one of *their* kind to do the sort of thing she talked about. Humans had the delu-sion that those beings were so wonderful, but some of them could be real assholes.

And one of them showing up down here could only mean one thing:

Problems.

He pulled out the map of the Fourth that Chase had given him and, at first, his brain didn't register what he was seeing.

There were no marks. The weathered parchment showed tunnels and caves, but no *X* marking Sorro's nest. "What the fuck?"

"What?"

He didn't look up at her. He flipped the scroll over; the back was blank. "Sorro's nest. It's not here."

She crossed to him and snatched the map out of his hands. "Why wouldn't it be on here?"

Arden couldn't understand it either. Chase had spent years collecting information to create these maps, and the only detail missing was the location of Sorro's lair? It didn't make sense. And what did it mean regarding his suspicions about Sorro luring them farther down?

"It's not like my brother to forget something like this." Could someone else have tampered with the maps?

"Now what do we do?"

"We move on."

"Move on to where?" She crossed her arms over her chest. "We don't even know where the fuck we're heading."

She had a point, but there was no way he would tell her that. "I'll figure it out as we go."

"As we go?" She stood up and stomped a circle into the cave floor. "This really isn't a learn-as-you-go type situation, and we don't have any time for you to play know-it-all."

"You don't know what you're talking about."

"Neither do you."

He'd gotten more accustomed to her bad attitude, but she was throwing off more than he could take at the moment. He stood and marched over to stand right in her path. "You're forgetting an important fact."

Frustration marred her delicate features when she looked up at him. "And what's that?"

"I'm a demon," he said. "Out of the two of us, I'd say I have the best chance at finding the way."

She stepped around him and paced away only to stop suddenly and spin back around. He could tell her frustration had morphed into anger; it was written all over her face. "You don't need to remind me of who you are. You've made it quite clear."

"What's that supposed to mean?"

"Don't play the innocent, Arden. It doesn't fit you." She moved away, but her angry glare was up close and personal. "You think I don't know what you did to me? Of course, you could probably convince me out of that too."

Convince her of...shit. This was about him using his Gift on her. "I didn't want you coming down here. I did it to keep you safe." Only part of the story, but it was true.

"You are so full of shit. Do you even hear yourself? You sound like Sorro when you lie."

He crossed the small space and, with his forefinger under her chin, forced her to look up at him as he backed her into the wall. "And *you* are out of your element. I suggest you back the fuck off. I did what needed to be done."

She slapped his hand away but didn't move an inch. "Don't touch me ever again." Her voice was like the steel of her weapon—cold, hard, and unrelenting.

He got a very good look into her eyes then and saw something darker than anger in their depths. This was about more than him using his talent on her, but he couldn't fathom what else was amiss. "Not too long ago, you wanted me to touch you." For emphasis he leaned in and traced the outline of her breast beneath her shirt. "I can still taste you on my tongue." When she tried to push him away he trapped her by putting his palms against the wall on either side of her shoulders. She didn't have an option except meeting his stare. "I want another taste."

He might as well have kissed the rock behind her head. Her lips didn't move. Her hands didn't wind into his hair to pull him closer. The pure, unbridled fire he'd found from her mouth before didn't flare into a blaze. So, he changed tactics and pulled her into his arms. She didn't resist. He smoothed the silk of her hair and then rested his hands on her back. A thrill passed through him as he realized how amazing it was to simply hold her.

As soon as he relaxed, she struggled free of his embrace. The warmth of her pressed against him faded and its retreat left him hollow. She walked away without a word and gathered up the map.

"If I had any choice at all, I would do this without you." She didn't look back at him. "But as it is, I need you."

He wanted her with a sudden, crippling fury. There had to be a way to deliver her to the Emissary and then come back to save her. And kill any demon who'd laid a hand on her. He would find a way.

"We should go," she said.

He would be a hero. Her salvation.

Because simply letting her go was no longer an option.

Chapter Twenty-Four

Nic didn't have the energy or the inclination to argue about his high-handedness anymore, so she let him lead the way.

She refused to think about how good it had felt to be in his arms again. It had only been a trick anyway. He needed her to cooperate.

And she would. Right up until Drew was safe. Then she would scrub the stain of Arden off of her brain and go back to living. She knew it would take a while to forget the heat in those icy emerald eyes and the way his smile stole her breath, but she *would* forget.

She'd get her brother into the best rehab she could find, no matter the cost. With time, and lots of counseling, he would overcome the illness they'd both lived with for so long. They would be happy again, even if the process killed her.

Of course, all of those things hinged on if she made it out of this place. She didn't know exactly how a demon obtained a "transformation." What happened to teen demon? Is that what Arden wanted? No. With him it would be something bigger. And she knew her blood would play a part, if not her soul.

If she hadn't gotten so pissed at him back there she might have gotten some answers. But no. As usual when dealing with him, her temper had gone nuclear and she couldn't keep her mouth shut.

The important thing was to find out what he needed from her. It hadn't been sex. That she'd already given him. He could have been done with her right then and there.

And damn it, why did it hurt so much? Why did his arms feel so welcome even after she knew the truth?

She'd always felt so smart, so jaded. Not in the number of relationships she'd had, but in her uncanny ability to *not* connect—to stay detached, unavailable. Shit, hiding herself away had been her trick for steering clear of getting too attached, too *involved* with anyone. So why had she let herself be tricked by him?

You fucking idiot, he's a demon. That's what they do.

Her conscience had it right. She'd been a fool. A stupid, love-struck—

No. Not love. Not for him. Ever.

She would find out exactly what he wanted from her. The knowledge might not change the outcome, but at least she would be prepared when the time came. For now, she would follow him deeper into the home of all lies.

The Fourth was more like what she had always pictured of Hell. No open fires or anything, but rocky and desolate; all the rock around her was dark, but with thin veins of red running through it like blood vessels. For all she knew it *was* blood.

On the other levels, it had felt like they were still above-ground. Down here, though, it seemed like they wandered along the edges of a huge, upside-down underground mountain, its peak crammed deep into the earth. The path led along its funnel-like interior. The only light in the place came from an unhealthy red glow emanating from the rocks themselves.

The cave had opened to a passage. The tunnel didn't look like it had been cut into the stone as much as worn into the landscape. The sides of the walkway curved up into the rock on either side.

At random intervals, the wall would open up to reveal another tunnel or cave. At each one, Arden would stop, motion for her to get back against the wall, and then peer in to make sure the coast was clear. When he was satisfied, he'd move on without a word.

Another tunnel opening came up and he flicked his hand in the air toward her. There was something cavalier and dismissive in the simple gesture; it pricked at her temper, and instead of stopping, she moved into the tunnel right behind him. He didn't notice her quiet disobedience until he turned to step back from the opening and realized she was standing right beside him.

She reined in the irritation. It wouldn't get her anywhere. "I think we need to stay as close to each other as possible." The double meaning in her words floated out into the air between them. "I mean, if we get separated. Or if someone sees us...or...something." Why, oh why couldn't she keep her mouth shut?

Even though he was the last person on the planet—last person in *Hell*—she wanted to be closer to right now, the weird, phosphorescent rocks were giving her the creeps. They pulsed with bloody red any time she neared the walls. She hated him for what he did, but she couldn't deny the comfort of his closeness.

He blasted her with a smile and she almost lost her train of thought altogether. "You're right. Stay close."

What? She'd expected a rebuttal, not capitulation, and the sight of his crooked grin caused a tiny thrill to rush up her spine. "OK."

If this became the new trend between them, maybe she could get answers out of him.

Her feet ached as if she had spent hours walking, but it didn't seem like they had gone very far. It had to be the landscape. Nothing changed, just the constant pulsing rock and tunnel walls. Arden hadn't paused, didn't even seem to be flagging. She began to wonder about the endurance of demons versus humans. If demons lived forever, could they walk forever too?

All of a sudden, her body seemed to register the fact that she hadn't slept much in the last few days. Two nights ago, before her world had been flipped upside down, she'd been plagued with insomnia after fighting with Drew. And since then, she'd had only a quick nap and a short bout of unconsciousness after the spider attack. A shudder passed through her with the remembered sight of his body stretching, growing, and the legs jutting out of his split rib cage.

Her muscles ached, her chest throbbed, and her life had twisted into something she no longer recognized; it was a rollercoaster she'd be happy to stop riding anytime now. Plus her jaw was cramping from her effort to keep quiet, to keep from drilling Arden for answers.

Plus the crazy spiral of emotions that had been her constant companion ever since she'd beaned him with Asmo's book. Nobody could have taken in as much as she had without feeling overwhelmed or just plain insane.

The acknowledgment and naming of everything that had come to pass weighed her down, slowed her down, and she stopped trying to keep up. "I think I need to rest for a minute." The wall made for instant support, and she laid her cheek against the creepy rock.

"You need more than a minute." He frowned. "I'm going to find a place to stop for a while."

"I'm OK," she lied. "I just need a quick break." What she really needed was a hot shower, a giant bed, and forty-eight hours of uninterrupted nap time. She took a deep breath and moved away from the wall; when she did, her knees turned into mush and refused to bear her weight. Her legs went wobbly and she hoped it wouldn't hurt too badly when she hit the ground.

Then the world tilted sideways and he lifted her up into his arms. "I'm fine. Really. Put me down."

"No." He glanced down at her, and if she wasn't mistaken, his eyes were full of concern.

Clearly she was delusional in addition to her other ailments. "I can walk."

"I don't care."

Nic didn't have the energy to fight anymore. His arms were too comfortable, too soothing. He kept her cradled against his chest and continued down the tunnel.

At the next intersection he hung a right, then a quick left into another passage. In addition to being carried, she was dizzy from the twists and turns and only being able to see above her. The ceiling was claustrophobic low, making Arden duck at times to avoid cracking his head.

She closed her eyes for a second. Bad idea—more dizziness. When she opened them again, she spotted something. "Wait a minute. Back up."

He took a couple of steps back and followed her line of sight. "What?"

"Right there." She pointed at a manhole-size circle in the stone. "Is that an opening or am I just seeing things?"

Like an optical illusion, the ceiling appeared smooth, but there were rough indentations around the edge.

"I see it," he said. "I'm going to put you down for a minute and check it out." He bent all the way over and set her down on her butt. "Don't get up. I don't want you toppling over."

She rolled her eyes but stayed put. He ran his fingertips along the ceiling, and when he got to the edge of the circular mark, his hand went up into the gap. It wasn't an optical illusion; there was a chamber up there.

"Be right back." He grasped the sides and vaulted off the ground, disappearing inside. After a couple of seconds, his feet appeared through the opening, followed by his legs and then the rest of him. "It's perfect. Totally secluded. If I give you a boost, do you think you could climb up?"

Secluded with Arden wasn't quite what she wanted. But she needed a moment—just a minute—of downtime. She couldn't help Drew if she was too tired to fight.

She nodded. "Yeah. Give me a lift."

He helped her off the ground, then grabbed her by the waist with both hands and lifted her up into the chamber. She got a grip on the ground inside, pulled herself up with a grunt, and slid the rest of the way in until only her feet dangled over the gap. It took a minute for her eyes to adjust to the new light, and when they did, the sight stole her breath.

Thousands and thousands of glowing green crystals sparkled at the base of the black walls like emerald-studded baseboards, twinkling and pulsing in time with her racing heart; their glitter was irresistible. The domed space wasn't tall enough to stand up in, so she crawled away from the opening to get closer to the glowing crystals. The abnormal texture beneath her hands finally sank in and she looked down to see a velvety layer of moss blanketed the ground. She ran her palm across the surface. With each touch, it too lit up with the same stunning luminescence as the crystals— quiet, green-white light like the heart of a candle's flame.

It was the single most amazing thing Nic had ever seen. "It's so...so beautiful," she said.

"I knew you had to see it." He smiled as he lifted himself up from the tunnel below.

"It's remarkable."

"And it makes a perfect hideout."

He was right. No one passing below them would notice the cave. Hopefully. "How is this possible?"

"No clue," he said. "Not exactly what I would expect on the Fourth. They're more the fire-and-brimstone crowd down here."

She laughed but couldn't take her eyes off the shimmering crystals. They clustered in random patterns at the base of the walls, some as big as her forearm and some smaller like the jewel that winked from the star on her necklace. A particular group caught her attention because the center crystal was huge and the grouping seemed to grow into the wall itself.

When she crawled closer, she saw that the cluster *was* growing into the wall. Not only that, but the wall was carved from floor to ceiling. The moss lit up under her hands and she dimly heard a gasp come from her lips. The wall was carved from floor to ceiling with...shapes?

No, what are those—?

Sex.

She rose on her knees and leaned back on her heels. Hundreds of figures stretched over the entire surface. Men with men and women with women, human and demon, contorted into every position imaginable. Some even had all four of both species together. The pair right in front of her was a male demon and a human woman. She could tell he was demon because of the tiny scales the artist—or whomever it was that made this place— had sculpted onto his body. Her skin heated. The female figure straddled the man, her head thrown back in obvious ecstasy.

It made her think of the time she'd spent with Arden in that basement, and arousal purred through her. For a moment she could feel his hands and his mouth against her skin. She shouldn't be feeling sexual heat in her veins; she should be feeling exhaustion. Was the cave doing something to her? Making her forget what he'd done and whatever it was he still planned to do?

He spoke from right behind her and she jumped. "Such fine detail." He reached around her and traced the curve of the woman's hip. His touch followed the surface up to her neck and down over the flow of her hair. The whole thing was no bigger than his hand, but lifelike in every way.

She felt him move closer—felt the heat of him—and watched as he repeated his trace of the figure. Where his fingertip brushed the woman, Nic's own body flared with need.

What was she supposed to be angry about? Why couldn't she get her thoughts together? There was something strange about the cave, and it went beyond the weird light and the carvings, but what?

Arden's breath whispered over her neck, and her pulse raced. Safe. They were safe here. She was safe here. He would never let anything bad happen to her. But...

A war raged inside of her. Anger and betrayal fought to dominate the longing and desire burning beneath her skin. He had hurt her, but that seemed insignificant now. His schemes had wounded her, but the pain dimmed in the crystal glow of the cave. She wanted him, needed him. Never before had her needs appeared so plain. It was all so clear. Everything she needed stood behind her. Everything. Even the love she had denied herself for too long.

Nic struggled to keep a grasp on the dangerous turn of her thoughts. The demon behind her didn't love her. She didn't even know if he was capable of the emotion. Or was he?

His heat moved nearer to her back.

Maybe he did love her.

And if she closed her eyes, maybe she could pretend it was the truth.

———

Something was happening, and whatever it was, Arden didn't want it to stop. His obsessions, his reservations, his greed—all of it was sliding away. The only thing he *could* get a grasp on inside his skull was the need pulsing through him.

Nicolette. Her body, her soft skin. He wanted her naked, wanted her back arched as he drove into her—needed to hear her scream his name in pleasure.

Get a grip.

He shook his head, trying to clear the muck that had become his brain.

He was so close, so close to having everything he wanted.

But Nic—

Electricity shivered through him when he ran his palm down her arm.

She's mine. She's always been mine. All I need.

He laid his other hand against her back. Her skin... she leaned into his touch. The air between them filled with something, some energy he couldn't name, and the crystals around them darkened. Full emerald.

He knew that's what the stones were now. Emeralds full of fire, and they were doing something to him, something to Nic too. She shook beneath his hands. His heartbeat filled his ears and his cock hardened until he thought it would break through his zipper.

Now. Have her now.

Arden grabbed her around the waist and pulled her back against him; her ass ground against his throbbing hard-on. She moaned and he heard an answering call from his own throat.

His mouth fell on the tender flesh of her neck and he bit down until he tasted her sweet blood on his tongue. Then he drew back and licked her skin, tasting the salt of sweat and the copper tang of blood. One hand found her breast and kneaded while he moved the other down her stomach to the juncture of her sex. He could feel how wet she was through the fabric and he dug his fingers into her thigh to force her legs apart. He palmed her and pressed the heel of his hand against her, hard, while he bit and kissed and sucked at her neck.

He was panting by the time he pulled her back onto the ground on top of him. He didn't let her turn around, just kept her body pressed against his while his hands assaulted her. He wanted her begging, needed to hear from her lips that she burned for him.

———

Nic knew there was a reason she shouldn't be doing this, but...fuck.

His hands, his fingers, his mouth. She couldn't think about anything else. She writhed against him, pressing herself into his hand and loving the friction.

The moss-light danced with the movement of their bodies. She couldn't bear it any longer and wrenched herself around to face him.

The sight of his face bathed in the emerald incandescence made the breath stall in her lungs. With her hands quaking like leaves in the wind, she reached up to touch his jaw. He captured her hands and kissed her palms, then laid her hands over his heart. His stare was frightening and molten hot. She smoldered beneath it.

Everything inside her morphed, changed, and made way for something more desperate, more primal.

Need.

Her fingers shook beneath his warm hands as she undid the buttons on his shirt. The fabric sighed when she pushed it out of the way to plant a kiss in the center of his chest. He was so warm and her lips tasted the smoky, raw scent of his skin.

In a heartbeat he was on top of her, his hands braced on either side of her head. She almost couldn't bear to look at him, but look she did, and a moment of despair cut her when she saw the indecision written all over his face.

His look cut right through whatever it was that had a hold on her.

And here was the truth of it all: she, plain Nic Wright, with the attitude and the toughness, a mile-wide chip on her shoulder, and enough heartache for a hundred people, was simply that; plain. Ordinary. Nothing close to good enough for him.

"You don't want me." Her voice broke and she looked past his shoulder at the ceiling.

"You're wrong, Nic." He captured her face between his palms. "I want you so much it terrifies me."

She looked back at him and saw the muscle in his jaw ticking in time to her pulse. He was probably lying, but she couldn't deny the truth. She wanted this. She wanted him. "Don't stop," she said. "Please. Not this time."

He leaned down until she could feel his breath on her lips. "I won't."

Episode Eight
Chapter Twenty-Five

The instant his mouth touched hers, a thousand flames birthed under her skin and Nic wove her hands into his black hair. When his tongue stroked her bottom lip, she opened to him.

The cave around them faded away. There was no Fourth Level of Hell. No desperate chase to save her brother, no unanswered questions, no confusion or hurt. No lying demons, no terrifying enemies.

All of those things still existed, filled her head with panic, but they were in shadow.

Because none of them could compete with the light in her current universe.

In this universe, there was only Arden.

He pressed his body into her, and she could feel his heat through her clothes. The hard length of his erection rubbed against her sex and she wrapped her legs around him to bring him closer. A purr rumbled in his chest and he broke away from her. She opened her eyes and found him looking down at her. He was on fire too; she saw it in his shaking hands and in his tensed muscles. She reached for him.

"Wait," he said, and disentangled himself from her legs. He rolled off of her and she felt the loss of his body like a death. But he settled next to her on his side and put his arm under her head. "I want to see your beautiful skin."

He lifted her shirt and she leaned up so he could pull it off over her head. Before she lay back he made quick work of unfastening her bra.

The whisper-soft moss caressed her back as he traced the mark from the spider attack. If there was still pain there, his touch evaporated it. She could feel nothing but him. He grazed her nipples with his palm and she felt them stiffen in response. The flat of his hand smoothed over her stomach and moved lower to the gathering heat between her legs. She was so wet, aching for him.

She kicked off her boots as he unfastened her jeans and slid them down over her hips, releasing her legs one at a time. Her panties went next and, after tossing them aside, he ran his hand along the inside of her leg, swirling circles over her skin until he reached her thigh. She wanted his fingers to move to the left and delve inside her, but he didn't put them there. Instead he took his arm out from under her head and shrugged out of his shirt.

His skin shone with beads of sweat under the crystal glow, and his tattoos danced with the movement of his muscles; his body was a marvel. He stood to take off his pants. The sight of his freed erection sped her pulse and her sex tightened. If she didn't feel him inside of her soon, she would die from the denial.

He knelt down but didn't touch her, only stared. "Nic," he breathed. "So stunning, so perfect. You are...breathtaking. Like mercury, loose and shining under the brilliance of the sun."

The compliment filled her with a longing so intense she thought she would be crushed under the weight of it. She froze up—could not move under the intensity of his stare—but when he extended a hand to her, she reached out to take it. He pulled her up until she knelt with him.

His hands came up to frame her face. Heat radiated between them in the moment before she felt his naked flesh against her own.

And when they touched, Nic drowned in fire. He pressed his lips to hers and ran his hands down her neck and over her shoulders to her back. The slow stroke of his tongue matched his movements and stole the breath from her lungs.

He trailed his kisses down her jaw to the side of her neck. She felt his teeth on the vulnerable skin of her throat and she tilted her head back to give him full access to her flesh.

Arden put his hands on her hips and lifted her into his lap, her legs stretched on either side. His cock throbbed between them as he fell to the ground, taking her with him. He rolled her onto her back and slid down over her body until she felt his teeth nip at her inner thigh.

A quiet moan escaped from her mouth when he ran his tongue over the soft wet skin that now ached for him. She felt his fingers open her folds, and his thumb kneaded the spot that had become the center of her universe.

An instant and violent climax wracked her body. He licked the juice from her, then slipped one long finger inside, and then another. With agonizing slowness he moved them, and before she'd begun to recover from the first, another explosion ripped through her.

"You taste so sweet." His voice was ragged. He moved up her body again and captured her mouth. She tasted herself on his lips.

She spread her legs and wrapped them around his hips. The feel of his cock against her was like a promise. She wanted him inside of her. All of him.

He planted one hand beside her head and the other reached down between their bodies to guide his shaft. He rubbed the tip down the length of her sex and then pressed it into her. She felt her inner muscles clench around him as he filled her, stretched her. She wrapped her legs around his waist, forcing him deeper. He braced his palms on the ground beside her, and with a hard thrust of his hips, he buried himself inside of her.

She heard him suck in a breath through clenched teeth, and his muscles vibrated beneath her legs.

It was not like before; the last time had been fast and over too soon. Now his strokes were slow, deliberate. Her hips rose to meet his. She wanted him harder, deeper.

With each stroke, a searing point of ecstasy built within her, beginning where their bodies met and spreading like a fever. Each time he slid into her, the sensation grew until she thought she would break into a million pieces. She grabbed his arms and dug her fingernails into his skin.

Arden rolled his hips and slowed his pace. "Not yet," he hissed as he pulled out of her and drove back in, inch by tortuous inch. "You're so wet and beautiful. Open your eyes and look at me."

She whimpered and obeyed. His eyes had changed once again. The emerald had gone pure black.

He went terribly still and she could feel him throbbing inside of her. "Come for me."

With his words, the edge she'd been teetering on fell away and she plunged into the depths. Lost. Shattered.

From somewhere in the haze, she could feel him moving again, thrusting into her. Some animal noise—from her own mouth or his she didn't know anymore—echoed off the walls. Shudders rocked her body. He lifted her hips and wrapped an arm around her back. He drove harder, deeper, and she fell into the void again.

"Nic." He said her name like an affirmation and then he came, his own climax spilling into her.

Arden rolled onto his back and pulled her to his chest, still inside her. She pressed her cheek to his skin and heard his heart thrumming. The only sound in the cave was the rush of their mingled, ragged breaths.

He lifted her chin until she could see his face. His eyes smoldered with ice-fire and some other emotion she couldn't name. "I don't want to let you go."

His words touched a sore place inside of her and she couldn't meet his gaze. She dropped her head back down to rest against his chest, and his thick arms wrapped around her.

Nic wanted to tell him the truth—she knew about his scheme. She knew letting her go was his intention all along. She knew he would hurt her in the end.

The cave had done something to force her guards away. She didn't doubt the place's power; it had done something to both of them. But when it wore off, where would that leave them? Where would it leave her?

The compartment deep inside of her where she kept all her secrets opened its door and a simple, but nefarious, truth was released.

There was a darker reason his betrayal stung so much. There was something she'd been running from, fighting and arguing with him to avoid. And she was an absolute idiot not to see it before.

She had fallen in love with him.

Her breath caught in her throat and tears clouded her sight.

All the time she'd been with him, that fact had been lurking in the back of her head, waiting to drown her in its truth. And even worse, drown her in the knowledge that it could never be.

She couldn't have a future with him, the demon Prince who held her. He'd go on with his plan, leaving her forever haunted by the memory of this moment.

Nic didn't know what the next few hours might bring, but at least she had this: the feel of his skin beneath her cheek and his hands resting on her back. It would be her sweet, crystalline memory to wash away the pain.

When the end approached, she would be ready.

Her desperate thoughts were sliced in half by the sound of running feet in the tunnel below. Arden tensed and tightened his hold on her just as the screaming started.

Chapter Twenty-Six

Arden peeked over the lip of the opening. There were at least twenty demons running away from something he couldn't see yet. Their screeches and screams bounced off the tunnel walls. He couldn't stick his head out any farther or he would be spotted, but he needed to see what pursued them.

Nic sat right beside him. She had gotten dressed with a speed that amazed him. "What is it?"

"Can't see it."

But then he heard it. Laughter echoed in the tunnel and the fleeing demons panicked. Some fell and were trampled. He saw limbs broken and faces smashed into the rocky floor. The ones who had fallen, no matter how severe their injuries, pulled themselves off the ground and hobbled or crawled to get away. The laughter grew each time blood spilled. It sounded like the raw, hollow call of a raven or the tittering giggle of a hyena.

He couldn't tell how far away the demon was, but a plan had started to form in his head. First, he needed to get dressed. It wasn't going to work if he was naked.

"What are you going to do?" She leaned over the edge of the opening, and he could see her jaw clench each time another demon was trampled below.

Again her resilience surprised him. The sight of the green and pulpy demon blood would make most humans sick, but she didn't even flinch. She amazed him. The vision of her body under him stilled his hands on the buttons of his shirt. He could still smell the fragrance of her arousal on his skin. And he wanted her again. Wanted to feel her and see the heat in her eyes when she came. His cock stiffened as he stared at the curve of her back.

No time for that, you idiot. Get dressed.

"What are you going to do?"

"I'm going to enlist someone's help to find Sorro's nest." He pulled on his boots but didn't bother with the laces. Timing was critical.

She picked up on his urgency and he could almost see the switch turn on in her head. Soft Nic was gone now, replaced by what he'd come to think of as her warrior self. All the struggles she'd faced in her life made her into an Amazon—steely and brutal. She crouched by the edge of the entrance. "I don't see any more runners," she whispered. "But I can hear footsteps. Whatever they were running from is coming."

He picked up his knife from the cave floor, pointing the business end at the ground. He crouched next to Nic, and to his surprise, she moved back, ceding to him without protest. Something had changed between them, but Arden had no time to think about it now.

The acoustics in the tunnel distorted the sound of the footfalls, but he knew the demon was close. The bizarre laughter rippled along the tunnel walls. Then he saw a shadow creep into view and he readied himself.

Just a little closer, asshole.

The demon came into sight below. A female Skinner. He had to play it perfectly or things would get real, real ugly.

252

He saw her stop and sniff the air, seeking her prey. She didn't look up, but he knew she could scent them. Too much emotion and sex filled the air for her *not* to notice.

Her head cocked to the side, listening, and he held his breath. The Skinner started to walk away and then stopped and backtracked.

They had been found.

As her head began to turn to look above, he threw himself through the opening into the tunnel below.

Nic saw only a struggling pair of bodies. She couldn't get a good view of the thing Arden wrestled with, but she knew it was vicious; it moved with the agility of a gymnast, and its feral screeches made her want to cover her ears. Its body was long and lean like a reptile or a rabid and starving stray dog. The dim light in the tunnel made it hard to see more detail, but she could see the dull, grayish-brown scales covering its skin.

They rolled out of sight and she jumped through the opening. She was itching for a fight to distract her from her own thoughts and wasn't going to let Arden have all the fun. Besides, maybe it would take away some of the pain burning in her chest.

When her feet hit the ground, she turned to where the fight continued ten feet away. He had the advantage of height and weight, but the creature fought him all the way, snarling and opening its mouth, looking to take a bite out of him. When it spotted Nic, it broke free from his grasp and leaped at her.

The demon rushed her, but she ducked at the last minute and Arden tackled the thing from behind. His arm wrapped around its throat, silencing its snarls, and he managed to get a leg around its midsection. He fell to the ground with the beast on top of him. After a few seconds its struggles slowed.

"That's right," he said, his voice calm like the purr of a cat. "Go to sleep, bitch."

Bitch? "That thing's a female?" The normal stuff to show gender wasn't there—no boobs—and since it wasn't wearing clothes of any kind, she could see no sexual organ visible between its legs. "How do you know?"

He didn't release his hold to answer even though the demon was out cold. "Her size and no wings. Skinner males are small and wiry like children and they have wings like beetles."

"What the fuck is a *Skinner?*" She knew it couldn't be good—the name told her that much—but she wanted to know which particular variety of bad he had in a sleeper hold and figure-four leg lock.

"They're like exterminators," he said. The female twitched and he tightened his arm around her neck. "It's our version of population control."

Nic moved closer to get a better look. "These things hunt their own kind?"

"Only the females. The males are for breeding."

A vision of a praying mantis came to mind and she figured their mating rituals were about the same, including the part when the satisfied female removed her partner's head. "But why does Hell need population control?" Wouldn't it be better to have more demons around?

"Demons tend to be a bit lusty," he said, grinning. "Why do you think I have six brothers?"

It hadn't occurred to her. A stray thought of him spreading her thighs and entering her came to mind. She fought it but blushed anyway. "Oh."

He laughed. "We can't help ourselves."

So it wasn't that he found her irresistible; it was just part of his nature. She tried not to let her disappointment show on her face. "That explains a lot."

"Sort of, but…" He paused, like he was careful in choosing his next words. "But with you, it's different."

Her heart fluttered a little, but she shut it down. She was a means to an end for him and nothing more. And no matter how her body responded to him, no matter that his arms brought her more comfort than she'd had in a very long time, she needed to remember he was using her.

The silence that fell reeked of so many things, but she could not bring herself to speak, afraid she would regret whatever came out of her mouth. She looked away.

He ended the standoff. "Take the laces out of my boots. We'll use them to tie her up."

She worked fast, not wanting the Skinner to wake up before she was finished. After she'd coiled his boot laces around the demon's scale-covered ankles and wrists, he pushed its body off and stood up. His proximity unnerved her and she took a step away from him. "How long will she be out?"

"Only a few more minutes," he said. "Then we make her tell us what we want to know."

She couldn't imagine the demon would be willing to cooperate. How did he think they would get the information? Pull out the female's fingernails? "This should be interesting."

He gave her a nod. "Wait a minute." He frowned. "The necklace. Where's the star?"

She clutched at her neck, grabbing for the chain. But she felt the closure and realized the pendant must have fallen back when—nope, she refused to let her mind go there. She pulled the star out over her collar.

Arden lifted his hand and pressed his palm over the charm, holding it to her chest. Their eyes met for a moment. He started to speak, then he shook his head, and his hand fell back to his side. She looked away to avoid his stare because she knew her face would give her away.

"You fucking moon-eyed lovers need to untie me right fucking now." Both of their heads snapped around to look at the Skinner. "Yeah, geniuses, I'm talking to you," she said. "Untie me before I call my sisters."

Arden stepped over to the demon and showed his knife. "I'll slit your throat and bleed you before you can utter a sound."

Her teeth gnashed the air and she fought her bindings. "Fuck you, Prince."

Why did everyone keep calling him that? For Nic, the word conjured up images of chivalry and charming men dressed in all white. He didn't really fit the bill. Especially with the evil grin on his face and the blade in his hand.

"Give me your name, Skinner, and I'll think about letting you live."

"My sisters will have your hide as a carpet to mate on," she said with a smile that showed off a very neat row of sharp teeth.

Arden dodged her mouth as she snapped her teeth. He ran his blade down the side of her face. She cried out as a thick line of blood flowed from the wound. "Your name or the next one will be deeper."

The Skinner spat at him, but he ducked out of the way. "We will gut your demoness and wear her entrails as jewelry." She laughed.

The charm had held—the creature didn't know she was human. But the threat made her angry and she wished Arden would just kill the thing and get it over with.

His knife met the side of the Skinner's neck, but the beast didn't stop. "Poor Prince, you can't see what's right in front of you. Your lover is hurt."

What? She hadn't even gotten close enough to get a punch in, let alone get injured.

Concern flashed in his eyes when he looked over at her. "Are you hurt?"

"Not on the outside, idiot," the creature hissed. "You forget our ability. I can see right through you both."

The creature could read her emotions. *Damn it.* How was she supposed to deal with that on top of the rest?

Ah. Anger. The only thing she'd ever been able to cling to when her heart ached. She thought of her brother and his captor and what she wanted to do to Sorro. Sweet fury filled her and she seized on to it, hoping it would mask the turmoil brewing within her.

The Skinner cackled. "You try to cover it, female, but your pain burns brighter than your anger. I will taste it in your blood when I rip out your throat."

The blade of Arden's knife twisted into the demon's flesh. "Give me your name." His voice was no more than a growl, low and savage.

"Oh, I see you too, High Born. You're full of conflict. You want something, but your need for the female is getting in the way. And there's something even more under it all that you are desperate to hide. Even from yourself."

Nic's breath caught in her chest. It had to be lies. The thing couldn't be telling the truth. But it had seen inside her own heart; could it also see into his?

He didn't move or look back at her, just pressed his knife deeper into the Skinner's throat. "Your name."

Three inches of the blade disappeared before she relented. "Wret." She squirmed under the cut of his knife and the wound opened farther.

Arden wobbled the blade and a screech poured forth from her mouth. "All of it," he said. "Your true name."

"Wretch—Wretched," she gasped.

"All right, *Wretched*." Arden emphasized the name and gripped his knife. "Here's how this is going to go. You will take us to Sorro's nest and maybe we'll let you go with your head intact."

The Skinner no longer fought. She lay quiet and her eyes never left Arden. "I will take you there."

"I knew you'd say that," he said to her. Then he offered Nic one of his devilish grins. "It's amazing what you can accomplish just by knowing someone's name, huh?"

Some important tidbit hovered at the periphery of Nic's brain, but like a snake, it slithered away before she could grab it.

———

The one kind of demon Arden didn't want to run across down here. Damn it. Female Skinners were empaths and she'd pull out every emotion she could from her enemy to weaken them. He'd have to keep himself on lockdown or who knew what Wretched might dredge up.

But the benefit of having her as hostage was that every demon within a mile would stay away like rodents fleeing when they heard the sound of the exterminator's truck.

"Move," he said, and the Skinner obeyed. He had untied Wretched's ankles to let her walk. The true-name tactic made her perfectly controllable. He shouldn't have used the forbidden trick, but he needed her cooperation. The culmination of his plan neared and he wasn't taking any chances.

He left her wrists bound to be safe. If only he had a gag to keep her dangerous mouth shut too. Not because of her teeth, but because of what she had almost given away—his plans. That wouldn't do. And the part about there being more to it than just his transformation?

Well, he wasn't even going to wonder what she was talking about. Just because Skinners were empaths didn't mean they knew everything.

But Wretched had said something else that bugged him—Nic was hurt, but not on the outside. What was that supposed to mean? Of course she was hurting because of her brother and the whole mess, but what did *he* have to do with her pain?

It didn't matter. Right now he had bigger issues to worry about. Because as they approached the point of no return, he found he wanted—no, needed—to see this out to the end. He would still get what he wanted out of the whole thing, but he would gut Sorro for the wrench he'd thrown into Arden's carefully laid plans.

However, a demon like Sorro would not go easy and neither would he lack defenses around his nest. There were bound to be all kinds of traps and guards, if not a whole battalion of lower demons watching the entrance. Damn it. If Nic hadn't been so insistent on finding Drew, he could already be done.

"You *should* be worried," Wretched said, clearly reading his emotions. "The one you seek is well protected."

"Shut up and keep moving." He needed to keep a tighter rein on his thoughts. She wasn't a mind reader, but if thinking triggered an emotional response, she would pick up on it right away. Arden didn't need the Skinner sifting through his emotions—especially where Nic was concerned. So he opted for a distraction. "What do you know about his nest, Wretched?"

At the sound of her name her shoulders slumped. "I've never seen inside myself, but some of my sisters have. He sometimes likes to use lower demons in his tortures and he calls one of us to dispose of them after he's used them up. The sisters say it's like a palace with room after room of luxury."

"Are there guards?" Nic asked. He realized it was the first she had spoken since before he'd fought with the Skinner.

Before Wretched had dropped her bombs.

Something was definitely going on with Nic. He glanced over and saw the way her jaw was set, and as she walked she didn't look anywhere but forward. Her hand sought the gun on her hip over and over. And not only had she not said a word until now, she hadn't even looked at him, which, for some intangible reason, pissed him off.

Wretched laughed. "Stupid Prince. Can't you feel her pain? It consumes her even now."

What the fuck was Wretched talking about? Hurt. What would hurt a human, but not physically? The same things that would hurt most creatures: loss or betrayal.

What had she lost? He knew Drew still lived; Sorro was trying to get *both* siblings, so he wouldn't kill one without the other.

Betrayal? No one had betrayed…

Except for him.

Which meant she knew about his plan. *Fuck*.

But how? He hadn't told anyone, not even his father. There was only one kind of creature in the universe who could know. It was their job to know what demons desired. It was how they kept things in balance.

And Nic had seen one in the room when she was attacked. She hadn't said it had spoken to her, though.

But if that creature was somehow involved in all of this, wouldn't it want Sorro to have that piece of info?

Damn it. Had to be Sorro. When Nic had been in that room, he doubted the demon would have wasted such a sweet opportunity to cause pain.

And now she knew he'd used her tragedy, her own desperation, for his own selfish purposes.

Betrayal at its finest.

All the time he had spent trying to protect her and he was the one hurting her. But in the cave she had given her body to him even though she knew the truth.

Hatred—utter disgust—did not come close to describing the way he felt about himself.

"Now you see, don't you, Prince?" Wretched smiled over her shoulder at him. "Your self-loathing is like sweet fruit on my tongue."

Nic glanced back at him. The look on her face cut him as if an expression could be a knife.

Wretched cackled. "And she feels so much more than pain right now, but I'm not telling."

He couldn't take any more revelations. "Keep moving, Wretched." Her name shut her up and her cawing stopped right away. Good, now they could get back to the matter at hand. "We need some answers. Are there guards around Sorro's nest?"

Chapter Twenty-Seven

"There has to be another way in, Wretched," Nic said. "We can't just waltz through the front door."

Arden was glad to see her engaged again even if she didn't direct any of her questions his way. It was better than her silence. The quiet let his mind wander and the places it went were areas he really didn't want to see.

Instead, he had kept Wretched busy with questions about Sorro's nest. She had filled them in on the guards—there were many and of all variety of demon. They had to find a way around his defenses, which led to Nic's question about a back door.

"His nest is like a big cave," the Skinner said. "Only one way in and one way out."

"How do we get in without being spotted, Wretched?" Nic asked.

She kept using the demon's name over and over as if testing out the power it gave her. It was a potent thing to have that kind of control over someone. No wonder his father had drilled it into him since birth to never give up his true name—it made a demon into a slave, and the result chilled him a bit.

"Too many guards, too many traps," Wretched said.

Nic rubbed her temples. "We have to figure out a way around them."

They walked on in silence. Every few feet he had to prod Wretched to keep her going or use her name to motivate her. It gave him a little time to think about their predicament, but he couldn't stop thinking about Nic. The way she had looked in the light of the cave. The way her skin felt. The way she tasted.

He'd make Sorro suffer for taking her brother, for hurting her, and for ruining his normally faultless ability to stay on task.

He couldn't stay focused because of a woman. A *human* woman.

Of course, she was an incredibly *beautiful* woman—not to mention brave, intelligent, funny, and when she was angry...those eyes, like sun-warmed granite—

What the fuck was wrong with him? Soon enough he would have everything he ever wanted. No more boredom. No more stupid half demon; he would be an Incubus, a full demon, whose only worry was how soon he could bed another warm, willing female.

And he wouldn't ever have to wonder about the half of him that was human, even if it meant severing his last tie to his mother.

"Such sadness," Wretched said. "What would a Prince know about sadness?"

Shit. Now Nic looked at him too, confusion like a cloud in her eyes. Almost as if his emotions mattered to her.

Enough. It was time to find out how much she knew. He could even do it without letting the Skinner know that Nic was human if he was subtle, and it would take only a second.

He grabbed her arm and spun her around.

She flung out of his grasp and her eyes flashed with angry lightning. "What are you doing?"

The only way it was going to work was if he could get her to meet his eyes just for a second. Then, he could get her to tell him anything.

He stepped a little closer to her. "Nic," he said. "Look at me."

"What?" She met his stare with a frown.

"I want you to tell me something," he said, not breaking the eye contact.

"What is it now?" she said.

Wait. What the hell? Her eyes weren't glazed, and from the set of her shoulders he could see she wasn't in a passive state. He tried it again. "Nic, I want you to tell me something."

Wretched started laughing. Her awful hyena tittering echoed off of the tunnel walls. "For a High Born you're a real moron. Didn't your snooty parents teach you anything? Your human isn't going to fall for your parlor trick."

Nic shot him a crazy look and he mirrored it. The Skinner knew she was human. But what about the Deceiver Charm? "What makes you think she's human?" he asked.

"I could smell her. As soon as she got close enough. She stinks of earth."

He had to know about the necklace. If the guards protecting Sorro's nest smelled a human, things could go bad in a big hurry. "But she wears a charm to mask her identity."

Wretched shook her head. "The rules were put in place to keep the Fallen from interfering down here or running amok."

"What rules?" If they didn't need the demon's help to find the nest, he would have strangled her for being so evasive.

"There are a lot of rules, but the one your sire didn't seem to teach you is the Rule of Proximity," she said. "Your sire should have told you. What an idiot."

"Wretched," Nic said, and at the sound of her name, the smile left the demon's face. "What is the Rule of Proximity?" Her quick thinking made him want to kiss her.

"Your power is strongest the nearer you are to home and when you are on earth. The lower you descend into Hell, the weaker your talent."

Shit. "And the charm?" he asked.

"Same thing."

Well, that put a whole new twist on things. "Anything else you think I might need to know about?" he said. When she started to cackle again he quickly added, "Wretched."

"One thing," she said. "Down here in the Fourth, you are as human as your lover."

Your lover. It did have a nice ring to it, and there had to be a way he could—

Fuck. He needed to get his shit together. Now he would be going after Sorro as a human *with* a human. How were they supposed to pull that off? And how would he ever figure out what Nic knew if he couldn't use his Gift?

"Is it possible for two humans to come down here and get lost or get away from their captors?" Nic asked. She didn't seem to be talking to him or Wretched, though. A frown wrinkled her forehead. "There are other demons down here who torture us, right?" This time she directed her question to the Skinner.

"Of course. Sometimes my sisters and I get leftovers." Wretched smiled and showed her pretty, pointy teeth.

"And Sorro's favorite thing is torturing humans," Nic said.

Arden could almost see the wheels spinning in her head. "What are you thinking?"

"Since we're both human now," she said, turning to look at him, "we'll make for good bait, if we can convince people we're dead, anyway."

He saw the sheer brilliance of her plan and gave her a grin. She offered him a tentative smile in return and his heart sped up at the sight.

He really wanted to kiss her.

— —

They were able to get Wretched to go along with the scheme. It took him only a couple more passes with his blade, saying her true name a million times, and swearing on the name of the Dark One to let her go as soon as they were in, but she'd agreed. They were even able to have her point out on the map which tunnel seemed most likely to have the lowest number of guards.

Nic's plan was genius. He had never met a woman with her level of whip-crack-fast thinking. It made him want her even more.

He just wasn't ready to let her go. Her mind alone would keep him from ever getting bored.

And her body?

Nope. Never bored again.

The tunnel they used to come up to the nest the back way was small, so Wretched walked in front and Nic walked next to him. He kept stealing looks at her, wondering how to find out what she knew.

In the end, he opted for honesty, and it was the first time in his life he'd ever been honest with a human. "I want to become something different. A different kind of demon."

"I know," she said. "Sorro told me."

Just as he'd thought. "I'm sorry." Another first for him.

"For what? Tricking me and then leaving me alone to find out the truth or for using me like a fucking pawn?"

That stung. He deserved it. "Would you believe me if I said I'm sorry for all of it?"

She laughed, but it was brittle and heavy, like trees after an ice storm. "I don't know what to believe anymore."

"Nic, I…"

"Let's just get through this, OK?" She shook her head, and her dark hair covered the side of her face, obscuring his view. "I guess our deal was a sham right from the start, huh? I mean, you already had sex with me, so your obligation is over."

Brutal to hear her talk about it that way. "I wasn't thinking about our bargain when we were back in that cave, or even in that shithole basement back on the Second." Again he owned up to the truth. He didn't have a choice. His sarcasm and charm wouldn't help him here. "I wanted you then. I want you now."

She stopped for a step and then moved on. "All *I* want is to get Drew, go home, and forget this happened to me."

Forget he *happened to her*? "We'll find him."

"When were you going to do it?"

Her question threw him. When would he abandon her? So she knew part of the plan, but didn't know when he would put it into action. And she had given herself to him in that cave *knowing* he would abandon her. If being human meant he would feel guilt and pain like this, he didn't want any part of it. But he deserved every cut she gave him and he was glad his demon side offered him no shield. "I'm sorry," he said again.

"I believe you *think* you are, but it remains to be seen whether you're human enough to really mean it or not." She sighed. "So, I have a proposition for you."

Now it was his turn to miss a step. "Proposition?"

"Well, the way I see it, we need each other. And no matter what, I want Drew back home where he belongs. If you will help me make that happen, and when I know he's safe, I'll do whatever I have to do to help you in return."

She didn't know what she offered him, or she wouldn't have asked. It would buy him time, though. Time to figure out how he could keep her. Maybe he could find someone else to use as his bribe for the Emissary. "Done."

Maybe he could get his way after all.

———

Sorro struggled to keep the glee from overwhelming him. The time drew near for him to receive his payment, and then he would be through with this place forever. No more stupid humans. No more red rocks that glowed with fear as their fuel. No more pain.

Everything would be perfect. For eternity.

And he would never have to hear the imbecilic whimpering inside his head when he awoke from the endless nightmares that had been his nightly parasites for as far back as his memory stretched.

Everything would be perfect.

But first, he had to get ready. The Prince and the female were coming and he had some surprises for them.

The guards he passed at the entrance to his nest stepped out of his way. Fear rolled off of them in waves. If it were a normal day, their fright would have earned them a punch in the face, but today it didn't matter and he let them slide. Not enough time for it anyway. He had things to do.

The human drug sucker had just about lost his ability to walk. By the Third level, he had to be dragged or kicked to keep him moving. It annoyed Sorro, but he didn't let it get to him. Both his and the human's worries would be over soon enough.

He stalked through the main chamber dragging the human behind him. All the time he had spent building his nest, all the little details he had added over the years for comfort, looked like trash to him now. Even the huge metal throne he'd sat in as King, reigning over his violent sanguine realm, stood on its dais abandoned and awaiting his heir. It made him a bit wistful to see it standing there empty.

The sharp steel hooks and chains of his suspension rig dominated the ceiling of the enormous room—a gigantic macabre chandelier covered in blood and bodies. When the victims were still alive enough to scream or kick, the whole thing moved like the mobile over an infant's crib. And he, the babe, lay underneath, cooing as dripping gore dyed his white hair red. But the centerpiece was still now, just a piece of oozing detritus hanging limp; the discarded decorations of a child's birthday party. He stopped for a moment to look up at it and smiled for all the joy it had brought him over the last four hundred years. At least he had found pleasure where he could.

He had so much to do, and he missed Flic because he really could've used his help with all the preparations. It would have also been nice to have someone fawn over his genius as he put the final touches in place, but no matter. The only witnesses would be the ones whose deaths were his ticket to paradise.

Several tunnels led off the main chamber, but the one he chose was the smallest of them all. It led down past the kitchens. As he breezed by, the smell of cooking flesh assaulted him. He wondered what would be for dinner when he got to his new home.

The citrine and amber eyes of the wiry guards stationed at intervals all along the corridor stared straight ahead. It wasn't the first time they had seen Sorro dragging a human down the hall.

But it would be the last time. The thought filled him with elation and suddenly he laughed, a burst of joy that sounded foreign and magical to his ears.

He took the next left and stopped in front of the double doors to his private quarters. Horren blocked the entrance with his massive bulk. His boulder-gray shoulders were as wide as the doors.

The demon's brother, Harrow, was dead. Sorro had left him back in the Third as a distraction for his pursuers and the Prince had slaughtered him. Such a waste, but having a personal guard was no longer necessary anyway.

No grief showed in Horren's apricot eyes—the Colossai saw death as an honor—as he waited for the password, the only thing that would move him from his post.

With the flick of a wrist, Sorro gave him the command and the beast stepped back to allow him access. "Dismiss all the guards. All of them, and everyone else," he told the Colossai. No reason for the guards to interfere with his prey. "I want this place empty."

He dropped Drew to the floor and flung open the doors. Once he had hauled the human inside, he took a moment to admire the place he'd spent so much time in. It was beautiful, really, from the smooth crimson walls alight with fear-fire to the carefully preserved legs and heads sitting on pedestals around the room. His gallery of death and pain.

Too bad he hadn't had time to choose another heir; it was a shame to let all his precious art go to waste. All of it would have gone to Flic, but his protégé wasn't going to be admiring artwork anymore.

Maybe he should give it all to Horren as reparation for the loss of his brother. He would think it over while he worked on his final project.

He smiled and the joy of it felt like it would crack his face open.

Time for the big show.

———

The long walk grated on Nic, not because she was exhausted—she was beyond physical exhaustion at this point—but because of all the silence. Silence gave her brain time to wander and she didn't like the places her thoughts took her.

She worried about Drew and wondered if his mind had finally snapped. All those years of drug abuse were bound to catch up with him sometime. It explained the way he had turned away from her in that brutal moment when he had chosen the hand of the enemy.

Whatever Sorro had told him, whatever empty promises he had given, she would make the demon suffer for all of it.

And if that meant sacrificing herself? Well, so be it.

Everything seemed so simple when she thought about it that way. Her life for someone she loved.

Arden had agreed to help her. She almost believed him too, but she waited for the other shoe to drop. He could still, at any moment, revert to his original plan.

She needed to be realistic. He was a *demon* and demons weren't exactly known for honesty. But now that they had all the cards on the table, what was left for him to lie about? He had her right where he needed her—desperate, vulnerable, and willing to do what had to be done. The knowledge did nothing to soothe the hollow feeling in her chest.

But what did she expect? Him to fall down on his knees and swear his undying devotion? The old saying about shitting in one hand and wishing in the other came to mind.

He told her he wanted her, but she didn't know what that meant. Chase had said something about her being a pet. The thought did not appeal to her.

She caught her own lie. If being his pet entailed spending the rest of her days with him, then she was all in. The way she felt in his arms told her everything she needed to know.

I love him.

His glacial eyes and his rebellious black hair. His crooked, sexy grin and his rock-star attitude. The way he moved like a jaguar and touched her as if she were a priceless jewel. And when she was in danger, he became a thing of pure violence and anarchy. He made her feel safe, protected. She had spent the last ten years of her life making sure everyone *else* was safe, not to mention the years she'd spent before that, trying to protect her parents from her brother and his illness. Arden made all of it go away, and for the first time in as long as she could remember, she knew peace in his embrace.

Yeah, if being his pet meant she got to feel that every once in a while, she would be happy.

First, they had to find Drew and get him the fuck out.

She focused back in on the here and now. Wretched said they were getting closer. They would have to stop soon to prepare.

Her plan was good; she just hoped it would work. The key was getting Wretched to cooperate long enough to get them inside the nest. Although, if any of the guards had time to look close enough and realize there was more to her and Arden than what they appeared to be, all bets would be off and they would opt for plan B.

Of course, she hadn't come up with a plan B just yet, but she was good at thinking on her feet. Maybe she'd let one of the guards take her and then stand back and watch as Arden slaughtered them all.

A bitter smile tugged at the corners of her mouth. If it came to that, she would enjoy every minute.

Perhaps she'd been spending too much time with demons. It made her wonder how she would ever fit back in with regular humans. She would do all the things they did, but in her mind she would never be one of them again. Her obsessive vigilance and isolation had kept her from feeling human for a very long time anyway.

But she wasn't a demon, or an angel, for that matter.

A picture of her parents ghosted into her mind. Were they sitting on a cloud somewhere in the sky, winged and jubilant, forever smiles on their faces? She hoped they were at least at peace. The old, familiar pain washed over her and she felt the first sting of tears. For all they had done for her, all the love they had showered on her like summer rain, she wished them peace.

Wretched stopped and looked back at her. "Stop it," she said. "You can't go to Sorro's nest with that kind of pain in your heart. If they don't eat you alive, I will."

Damn empaths. She brushed the tears from her cheeks. "I'm cool."

"You sure?" Arden asked. Concern creased his brow.

"Yep," she lied. "Fine."

"We're near the nest," Wretched said.

For good or ill, Nic got the sense that all her life had careened toward this inevitable battle. Now that the moment had come, she could only hope she was ready.

This would decide her future…

If she had one.

"When will you let me go?" Wretched asked her.

"Once you fulfill your obligation," Arden answered. "If you try to run before then, Wretched, I will deliver your head to your sisters myself."

"And they will pluck those pretty eyes out of your face and feed them to our young."

Nic reviewed the details of her plan with Arden. To keep control of Wretched, they would have to keep repeating her name, but only in a whisper to prevent the guards from hearing. The Skinner would offer up the humans for Sorro. Arden would keep his head down to keep from being recognized. Once they were inside…well, the plan got a bit fuzzy after that.

She watched as he untied their hostage, and then she held out one of her own wrists for him to wrap. He smoothed his hand over the skin of her forearm and a shiver ran through her. She looked up at him and his expression was as hard and fierce as a freshly sharpened blade.

"Do not get separated from me," he said. "I will not let them hurt you." The intensity of his stare made her heart ache. He bound his left wrist with her right. "I don't know what I would do if I lost you."

His plan. The transformation. Of course that's what he was talking about. Without her, he wouldn't get it. "Don't worry, I'll keep my promise. You'll get what you want."

"I'm not talking about..." He trailed off, then shook his head and looked away. "Nevermind."

Then what are you talking about? she wanted to scream at him, but kept her mouth shut. There wasn't time for bullshit, and some things were better left unsaid.

Their second of distraction almost cost them. Wretched was backing away, back down the tunnel in the opposite direction. "Wretched," Nic said.

The demon stopped in her tracks and hissed. Hatred shone in her black eyes. "Before we kill you, female, we will let our males mate with you. Their seed will rot you from the inside out."

"Shut up, Wretched." She saw the Skinner's shoulders slump. The violence remained in her expression, but the beast was helpless. The name meant total control.

Then Nic remembered. She could've smacked herself for forgetting, but so much had happened since she'd read the passage from the book by Asmodeus. It had said a human only needed to use a demon's names to control them. The pieces fell together like a puzzle inside her skull.

If she could learn Arden's true name, she would be free. In the beginning, it had been the one thing she thought would get her out of their little arrangement. But Wretched had given it up only with a knife shoved into her face. What would it take to learn his?

She looked down at their wrists, his skin against hers. There was still a possibility she could leave all of this behind.

Once Drew was safe, she would keep her word. But maybe she could bargain with him again, this time for his secret name—only if he told her would she do what he wanted. It was a slim chance but all she had to cling to in hopes of being freed.

His arm was warm next to hers, and he stood so close that the fiery, smoldering spice of him filled her nostrils. Images of his body bathed in green crystal fire writhed through her mind, a slow and creeping serpent leaving a trail of heat in its wake.

The real question—

Did she want to be free?

Episode Nine
Chapter Twenty-Eight

Nic and Arden took turns whispering Wretched's name. The tension, a living thing, expanded inside of Nic until it threatened to take her over, but she refused to be taken. Except for the whispered name and the shuffle of feet, the only other sound came from the steady beat of her heart.

Wretched had been a boon...well, except for the emotional bombs she'd dropped on Nic. She knew the fallout had shrapnelled Arden too. The Fourth Level of Hell had been devastating so far, which fed the hungry red rock around them, rock that fed on the pain in the air. Not to mention the terrible gamut of emotion and the war going on within Nic's heart that only increased with every step. She couldn't do anything besides try to maintain some level of composure against all the battles she had yet to face.

The rock of the tunnel had changed. Before, the dark shiny crags had been backlit with a soft crimson hue, and now it shone with the brilliance of a hellish sunrise. It pulsed and breathed as they passed, and with each of their steps the light grew brighter.

"All the suffering," Wretched said with a moan. "The rock is alive from all the suffering. It feeds me like mother's milk."

"Quiet, Wretched," Arden said. The muscles in his neck tensed in time to the rhythm of his steps.

Like phantom limb pain, Nic's hip ached for the weight of her Ruger, but it was tucked into the back of her pants. She felt the steel bite into the skin of her lower back each time she moved.

The temperature had risen at least ten degrees. Sweat trickled down the side of her neck. She stole a look at Arden and saw beads of perspiration on his forehead. "It's getting hotter," she whispered.

"The farther down we go, the closer we are to the Lake of Fire," he said.

The fun little fact didn't do much to ease her nerves. She was glad they hadn't come across any other tunnels. The black openings held a million secrets and she didn't want to learn any more about this place. She'd learned enough.

They walked on in silence and took back up the pattern of whispering the Skinner's true name.

It wasn't long before Wretched slowed. "Just ahead," she said over her shoulder.

"Do not disobey us, Wretched," Arden said.

The tunnel curved to the right and then opened to a huge cavern. Nic thought it would have easily held her entire hometown. Massive splinters of rock jutted from the ground at odd angles, forcing them to zigzag through a maze of stone. Behind each one, she was sure a new terror waited, like the actors in a gigantic haunted house waiting until the kiddies got close enough to scare.

Her breath came in quick puffs and the inside of her lip bled again from the work of her teeth. Arden's palm was warm against her own. She laced her fingers with his and he gave them a tiny squeeze.

The soaring rock formations got smaller and smaller. When they stepped out from behind the last one, the sight in front of them stole the air from her lungs.

A matched set of enormous boulders rose forty feet into the air, the red rock carved into the shape of two serpents, tails intertwined, pointing upward, ever upward. Their fanged faces pointed out over the stairs to welcome guests with their toothy grins. Rubies the size of her head sat in each of the eye sockets, and the gems glowed, lit from the fire within. The incredible detail in the carving made it seem as if they would break free from their stone prison at any moment and swallow her whole.

At the top of the steps, between the two giant heads, was a set of immense double doors thrown open and gaping as wide as the ominous mouths of the snakes.

Sorro's nest.

There were no guards standing watch at the entrance, which Nic knew could mean only one thing.

Arden mirrored her thought with words. "He's inviting us in."

Chapter Twenty-Nine

Nic did *not* want to go through the doors but knew it was inevitable. The unhealthy garnet glow and the stench of death that flowed from the threshold made her feet not want to move.

Arden undid the laces binding them together. He drew his blade from his boot and she followed suit with her nine. She looked at him and hoped her hesitation didn't show on her face.

He smiled and it was so out of place with their surroundings she couldn't help but smile back. "No problem," he said.

His arrogance knew no bounds and she loved him for it. The sudden, shocking intensity of the knowledge made her want to tell him how much. She nodded instead.

At the sudden sound of wild laughter and running feet, they spun to see the disappearing figure of Wretched swallowed by the maze of rock. Her threats of slaughter were empty ones when confronted with Sorro's open invitation.

Well, at least someone got to run away. She flexed her hand around the grip of her gun and dug deep inside herself to touch the reserve of steel lying in wait for battle. It strengthened her resolve as she approached the steps with Arden at her side.

When she reached the top he held out a hand for her to stop. He leaned his back against the open door on the left and peered inside. The bloody light from inside washed over his features and she saw him grimace. "Anyone?"

"No one alive," he said. "No guards either."

Arden eased inside and she followed with both hands on her weapon.

The small entryway opened to a huge chamber. The ceiling soared as high as the serpents' tails outside. Her stomach churned at the sight of the brutal fixture hanging above the blood-soaked floor.

It was in the shape of a hollow, tiered wedding cake. The rings making up the frame were draped with chains. At random intervals on the pseudochandelier, disemboweled and decomposing corpses hung like freakish charms.

She pressed her fist against her mouth and nose. The stench of decomposition was unbearable and she had to swallow several times to keep her stomach from playing reversal of fortune.

All along the walls, more bodies lay in ruin. Some were missing limbs, and others, their skin.

It was the Hell she had always pictured—hot, red, and full of unspeakable rot.

At the back of the chamber there was a dais with an unembellished metal throne in the center. Something about its simplicity made it even more threatening.

She guessed the throne was where Sorro sat to watch his vile drama of soul suffering while the rock around him—and he, himself—drank it up like wine.

Her knuckles tightened around the grip of her nine as anger, heavy and menacing, filled her heart, and dread as potent as a swig of arsenic tea swept over her.

"If Sorro wants us here, why doesn't he come out and face us?" she asked Arden.

"Don't you see?" His grin was gruesome. "He wants to play with us first."

It rang true with what she'd already experienced of the demon whose blue eyes swam with horror. He would want to give them all the pain he could before he took them out.

She scanned the breadth of the cavernous space and saw there were ten different tunnels cut into the walls. Their openings stared at her like empty eye sockets. "He wants us to look," she said, "so let's look."

They started with the farthest one on the right. The rock put out enough light for Nic to see. The smooth floor led upward and the path ended in a fork. She peered into the depths of one side and strained to hear. There was no sound, no movement, but the burning odor of offal and death wafted out from the dark depths. Arden checked the other side, and from the way his mouth drew down into a grim line, she figured the smell must be the same on that end.

"I'll go first." He maneuvered around her and headed into the tunnel. After two steps in, he turned back to her. "Breath through your mouth and stay right behind me."

"Right." She tried to grin, but the smile wouldn't come. They could be walking right into a trap.

He moved down the tunnel ahead of her. The farther they went, the stronger the awful stench became. It burned her eyes until tears streamed over her cheeks. The passageway ended and opened onto the edge of a crevasse. The contents of the wide, deep canyon beyond the lip of their perch explained the smell.

Like a holocaust grave, the canyon was filled with bodies.

And some of them were still moving.

She scrambled to get away from the horror and practically dived into the other tunnel opening a few feet away. Once inside, she paused, doubled over at the waist with her hands on her knees, and gasped for air.

Arden stepped into the passage behind her. She heard him suck a couple of gulps of air in through his mouth. "Let's get out of here."

Her thoughts exactly. She went first. This tunnel was smaller and lower than the other had been, and it curved instead of going straight ahead. It felt like they were turning away from the fork instead of heading back toward it, and the passage was so narrow her elbows brushed against the walls. There were obstacles—as if the builders had met with an unfortunate accident on the job—and several times she had to turn sideways and shimmy past a rock outcrop to keep going. A few feet ahead she saw another one jutting out from the tunnel floor. There were only a few inches on either side. Not enough room to squeeze between it and the wall. She couldn't fit and there was no way Arden could get through either. "Problem," she said.

He leaned over her shoulder to look. "There's a gap above it, though. We'll just climb over."

The gap was a two-foot space between the boulder and the ceiling. He lifted her up and she pulled herself onto the large rock. She couldn't even sit up in the cramped space. To get across it, she would have to armycrawl all the way.

The rough surface rubbed the skin off her elbows. Sweat gathered on her forehead. From the ceiling, jagged rock poked down, cutting into her sore shoulder where she still had marks from the door she had busted through. She wormed sideways to avoid the ceiling. Her back connected with the wall beside her and the awful sound of rock giving way filled her ears.

The wall opened up and she fell. A rock smashed into her side and the air whooshed from her lungs. She landed with a violent thud and cracked the back of her head on the hard ground as debris fell all around her.

Chapter Thirty

Someone called Nic's name. It sounded muffled, as if the speaker had a cloth over his mouth.

Her eyes flew open and she scanned the room for threats but found she was alone in a round pit of sorts, only about six feet by eight feet at the bottom. On one wall, near the ceiling, she saw the ragged hole where she had come through. A man leaned out of the opening and yelled at her. She shook her head and enough of the fuzz cleared out for her to recognize who it was. Arden.

"Nic!" he shouted.

"Yeah. Here." She sat up and the room spun like a merry-go-round. "I'm OK." Except for the pounding inside her skull and the stabbing pain in her side.

"I'm coming down to get you," he said, and started to climb through the hole.

"No." There was no other way out. "We'll both be stuck down here." Her brain raced to come up with an alternative. He couldn't come down and she couldn't climb up unless they had a rope or something.

"I'll be right back," he said. "I'm going to go get some chain to lower down to you."

A poison flower of panic bloomed in her chest. Now was the moment when he would do what he had intended and leave her to rot in this hole. "No." She hated the plea she heard in her own voice. "Don't leave me."

Her heart stuttered and fear closed over her like the lid of a casket.

His fingers dug into the rock at the lip of the opening, and even from her spot she could see all his muscles tense. "Don't be afraid, Nic. Please."

She caught the slip and struggled to correct it. If she let the fear overcome her, he wouldn't be able to resist and would come vaulting through the gap in the wall.

Breathe, Nic. Breathe. She willed herself to be calm, to be still. After counting to twenty, she felt better.

"OK." She took as deep a breath as she could manage with the bad rib situation. "Go."

"I'll be right back."

The words brought her little comfort considering all that had taken place since she had first laid eyes on him lying unconscious on her brother's bedroom floor. But it wasn't as if she had much choice at the moment except to let him go get the chain.

"Just hurry," she said.

"Nic," he said. His voice made her name sound beautiful. "I won't leave you."

He disappeared and she was alone.

She could only wait and hope that her demon would keep his word.

———

The stench of rot polluted the air, but above it all he smelled the female—alone and trapped. If Flic could still smile, he would have. But spiders' mouths were designed for an altogether different purpose, and it did not involve joy.

He stretched his long limbs out, loving the feel of his tiny, sharp feet on the rock. His vision was still spectacular despite the two eyes that had yet to heal thanks to the human bitch's gun. The new abilities that came with his maturing had been invaluable in tracking the pair through the endless passages of the Fourth. He had been waiting for them outside of the cave where they fucked. But then the stupid Skinner had shown up and he'd been forced to hide and wait for a better moment to get his revenge.

The female would pay for what she had done. He didn't care if Sorro got mad at him or not.

He didn't understand how her bullets had done so much damage. He remembered seeing the gun, seeing it fire, and then feeling the aching burn in his eyes. He'd lain there, unable to move, wondering how long it would take for him to grow a new set. When Sorro had left with the male, and then the gate had opened again and the Prince and the female had gone through, he had willed his limbs to move.

Good thing they had forgotten to close the door or he wouldn't have been able to get through. Having eight legs made for easy climbing, but when it came to opening doors the extra limbs weren't much use.

The mystery of the magic bullets would wait for another time. He needed to get to the female.

He skittered along the ceiling of the cavern and then crawled over the serpents marking the entrance to Sorro's nest. It was a little disorienting to be able to see in front of him and below him at the same time, but he'd gotten more used to it now. Once he made it inside, he saw the place was empty and quiet. Then he saw a figure run out of one of the tunnels, give the main chamber a quick once-over, and then disappear down another passageway.

The Prince without the female. Which meant his moment had come.

He loved his new body! He felt powerful and his missing eyes didn't make a difference. His pointy feet whispered over the rock as he made for the tunnel.

The passage was a tight fit for him but he found that if he stretched out, his body narrowed and he could still move. He crept along until he got to the spot where she had fallen through the wall.

When he peeked into the opening, he could see her down at the bottom of the pit. She sat against the wall with her arms wrapped around her knees.

Maybe he would play with her a bit. Her fear was delicious, and when he struck he would be robbed of the sweet flavor. A few minutes wouldn't matter.

She was trapped and alone.

And soon, she would be dead.

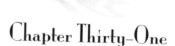

Chapter Thirty-One

It took Arden a few minutes to unwrap the chain from around the body, but the last of it came loose from the flesh with a slobbery sound. He draped the length over his shoulders and ran off, back down the tunnel he'd come from—or so he thought. He picked the wrong one and had to backtrack, made a wrong turn, and ended up right where he had run across the trussed-up corpse.

"Fuck."

Nic's panic made him careless, made him want to kill. It was different from her fear—that he could handle—but the panic just made him want to slaughter everything in sight, and right now he needed a clear head.

He forced himself to stop for a minute and calm down. A few breaths later he was moving again. This time he came back out into the main chamber, and he rushed back into the acrid air of the passage leading to the canyon of bodies. He slowed a bit along the edge of the cliff. If he fell down into the mass of the dead and the dying...*nope, not even going to think about it.*

Then someone called his name. At first he thought it was Nic, but she was too far away for the sound to carry this far and it was too clear to come from the bottom of the pit she was trapped in.

And then he heard it again.

It didn't come from the tunnel; it came from the canyon below. The voice was familiar and the hair on the back of his neck stood on end. He hadn't heard it in more than one hundred and eighteen years.

"Arden, I'm here."

No. He refused to believe his own ears.

It just wasn't possible.

"I knew you would come."

His mother's voice carried up to him from the depths like fog creeping over damp earth. He didn't want to look but was powerless to stop himself.

"Yes. Come to me, my son. I've missed you."

The bodies in the crevasse shifted, some of them whimpering as his mother crawled out from underneath.

With little-boy eyes he saw her—the flowing blonde hair, the curve of her lap, the soft look in eyes shaped exactly like his own. Time had not touched her.

He froze in place on the edge of the cliff.

"Lend me your hand," she said.

After a moment's hesitation, he lay down on the ground and reached out to her. When she took his hand, he felt her warmth. He pulled her up and helped her to stand.

"I knew you would come. All of the suffering never made me doubt it. You were always the strongest of my boys." Her smile lit up her whole face. She smoothed the filth from the front of her white dress.

"How?" He wanted to say so much more, but the simple question was all he could manage.

"Oh, let's not talk about it," she said, flipping a hand through the air as if she swatted away a bothersome mosquito. "I have something to tell you."

"Not right now. I'm going to get you out of here and home. But I have to help Nic too," he said. "Wait 'til you meet her. She's remarkable and—"

"No, my darling, you have to leave her."

"No, you don't understand. I have to save her."

"You can't. You must leave right away," she said. "That is what I have to talk to you about."

"I can't leave her here." His voice had an edge to it he wasn't comfortable with; it almost sounded like panic.

She shook her head and put a hand to his cheek. "She is *human* and weak just like me. She will not survive."

"No, she's strong. So much stronger than any human I've ever met."

"The part of me in you is what makes you think this way. But you must leave her or you too will be lost."

Time became a slippery thing—it felt like he had been standing on this cliff forever. He needed to get back to Nic—

Wait. How did his mother know about Nic in the first place? *Nic.*

"Arden, listen to your mother."

There was something strange about her eyes when she issued the command, and it fed his urgency. Suspicion crawled up from his gut to lodge in the back of his throat. "I can't talk about this now. I have to go get Nic." He started to back away from her and then felt her fingernails dig into the skin of his forearm.

She clutched his arm with the strength of a man. "Do as I say."

"I will not leave her."

"You sound like a child. Don't let my blood make you weak."

"Let go of my arm."

"You are such a disappointment. You do not deserve the title of First Born," she said. Anger glinted in her pale eyes. "All this for a pathetic human."

"I love her." The sudden admission stunned him and the truth of it rocked his soul. He loved her and he had to go get her out of that pit. "I have to go."

"You aren't going anywhere, Prince."

Reality swam and his mother fell apart, revealing the thing in front of him for what it truly was...

An illusion.

"That's right, no more mommy." As it spoke the skin slipped away from its face and off of its body. Underneath was a horror of corrupt flesh and white bone. "Sorro said you would like me."

He wrenched his arm to break free, but the creature anticipated his move and dug in further. It reared back and then lunged at him.

There was no space on the ledge to maneuver, and he spun to crush the thing clawing at him into the wall.

With a laugh it kicked against the wall, and his momentum acted as a counterweight. They tumbled over the edge.

Down, down they fell until he was lost in the sea of death.

———

Nic's ribs hurt. Hugging her knees to her chest was the only comfortable position she could sit in. Along with the pain in her rib cage, she couldn't get her brain to stop being oversensitive. The only sound was her breathing, but Nic swore she kept hearing soft scratching sounds on the rock wall above her. She looked up and again saw nothing.

Where in the fuck was Arden? She had never worn a watch in her life and right now she was thankful. Just because you could see the minutes ticking by didn't mean they would move any faster.

She let her forehead fall against her knees and then she heard the unmistakable sound of footsteps in the cave.

Her breath hitched. She really wished she hadn't tucked the Ruger away. Slow, like the gentle lifting of a bridal veil, she looked up.

And saw her parents standing in front of her.

Hand in hand they stood, smiling at her, just how she remembered them. She couldn't speak, couldn't move, but wanted to jump up and run into their arms. Her heart ached.

Then the force of the situation hit her. They were in Hell. Her loving and murdered parents were in Hell; not the place where the innocent were supposed to end up. The vision she had earlier of them as cloud-sitting and winged resurfaced, and she felt the undeniable burn of tears begin in the corners of her eyes.

"It's OK, Nicolette," her father said. His wide grin and tender voice untied the knot in her chest. She had almost forgotten how much he and Drew looked alike: the same short, wayward, coffee-colored hair and light eyes she shared with them. "We're here for you."

"Mom." Only one word, but it felt like a whole dictionary coming from her mouth. The tears rolled over her cheeks and she didn't wipe them away.

"Hi, Nic." Love filled her expression and she reached a hand out. "Come here, honey."

The endearment thawed her frozen limbs and she stood up. She swayed and had to push off the wall to get her legs to move. Her parents' arms opened for her and she fell into the sacred cradle of their embrace.

All the years of yearning and loss melted away. She could smell her dad's cheap cologne and the delicate lavender bouquet of her mom's favorite perfume; a balm for her broken heart. A sob broke from her mouth and she let it happen. This was what had been stolen from her when the flame of their lives had been snuffed out.

Memories flashed through her mind. The taste of her mother's pancakes. The deep rumble of her father's laughter as she carefully explained to him why it was essential that she get a puppy. The patience they had showed Drew and their hurt every time he had disappointed them. The way her mother's forehead had creased when Nic had told her she wanted to take birth control and the flare of worry on her father's face when she left for college. All of it came wrenching out of her while they whispered soft reassurance in her ears.

Her mom's hand stroked over her back. "Oh, sweetheart. We're here now. You're safe."

When it felt as if her well of tears had run dry, Nic stepped back but didn't let go of their hands. "I don't understand," she said. "Why are you here?"

"We came to take you with us," her dad answered. "You don't belong here."

"But Drew's down here too. We have to go get Drew." She glanced up at the fissure where she'd fallen through. "Arden. I can't leave him without saying good-bye." In fact, she didn't think she could leave him at all, and the thought of it resurrected the panic their arms had destroyed. It rushed through her and spurred her to action. "He'll be back any second. We have to wait for him."

"There's no time for that," her father said, his voice growing stern. "He is evil and he will hurt you."

"No." She shook her head. "He has good in him. I can feel it."

"He's tricking you, honey." The mellow tones of her mom's voice made Nic's fear all the more real when spoken aloud. "He is a demon."

She couldn't meet her parents' gazes because the truth would hurt them and she didn't want to see the disappointment in their eyes. "I can't leave him. I love him."

"You have to, Nic. It's the only way."

It didn't matter which of them had spoken; her answer was for them both. "No."

"Enough, damn it." Her father's response was sharp. "You are coming with us right now." The harshness of his words was out of character for the ever-patient dad she remembered. She looked up at him and his expression heated with anger. Something was strange about his face; it looked darker somehow, blanketed in shadow.

Nic glanced at her mother and saw the corners of her mouth turn down when she spoke. "We are all leaving. No more arguments, princess."

Princess? Never had her mother called her "princess." There was an odd note to the word, like she didn't enjoy the flavor of it, and her face had the same shadow-cast as her father's.

Their hands tightened around Nic's, and when she tried to pull away they drew her closer. The beloved fragrance of her parents flowed away and she felt their breath break over her in a foul wave. Their faces began to change and distort. The flesh loosened from their bones and peeled away. Underneath, the sinew was gray with decay.

She fought, kicking at them and flailing her arms, but their grip on her did not relent; a scream tore from her throat.

The thing that had shed the last of her father's skin smiled to show a row of broken, blackened teeth. "Sorro was right. You made it so easy."

———

It felt like drowning, but instead of water, Arden was awash in an ocean of blood and flesh. Arms clawed at him, pulling him deeper. The chain still around his neck weighed him down. The mother-thing gripped his arm with the strength of a vise and he couldn't break free. He lay on his back among the shifting mass of bodies and he was sinking as the imposter dragged him farther into the depths.

For a split second the sinking motion slowed and he kicked away from the creature. She howled and raked her nails across his arm. He felt the flesh open up, and the warmth of his own blood ran down into his palm. But the moisture loosened her grip and he wrenched his arm free.

She scrabbled to grab him again. He tumbled forward, out of her reach. She howled and Arden looked back to see her using mouths and rib cages as handholds to climb toward him.

The footing was treacherous; torsos and thighs gave way under his weight and his feet sank right through them. He tried to stand but lost balance and fell face-first onto the back of another body—one of the fresher ones, so when he grabbed the shoulders the skin stayed in place. He dragged himself over it on his belly and gained another foot of distance between himself and the howling creature.

The moans and cries around him were a cacophony, like the inside of a slaughterhouse. The noise fed his desperation.

He used the fresh body to get his footing, glancing back to see the mother-thing crawling, clawing to get closer. In front of and above him the cliff rose up to the edge where he and the creature had fallen over. It was twenty feet high, but if he could get to it he could climb.

Nic.

Like jumping from rock to rock to cross a raging river, he leaped across the bodies to the rough, red surface of the cliff wall. He found handholds in the pitted and pebbled outcrops and stepped one booted foot into a shallow depression in the rock. The writhing corpses below him grabbed at his ankles and he kicked them away, stretching to reach up and pull his weight up the wall.

Fissures littered the jagged surface, and soon he made it above the reach of the questing arms and fingers and faces. He repositioned and gained another couple of feet of distance from the deadly mass below.

Then he heard a screeching cry and the mother-thing was on him again. She wrapped her arms around his waist. The added weight tugged him down and he struggled to maintain his precarious hold on the rock. His arms shook from the strain.

A stab of pain ran up his side. He looked down and realized the bitch had bitten him. Her sharp teeth and chin were stained with his blood, and she reared back to take another bite. With one hand clinging to the jagged wall, he used the other to smash a palm into her face, pushing it up and back until he thought for sure her neck would crack.

When she moved to knock his hand away, he bent his knee and kicked back against her. His foot connected with her chest and he felt her other arm lose hold of his waist. Another kick and she fell away backward, her arms pinwheeling in the open air. She landed with a sickening thud. A wicked, primal scream flowed from her mouth and filled the canyon.

He climbed faster, his breath rushing in and out of his lungs. The serrated rock ground into his palms and his blood painted the cliff an even darker shade of crimson.

The chain had loosened in the struggle and he felt the long length leave a trail of bruises over his shoulder as it fell. He watched it go and cursed. He would have to figure out another way to get Nic out of the pit.

After a few more reaches, his fingers met the edge of the cliff and he pulled himself up onto the ledge.

He did not stop to catch his breath before racing into the tunnel. The long curve led him around to where she had fallen through the rock.

A feral scream pierced the air, and when he rounded the bend, he saw the huge spider. It drew its spindly legs up against its body and then crawled through the opening in the wall.

Chapter Thirty-Two

Nic braced her palms against the demons' chests and pushed back, throwing all of her weight into the motion. The slime from the skinless arms wrapped around her made her slippery enough to break free. She rolled away across the ground, and as she came back up to her knees, she drew her gun.

As one, they rushed her and she fired. Her first round connected and she saw part of a jaw blown away. The male staggered and crumpled to the ground. She fired again, hitting the female who'd posed as her mother in the shoulder. The female screamed, a guttural, animal squeal, and Nic could see the rage in her black eyes.

The female lunged for her, and when she sidestepped the demon's attack, she saw an eight-legged shadow looming from the ceiling above. The two demons didn't notice as the spider scrabbled down the wall and crept up behind them. Her chest hurt again as if the proximity of the thing that had bitten her awakened the wound.

The creature leaped with an eerie and terrifying quickness. The male demon with the missing jaw howled as one long, thin leg stabbed through his chest. The female turned at the noise and then started backing away.

The spider freed its limb and skittered sideways, tracking its prey. The demon dodged back and forth, but there was no escape.

Nic watched the spider grow still. She had seen him do this before, right before he had attacked her, and she knew what would come.

The demon took the creature's stillness as a break and made for the other side of the pit. She took only three steps before the spider struck, sinking its fangs deep into the soft flesh of her torso. She cried out but was silenced when the creature flipped her over and began spinning a tight net of silken web around her face, and then the rest of her body.

While the creature bundled its meal, Nic backed away along the wall until she was as far away as she could get in the small space, hoping it didn't notice her as it finished its business. It repeated the gift wrap treatment with the other body.

Her pistol had worked on the spider before. The bullets obviously hadn't killed the creature, but she hoped they would at least stun it enough so she could try to get up the wall, through the opening, and away.

The spider sealed its—his—meal. Flic had been male and maybe still was. He wrapped his packages and then turned toward her. He crept one way and then the other, weaving a path across the ground. If she didn't know better, she would have thought he was toying with her, but spiders didn't do that, did they?

No. Not other spiders. Just this one.

She waited for him to get closer. She pulled the trigger.

Nothing happened except for a hollow click. Out. Why the fuck had she settled for food when the extra mag would've been more help?

His thin legs stretched out, ticking against the floor. She pressed herself back against the wall, her heart pounding in her throat. She didn't dare take her eyes off the creature to glance at the one escape route twenty feet above her head.

He inched closer. The soft clicking of his pointy feet made her skin crawl.

Then a cloud of dust drifted down from above.

Arden.

The spider looked up and realized they were no longer alone. He reared up on his back legs and she ducked underneath his rounded abdomen, between his outstretched limbs, and away to the other side of the pit.

She spun back around and saw Arden fly through the air and land on the spider's back. His blade came down in a shining arc and cracked through the creature's carapace. The spider shuddered and reared again to dislodge his adversary.

Arden fell to the ground and came back up in a crouch. He flipped the handle of his knife around as the spider made to come after him.

The creature paused, looked over at Nic and back at Arden. He crept backward until his rear legs met the wall, then he scrambled up and, after a final look, crawled away through the gap in the rock and vanished.

She wanted to scream for him to come back so she could watch as Arden finished him off. Instead, she crumpled to the ground like a wilting flower. Her gun fell from her hand and landed with a metallic clank. She doubled over and sucked air into her lungs.

When she looked up, Arden was standing a few feet away, staring at the hole where the spider had disappeared. "I don't think we'll be leaving the same way we came in."

She laughed, a ridiculous notion considering the situation, but a tiny bit of tension eased from her muscles. "Nope. Guess not."

He walked over to her and held out his hand to help her stand. She felt the warmth of his skin against her palm. It felt like home.

His arms wrapped around her and pulled her into his chest. "I told you I would be right back."

———

It took some time, but Nic eventually found the hidden passage where the two demons had entered the pit—a long, thin fissure in the rock. If she hadn't been running her hands over the surface, she never would have discovered it.

"Yes," she said. She couldn't wait to get out of the pit where the imposters' bodies lay wrapped on the floor; a haunting reminder of cruelty and pain.

Arden pushed on the wall and the pocket door slid open. He stepped back as a wave of noxious fumes wafted out of the room on the other side.

Great. If she had to keep breathing through her mouth, she might hyperventilate. The scary part was she was starting to get used to the smell of death.

The heat, on the other hand, was another story. She could feel the back of her T-shirt sticking to her and sweat stung all the raw patches on her skin. Her jeans were covered in dirt and gore.

After a quick look to make sure the room was empty, Arden took her hand and they stepped through into...

A kitchen. It was equipped the way a normal kitchen would be, if a little medieval. There were stoves, cupboards, and cutting boards. But judging by the rest of the place, she guessed the fare leaned toward the Dahmeresque variety.

A spit hung low over an open fire; pieces of flank still connected to thigh bone rotated, and the fat popped and sizzled as it dripped into the flames.

There was no one around, but apparently the cooks had left in a hurry. Open pots still bubbled on the stove and knives lay where they had been dropped.

"Guess dinner's going to be late," she said.

"I know he wants us to find him, or else he would have left more obstacles for us, but I get the feeling Sorro isn't planning on sticking to his nest."

"You're right. It's too empty. Which means we have to find him before he decides to fly." She walked over to a countertop, grimaced at the bits of meat there, and picked up two long fillet knives. Her empty pistol was still stashed in her waistband, but she refused to go weaponless. "Ready when you are." She waggled the knives at him.

He smiled and his frosty eyes were full of warmth. It gave her a little rush. She remembered the fear that he would not return and it left a question unanswered in her mind. Before she could stop them, the words flew out of her mouth. "What took you so long?"

"I ran into a...complication." His lips tightened as if he'd eaten something sour and he looked away. "A little gift from Sorro."

So he'd had a visit too. "I got my own present," she said. "Who did he send for you?"

His response was so quiet she almost didn't catch it. "My mother."

Sympathy burned in her heart for him and for herself. "He sent my parents."

"I'm sorry," he said. "I know how much that must have hurt you."

She wanted to go to him, feel his arms around her, but she didn't move. "The imposters tried to kill me, but the spider came." She shivered. "Did your demon try to kill you too?"

"We had a little chat first," he said. The expression on his face was dark. "And then we went for a swim in the canyon."

In the bodies? That explained the state of his ripped and bloodied clothes. The nightmare of it overwhelmed her. She wondered if his conversation had hurt as much as the one she'd had with her false parents. "We should go," she said.

He reached out and brushed a strand of hair from her forehead. The backs of his fingers trailed over her cheek before dropping away. "Yes," he said. "Let's go thank Sorro for the gifts."

They headed left from the kitchen but ended up back in the main chamber. Nic's sense of direction had deserted her altogether.

A couple more turns led to dead ends or empty rooms. The quiet unsettled her, but squeezing the handles of her new weapons made her feel better. Knives were so much more intimate than a gun anyway.

The next tunnel they chose was big enough for them to walk side by side, and it sloped down before leveling out. The rock burned bright red with pain-fire, and she suspected the tight knot in her stomach was her intuition telling her they were getting close.

They turned a corner and came to a stop. A set of massive double doors marked the end of the tunnel and she knew without question who was on the other side.

Drew and the monster who had taken him.

She leaned into Arden for a second, wanting to feel him against her one more time. Then she stood up straight, squared her shoulders, and opened the doors.

"Welcome, friends," Sorro said. "So nice to see you."

Nic made sure not to look into his eyes.

Chapter Thirty-Three

Nic saw everything at once. The disgusting sculptures scattered around the room. The small, vile chandelier hanging from the ceiling. A long, mirrored wall reflected the whole scene back at her, including Drew, curled in the fetal position at Sorro's feet.

"He's been out for quite some time now, poor darling," Sorro said. He knelt down and ran a hand over Drew's head. "He served his purpose well, but I'm afraid this is the end for him."

"Get your hands off him." She gripped the handles of the knives. "I will gut you for what you've done to him."

"I am sure you would, my dear, given the opportunity. Your fury is delicious, by the way, but this is the end for you too." He stood and stepped over Drew. "And as a bonus, I get my first taste of royal blood."

Arden was at her side. She could feel the anger radiating from him. "My father's Master will have your head for that."

"You are so fucking arrogant, First Born. A spoiled brat too soon removed from his mother's swollen teat." Sorro weaved back and forth like a snake when he talked. "Did you like her? I just love using Watchers. They make spying so much simpler."

Watchers? Nic suspected Sorro was talking about those abominations back in the pit. And that meant he had heard everything. Even her confession of love. She struggled to cover her thoughts, not wanting to give him anything more.

"Too late for that, darling," Sorro said. "I know what froths in your little human heart. The fact that you have fallen in love with a demon you cannot have makes this all the more fun for me." From the corner of her eye she saw Arden's head snap around in her direction, but Sorro wasn't done. "Oh, Prince, I heard what you told Mommy too. How sweet."

"Shut up and give us the male, Sorro." Arden's voice was like ice. "Do it and I'll forget you ever threatened me."

Sorro shook his head, his long white hair rippling over his shoulders. "Don't bother me with idle promises. None of that business will matter once your little pet is dead anyway. Can't you see? It's the perfect ending. I lured the female down here with this thing," he turned and kicked Drew's still form, "as my bait. And getting you down here with her? Well, I consider it my finest work to date. Now that I know for sure you've fallen in love, I can kill you and get my reward."

He was too busy gloating to notice Drew had awakened behind him and pushed himself up into a sitting position. "Sorro?"

The demon turned around and smiled. "I'm so glad you're awake, my dear boy. I didn't want to kill you without being able to look into your eyes when I did it."

"You're going to kill me?" Drew asked. His quiet words hurt Nic's heart. "But you can't. Not until you take me to the Well to get my parents. I said you could only have me after I knew they were safe." He turned to Nic and Arden. "I'm going to die but Mom and Dad get to come back. Nic, they get to live."

"Drew, no," she said. "They can't come back. They're gone." *So this was why he let the demon take him.*

"You shouldn't have come after me," Drew said.

"The emotions are tantalizing, but all the human drama is boring me." Sorro sighed and pulled a long, tapered dagger from under his jacket: a pencil-thin blade stained red. He smiled as he watched the light play along the length. "Well, Drew. Let's make this quick, shall we?"

Drew rose and backed away. Nic saw the confusion on his face. "You lied to me?"

Sorro must have reached the end of his patience because his whole demeanor changed in an instant—no more plastic smile, no more relaxed attitude. "Of course I lied, you stupid shit. I'm a demon."

"There's no Well," Drew said to no one. "I can't bring them back." As he spoke he crept farther away from Sorro.

"Drew." Nic hated letting the white-haired demon hear the desperation in her voice. "Get away from him. Come here, to me." Relief flooded through her when he stood and walked backward toward her, his eyes never leaving Sorro.

The demon laughed. "So obedient, like a good doggy." Sorro flipped his dagger back and forth between his hands. "But I'm still killing all of you."

When he waved a hand in the air, the doors behind her slammed shut. Nic spun around at the noise and lost her footing. Arden reached out to grab her but didn't make it in time. She hit the floor and the knives spun out of her hands and slid across the ground. Before she could grab them, Drew bent down and picked them up.

It all happened in a flash: she saw her brother pick up the knives and smile at her, saw Sorro coming toward her, saw Arden step in front of her. In the giant mirror she saw the reflection of Drew's face and the flash of metal as he drew the blades up above his head.

Episode Ten

Chapter Thirty-Four

Nic's vision zoomed down to a tunnel, focused solely on her brother, the knives, and the monster, Sorro. Time distorted. Sound ceased. She couldn't hear beyond the thunderous clap of her heartbeat.

She'd made it all the way to the nest of her enemy. She'd gone through Hell to rescue her brother and finally had his safe return to earth within range. She had made a deal with a demon, risked her life, her soul, and her heart. And the next four nanoseconds would determine what kind of future she would face.

Sorro kept coming, so focused on Nic he didn't notice Drew running toward him. With an agonized cry spewing from his lips, her brother jumped onto Sorro's back, bringing both knives down into the tops of the demon's shoulders, wedging them into his muscles. Sorro staggered under Drew's weight and they both fell to the floor.

She watched Drew yank the blades out and stab the demon over and over, Sorro's black blood splattering the ground and leaving dark splotches on the rock.

Arden grabbed her to hold her back, but she broke free and ran over to pull Drew away from the sopping mess of Sorro. He stabbed again and again and she saw the stygian darkness of the demon's blood forming a pool around Sorro's body. Moist gurgling sounds came from his throat, and his scaled, porcelain face contorted into a look of disbelief.

She snatched her brother around the waist and pulled. They rolled away and landed in a heap. Drew sobbed as he continued to stab at the air in front of him. "He lied. He lied."

Nic gathered him up into her arms, turning him away from Sorro and holding him as he wailed. "It's OK, Squirrel. It's over." She looked over his head at Arden. "It's OK."

Arden walked around them and stood over the still-gurgling Sorro. "Guess you aren't getting your prize after all."

Sorro coughed and black blood ran down the sides of his face. "This isn't the end, First Born. My employer will not stop until you and all of your brothers are dead." He spat at Arden and it hit the knee of his jeans. "All the sons of Asmodeus will die."

Drew struggled in Nic's arms and she fought to hold on to him. If there was still meth in his system, he could do real damage. "Arden," she shouted as Drew wrestled out of her control. "We need to get him out of here."

Arden spun and ran to intercept Drew by snagging the edge of his shirt. Her brother tore at Arden's arms, flailing around until Arden grabbed him by the neck and pushed him back toward Nic. "Listen to me. Listen. Calm down." Drew's head listed to the side. His limbs twitched and vibrated. "Can you get yourself under control or do I need to knock you out?"

Drew's answer was garbled, unintelligible.

Nic stood up and seized Drew around the waist, pressing her head into his shoulder blade. He shoved at her arms and almost broke free again. "He won't quit. Knock him out!"

She heard a thump and Drew sagged in her arms. Arden held him up and Nic stepped away, panting, relieved.

Until she saw the reflection in the mirror across the room.

Sorro was gone.

No way would she leave without making sure the demon was dead. She'd come all this way, suffered and bled to get her brother back. And now she wouldn't be able to punish the one responsible? Unacceptable. "We have to find him."

Arden looked at the pool of sticky blackness where Sorro had gone down. She could see he was torn. He had as much reason to want the demon dead as she did. "He will be found," he said. "He threatened my life and the lives of my brothers. He will be found and he *will* be punished for it." His arctic eyes blazed with anger, then softened when he looked at her. "But my priority right now is making sure you are safe."

Of course he wanted to make sure she was safe. He still had the transformation to think about. "Help me get Drew out of here and I'll keep my word to you." Her voice shook, whether from adrenaline or anger, she wasn't sure. But she *was* sure of the ache in her heart. "I haven't forgotten your plans."

If she didn't know better, she would have taken his flinch and the expression on his face for hurt. Then, like the door of a bank vault, he closed up. "Let's get out of here."

Chapter Thirty-Five

Arden kept guard while Nic helped her brother along— Drew hadn't been unconscious for long. The map that hadn't been helpful in finding Sorro's nest proved useful on the way back at least. He still didn't understand the coincidence of Sorro needing to get Nic down to the same place that Arden himself needed to take her, and who knew if he'd ever figure it out.

He could still do it too—find the Emissary and hand her over. It disgusted him to think about it. He'd been so eager to use her, so blinded by his own desperation. What the fuck was wrong with him? Self-loathing churned in his gut. The faster he could remove himself from Nic's life, the better.

He scanned the tunnels for attackers, but no demons trailed them. The paths along the way were quiet, but his thoughts were too scattered for the eerie emptiness to bother him. After a while, they arrived at the gate back to the Third.

Arden helped to get Drew up and out of the basement. Night had come and gone while they were in the Fourth. The sky in the east pinkened with the approaching sun. After all that had happened only a night had passed. It felt like ten years. Or thirty.

The Third was as deserted as it had been when they'd left it. He wondered if any of the residents had survived their brush with Sorro. Lesser demons had slimmer chances of regenerating. If there were survivors, they paid no mind to the three travelers passing through their desert fortress and their shantytown streets.

As they passed back into the Second, Nic clung to Drew through the crossing and Arden kept a grip on her arm to keep them from getting lost. He asked her if she'd felt anything in the swirling chaos trying to take her like before and she said no. She didn't look at him much, and it stung. The time would come soon enough for him to tell her he would let her go home, but he wasn't going to delay their progress by bringing it up. He knew she would be happy to be done with him after all she had been through.

He only wished it didn't feel like letting go of her would be the end of him.

Their packs were still stashed behind the Dumpsters where they had left them. He got out a bottle of water and handed it to her, then shouldered both packs himself. The onset of day meant all the druggies, pimps, and whores that populated the Second would be in bed sleeping off the night's revelries. Hopefully.

Not having to deal with any interruptions meant quick progress, and before long he was climbing up the rickety steps and opening the door to the back room of Big Jackie's convenience store. He pounded on the door until the proprietor came to unlock it. Jackie didn't blink an eye at the fact they'd brought someone back with them. Arden spotted one red shoe next to the cash register. He figured they'd already paid for a second safe passage.

He found a pay phone outside and called home to have them send a car. Remy was formal on the phone, as usual, but Arden detected a hint of relief in the butler's voice when he realized who was calling.

They were sitting on a bench across from Jackie's when the shiny vintage limousine pulled up to the curb. Drew had passed out again, so Arden picked him up and hefted him into the backseat. Nic climbed in and he shut the door behind her before hopping into the front.

The first crimson rays of the sun peeked over the horizon as they passed the shabby houses on the low end of the First. Suburbia soon gave way to affluence and the next he knew, the driver turned the big, long car into his father's driveway. The cast-iron angels parted and the car glided up the drive to stop in front of the huge stairs leading to the front door.

The front doors flew open and his father came out, his expression mysteriously full of pride and a wide grin spread across his face from ear to ear. He wouldn't smile for long when he heard the news Arden had to deliver to him, but it would have to wait until he could speak to him alone.

Next out of the door came Chase and, to Arden's surprise, Civious and Malevo. Which meant he would have to debrief his father with three of his brothers present. He supposed it would be best if as many of them were aware of the situation as possible. The others would get called home as soon as he relayed what Sorro had told him anyway.

Remy took charge of the Drew situation at once and called for footmen to come and carry him up to one of the guest rooms.

He stood at the bottom of the stairs next to Nic. There were so many things he wanted to say to her, but it would have to wait. "I need to talk to my father." It was better than the other options, like "I love you," or "You have to go home."

She nodded. "I'm going to make sure Drew's OK, and then I'll come find you." Something similar to sadness haunted her hard gray eyes and it cut him the same way a straight razor would.

"All right," he managed. He watched her smile on her way past his father and brothers and then she disappeared, swallowed up in the vastness of his father's house.

His father clapped him on the shoulder. "I'm glad you're home, son."

"We need to talk." He turned to his brothers. "And you guys need to hear this too."

———

Nic watched Remy fuss over the details of the room. He pointed her to the bathroom and she was a bit stunned when he showed her the tasseled bell pull. She didn't think those things actually existed.

A maid came in with fresh clothes and a small tray with food. The servants moved around like ants on an anthill and then, when everything seemed to be in order, the short butler clapped his hands and they all disappeared.

The room they had settled Drew in was just as lavish as the rest of the house: a huge bed, a sitting area, a giant fireplace, and tall windows. The curtains were closed to keep out the daylight, and for that she was thankful. She didn't look forward to facing this particular day, but seeing her brother asleep under a mound of soft, fresh bedding made her feel better. At least he was safe. She would make sure he got the help he needed no matter if it cost her everything. Besides, she wouldn't need the money anymore.

She would sacrifice herself for him. Her parents would have done the same if they'd had the choice, and in a way, they had already given their lives to the cause. Her decision was final and almost a relief.

She had to hop up to sit down on the tall bed. Drew stirred and opened his eyes. For once, they were somewhat clear. "Hey."

"Hey."

He rolled over to face her, and it had been a very long time since she'd seen him this lucid. Maybe his journey through Hell had been like a detox. Wasn't that what junkies called detox? Either way, it had done him good.

"Where are we?" he asked.

"This house belongs to Arden's father."

"Is that the guy you were with down there?"

"Yep."

"His dad's pretty rich," he said, looking around.

"You could say that."

He finished scanning the room and then his eyes came back to her. "I'm a little fuzzy on the details. Who is Arden and what the fuck happened to me?"

She gave him the short version but left out the part about her falling in love with a demon. He cringed when she told him about the part in the basement when he'd taken Sorro's hand. In a couple of places he filled in some of the gaps with his own memories, including the part when he had stabbed the demon. The whole ordeal had felt like a lifetime, but the story was over before she knew it. "Then he called for them to send a car for us."

"Whoa. I feel like it's all just part of a really twisted bad dream." He shook his head a few times. Nic could relate. "But what about Arden?"

"What about him?" She was pretty sure she knew the direction his question led to and she did not want to go there.

Drew smiled. "The way you look when you talk about him? Man, you're so in love. It's written all over your face." He laughed. "Well, his family's loaded, he looks like a rock star, and, from what you said, he fights like a total badass. I say good for you."

His smile was contagious and she shared it, even if it felt a little fake. She didn't have the heart to tell him what she'd agreed to for his safety. "Drew, I—"

"Wait, let me say something first. I know I've been a fuckup all my life and I want you to know that I'm done." He reached over and put his hand over hers on the comforter. "As soon as we get home, I'm going to rehab. I'm going to do it. I don't want to disappoint you anymore. You need to be happy and I know you won't be until I get my shit together."

It was exactly what she had always wanted him to say, but it meant more to her now than ever. "I know you can do this."

"You've always believed in me no matter what," he said. "I always thought you were stupid for that."

"I believed in the Drew I loved, and I knew one day he would come back." She brushed tears off her cheeks. He didn't know they would be saying good-bye. For good.

He sat up and hugged her. "Love you, Nic."

"Love you, Squirrel."

"Now." He took her by the shoulders and looked her in the eye. "Go be happy." When she looked at him a little puzzled he rolled his eyes. "Hello? Your new kick-ass boyfriend?"

She laughed at the thought of Arden as her boyfriend and the possibility of that kind of future. But she wouldn't say anything to take the smile off of her brother's face. "Right. There's a bathroom through that door, and if you need anything just pull on this." She pointed to the crazy bell pull. "They left you some fresh clothes too." She gave his hand a final squeeze and rose to leave. "Get some rest. Everything's going to be better now."

It was only half of a lie. *He* would be better.

It remained to be seen if she would be better too.

———

Drew felt like shit, and since he couldn't remember the last time he'd done it, he decided to take a shower.

He got out of the awesome bed and trudged over to the bathroom. It was almost as big as his whole apartment— the glassed-in shower big enough for five people. At first he couldn't figure out how to get the water to turn on, but then he found the right way to turn the handle and he held his hand out to test the temperature.

"Perfect." His words echoed back at him from the tiled walls.

The mirrors over the sink showed him he looked as bad as he felt.

Actually, he couldn't remember the last time he had really *looked* at himself. The person in the reflection was like a stranger; thin, sunken cheeks and hollow eyes, dirty clothes. The skin of his face speckled with scabs and sores from where he'd picked at nothing.

It killed him to see what he'd become. What he'd let the crap he put in his veins take from him. What he'd let it take from Nic.

A life. Happiness. A mother and father.

He closed his eyes and took a deep breath.

The clothes they had left were just jeans and a tee, but they were clean. He made up his mind to burn the ones he was wearing as soon as possible. It would be like a sayonara to his old life. Like a phoenix or something, he would rise from the ashes of the mess he'd made.

No more. No more dope. The Drew in that mirror would go away. And just like the clothes burning, the shower would wash away the grime and filth he'd been covered in for too long.

He pulled his shoes, socks, and shirt off, then shrugged out of his pants. When they hit the floor, something clinked.

"What's that?" he asked his reflection.

He dug into the pockets and his fingers touched something narrow and plastic. A sinking feeling began in his chest as he fished around and felt cold metal and heard a very familiar crinkling noise. His ears filled with a dull buzz, like static, and his hands shook.

A fuzzy memory came back of Sorro leaning over him and whispering in his ear. What had he said? Something about a backup gift?

He swallowed hard, his mouth suddenly desert-dry, and pulled the stuff out of the pocket. He set the ugly collection down on the white marble counter. The needle was capped and the spoon sterling; the wad of meth in the baggie the size of a quarter.

Nic's face danced across his mind and he braced his hands on either side of the treasure. He would go to rehab. He would not disappoint her.

The scabs and scars up and down his forearms danced as he flexed and relaxed his fingers. He wanted to be the brother she deserved—wanted it so badly his heart hurt.

But he stared down at the crank and told his reflection the same lie he had told himself so many times before. The lie that every junkie whispers in the earliest hours of the soul.

"Just one last time."

Chapter Thirty-Six

"He said 'all the sons of Asmodeus will die.'" Arden had relayed the rest to them, but he knew that detail was the most important. "Any ideas?"

Chase was the first to speak. "I will track him. Once I get to him, I'll make him talk."

"I'll go with you," Civious said. "It'll be fun."

"Your idea of fun usually involves four strippers and six bottles of champagne," Arden said. "This is serious." He looked across the wide desk at his father. "What are we going to do?"

Asmodeus crossed his arms over his chest and leaned back in his chair. "We wait." When his sons all started up arguments at once, he held up a hand. "Sorro will surface sooner or later. I think you're right, though, Arden. We need to call everybody in. All of you need to watch your asses."

Arden couldn't believe what he was hearing. He agreed with Chase. They needed to find Sorro and find out who he was working for. And something bothered him about his father's quick dismissal of the threat. Maybe he was just playing it cool to keep them all from running out and ending up in more trouble.

Asmodeus pointed to Malevo. "Hedon and Devian are up top on a Call together. I want you to go get them and bring them back."

Malevo nodded. Arden thought it odd to see his moody, quiet brother in the main house. He usually stuck hermit-like to his own house. But, if anybody could call Hedon and Devian off a job, his six-foot-six, built-like-a-tank brother could. Those two brats wouldn't have a choice.

"Civious, you'll have to go find Sation and bring him home, but don't get caught up in his games. You two are a real terror when you get together, and we don't need the trouble right now."

Civious frowned with mock hurt. "Ruin all my fun."

"What about me?" Chase asked.

Asmodeus gave his second born son a look that confused Arden. A ghost of a smile played around his father's mouth. "You stay here. I need you to do something for me."

"Fine, I guess." Chase tucked his blond hair behind an ear. "It better be good."

"Don't worry, it will be." Asmodeus rocked forward and put his elbows on the edge of the desk. "Now, go. I need a word with Arden. Alone."

Arden did not like the sound of that. He had his own issues to deal with. Not that he was anxious to tell Nic she could leave, but the faster the cut, the less it would hurt, right?

His insides begged to differ.

His brothers filed out of the library and shut the door behind them. His father didn't say anything for a minute and the silence grew heavy. "Can we move this along, Dad? I have something I need to take care of."

"That's what I have to talk to you about."

"I know." Arden sighed. "Don't worry, I'm sending her back."

"No!" The shout was too loud in the empty library. "I mean, you can't," his father said.

"She doesn't belong here. I was selfish to think I could keep her." It pained him to say it out loud, but it was the truth. "I thought she would be my way out, but now..." He let his words trail off. He didn't want to admit the rest.

"But now you find you can't use her that way?" Asmodeus leaned farther over the desk. "I know about the transformation."

What? "What?"

"When you discussed the matter with the Incubai King, I was told right away." He sighed and Arden saw a shadow pass over his face. "It doesn't matter now though, does it?"

"Not really. No." Arden wasn't sure how he would go back to where he had been before Nic. The endless cycle of boredom, Call, boredom, Call, would start up all over again. He would still be half human. He would remain dissatisfied. But the worst? She would be gone.

"Tell me something," Asmodeus said. "You wanted out of here so badly. You were sure Nic was the key to having what you always wanted." He was leaning so far over the desk, he was almost standing. "What changed your mind?"

Arden didn't want the confession to come out of his mouth and he barely recognized his own voice when it did. "I love her. And that means I have to let her go."

His father laughed. Laughed. "You can't imagine how glad I am to hear you say that." He relaxed back into his chair, but his smile did not diminish.

First the laughter and now this? The conversation made him dizzy. "You're *glad* I have to let the woman I love go away?"

"Oh no, not that part. The love part."

Arden could only stare. Words escaped him.

"And she will remain here."

"What?" Shock mixed with restrained joy boiled in his veins. A hundred questions about his father's behavior stepped aside in light of the news. "She has to stay?"

"It won't be safe for her up there. Not with Sorro MIA. If she's down here, we can protect her."

Arden thought his heart would jump out of his chest. "She has to stay?"

The smile hadn't left his father's face. "Yes."

He launched out of his chair and planted his hands on the desk. "She has to stay." Then the words sank in. "I have to go."

His feet wouldn't move fast enough. He took the stairs two at a time and could still hear his dad laughing when he reached the top.

Nic.

She *had* to stay. With him.

He only hoped she would agree.

———

Nic stepped out of the shower, dried off, and put on the black shirt hanging from a hook by the door. No way would she put the other clothes back on. They were soiled by more than dirt.

The button-up shirt had to be Arden's. She lifted one lapel to her nose and breathed in the smoky scent of him. When he was done with her, she hoped she would still be able to smell it.

She pulled the tails over her hips. It fell to her knees and the soft fabric reminded her of the way his skin felt under her palms.

That's enough. You're only going to make it worse.

Her foggy reflection in the mirror showed her she was clean, but not much more than that. She looked tired and her wet hair was matted to her head like a swimmer's cap. Not to mention the lovely collection of scrapes, cuts, and bruises. It all boiled down to one thing—

Did she really think someone like him would fall for someone like her?

She wiped a hand across the mirror and smeared the face she saw there. That part of her life was over, and the sooner she let it go, the better.

Drew was safe. Time to pay up.

Arden's bedroom looked the same but did not feel the same. Before, it had been dark, moody, and intimidating. Now it seemed warm and lush. She ran a hand along the black velvet wall, loving the sensation on her fingertips. The curtains were open and the red morning light filtered in through the windows, changing the colors in the room from jet to warm burgundy wine.

The enormous bed beckoned her. She climbed up and settled back against the pillows. Her memory of the last time she had been in this bed catapulted to the front of her mind and she closed her eyes, clinging to the images in her head like a lifeline.

The outer door to his rooms slammed and then the bedroom door crashed open. Her eyes flew wide and she vaulted from the bed.

It was Arden, and she could see his eyes flash with ice-fire like she had never seen before.

He had come to collect.

She looked at the floor and leaned back into the side of the bed, waiting to hear what would be asked of her. The time for negotiating was over. And she was tired of fighting.

Instead of him speaking, she heard him close the door. The quiet snick of the latch sounded and then she heard his footsteps coming toward her. She saw the toes of his boots in front of her downcast eyes.

"Uh, how was the shower?" His words were stilted and awkward, like he couldn't figure out what to say.

After everything, after all the drama and bullshit, all he wanted to know was if she had enjoyed her shower?

Oh, that's it. "You want to know if I had a good shower?" Tired of fighting? Not now. "Well, golly gee, it was the best shower of my life!" When he didn't say anything, she went on, stepping away from him and pacing the length of the room. "I just went through Hell, literally, to save my brother. Almost got sexually assaulted in a back alley, was manhandled by some kind of goliath, watched a teenager turn into a giant spider that bit me, got a visit from some demons posing as my dead parents who tried to kill me, and the topper? I did it all in the company of someone who was *using* me for his selfish fucking schemes." She shook with pent-up rage and stomped over to glare up at him. "Yes, Arden, the shower was just fucking fabulous."

He laughed and she wanted to slap him. The look on her face must have changed his mind because his crooked grin went away. "I just wanted to make sure you were all right."

She sighed and the molten flow of her anger stalled. "Look, I gave you my word that once Drew was safe I would help you. I trust you'll get him home from here, so if you don't have any objections, I would like to get this over with."

"You don't have to help me."

Huh? "What?"

"I said, you don't have to help me. I release you from your obligation," he said. "But you do have to stay."

At first she was a little too shocked to say anything. She had to stay? Clearly he was trying a new tactic; maybe so she felt more in control. It wouldn't work. "You think if I stay you'll have more time to figure out a way to use me anyway?" Anger crept back into her words, but not just anger—pain. So much pain. "Another ploy, another trick to make me—" Her rant broke on a sob. "To use me to get what you want and then throw me away. You don't have to lie to me anymore, Arden. I'll give you whatever you need."

"I'm not fucking lying to you."

"Then what do you want from me?"

"You have to stay here so I can protect you."

His words made her heart thud inside her chest, but the old Nic spoke up anyway. "I can protect myself."

"It's not safe for you to leave and I won't let you go."

"Why?" It was a simple enough question, but her breath stopped as she waited for him to answer.

"Because, I...you just can't leave."

"There's no reason for me to stay." There *was*, but she wasn't ready to give up the secret.

He grabbed hold of her arms and leaned down to look her in the eye. "I want you to stay—no, I *need* you to stay."

"Why?" she asked again.

"I love you."

Of all the things she expected to come out of his mouth, that wasn't even on her radar. *He loves me?* She could see him holding his breath, hoping she would buy it. But another, darker fire burned in his eyes, as if what she would say next would free or condemn him.

Could it possibly be true? Her own heart filled with joy hearing the words, but there was still that tiny spot of disbelief inside of her. How could she believe him? "Prove it."

Dismay flitted across his features and then he smiled. Again he reminded her of the cat with a mouthful of canary. He pulled her closer until their noses were almost touching. "Ardent," he said. "My true name is Ardent."

The one thing that gave her total control over him, the thing she had hoped would be her key to freedom, and he had given it to her. She could see the shadow of doubt on his face. He thought she would use it to leave him.

Not in a million years.

"Well then, Ardent," she said, watching him close. "I think there's something you should know."

His hands came up to frame her face. "Yes?"

"I love you too."

She felt her feet leave the ground as he picked her up and deposited her on the bed. He settled himself above her and started kissing the side of her neck. "What do you plan on doing with my secret?" he purred in her ear. His hands lifted her shirt and he brushed the fabric out of the way so he could trail his palm over her breasts, followed by his mouth.

A chill crept over her skin, followed by fire wherever his lips met her flesh. "I'm going to use it to get what *I* want."

"And what do you want?"

"You, Ardent. I want you."

He growled low in his throat, and her shirt became a tattered rag.

She said his true name four more times before he robbed her of all ability to speak.

— —

Arden had lost track of how many times he had climaxed. The sound of his name from her lips drove him over the edge again and again, and she had tumbled off the cliff with him each time.

Her body was pressed into his side and she slept. He smoothed his hand over her silken skin and kissed the top of her head.

She was *his*. The thought filled him with a sense of peace he hadn't realized he needed.

Nic gave him life.

He sighed and hugged her closer.

And that's when he heard the shouting start from the other side of the house.

Chapter Thirty-Seven

She raced down the hall right behind Arden. Nic didn't need anyone to tell her where they were running; the tight knot in her stomach and the undeniable flood of adrenaline coursing through her veins told her everything.

Drew.

Remy stood just outside the door with his arm around a sobbing maid. He gave Nic an apologetic glance as she brushed past him and into the room.

The tray of food the maid had brought in lay on the ground, its contents scattered across the carpet. Arden blocked her view of the bed for a moment, and when he stepped away, she saw what was hidden there.

Her brother lay on the bed half under the covers with his head nestled into the pillows. A syringe hung limp from his arm.

She staggered over to the bed and took the needle out of his vein. It fell from her hand, but she didn't notice.

"Drew." Flashes of their earlier conversation danced in her head as tears fell from her cheeks to darken the white sheets.

She sat down on the bed next to him and felt all the things she wished she would have done wash over her. She should have stayed with him longer. She should have checked his pockets. She should have...

None of it mattered now. Her brother was gone.

Arden came up behind her and put his hand on her shoulder. She leaned her face against his knuckles and closed her eyes.

Beneath her cheek she felt him tense, and she opened her eyes. A brilliant white light filled the room. She had to blink to see the source.

The light came from her parents.

On the other side of the bed they stood, shining as bright as a lightning strike.

The memory of the demons from the pit brought her to her feet, but when she made to lunge across Drew's body, Arden held her back.

"It's all right, Nic," Asmo said. She hadn't even noticed him standing near the fireplace, his face full of sympathy. "They've come to take him."

She looked back at the glowing figures and some last link clunked together in her brain. "Mom?"

The long wings on the angel's back fluttered. She didn't speak, just gave a short nod of her head. A sense of rightness shone from her eyes.

The other angel—her dad—smiled and then bent down and ran a hand over Drew's face.

Nic watched her brother's form shift, and a second Drew rose up from his body and took her father's hand.

The three figures looked at her with serene smiles, and tears blurred her vision. A sob twisted from her mouth.

Then, like the slow diminishing of the setting sun, they faded and faded away. The room darkened from the absence of their light.

She turned into Arden's arms and loved him more for the warmth there. Her tears were gone, dry. Drew was safe at last, carried away on the wings of her own personal angels.

With him went the last of her ties to her old life. It felt so *right* somehow, as if it were supposed to be this way all along.

And in her heart, she saw the truth of it.

Epilogue

Sorro hunkered over his cup of coffee, feeling the warmth through the cup. The shitty diner was empty except for the cook in the back and the haggard waitress who flirted with a trucker at the counter.

Outside, rain came down in sheets. He hoped it would clear up soon. He couldn't stay in one place for long and he really hated the rain.

The diner made for a shelter, even if it was dirty and run-down. The booth seat creaked each time he moved, and it irritated him.

He guessed it didn't matter where he was. As long as he kept moving there was a chance he would survive.

The coffee tasted more like an oil slick than a refreshing pick-me-up, but beggars couldn't be choosers. He reached for another packet of sugar in hopes of drowning out the bitterness; it tasted too similar to the tang of failure for his liking.

One thing was certain: if he survived, he would never waste his time with humans again. Or the children of the Fallen, for that matter. That lot was nothing but a dagger thrust into his side.

Another certainty was the fact that all of his work, all of his ridiculous fantasies about roaming free in paradise, had blown up in his face. He would never be free.

His employer would find him whether he used his glamour or not.

The bell on the door chimed, and he looked up to see who else sought shelter from the storm howling outside.

If he'd had a heart, it would have stopped when he saw the tall, blond man glance around and then settle his clear eyes on Sorro.

The Archai's black wings were hidden under his overcoat, and his hair was soaked from the rain. He didn't look at the two people at the counter as he walked past and settled himself into the empty seat across the table.

Sorro did not speak. There wasn't much for him to say anyway. He took a sip of his coffee, suspecting it would be his last.

"You failed, but this isn't over," the Archai said. "I have another job for you."

Acknowledgments

A huge chunk of my unending gratitude belongs to my agent, Nalini Akolekar, who believed in this story as much as I did. And she never laughs at me when I ask dumb questions. Enormous thanks to my editor, Kelli Martin, for turning my dreams into my reality. Thanks also to everyone at Montlake Romance who used their wizardry to make my baby pretty.

I owe Kimberly Meyer, my braintwin, constant cheerleader, and bfff, more thanks than I could ever express in words. Huge thanks to Abbie Roads for asking tough questions and forcing me to answer them. 6C forever!

Thanks to Linnea Sinclair and Stacey Kade for being so generous with their collective knowledge and for being awesome in general. And thanks to Judi McCoy for her humor, her wisdom, and for teaching the class that changed my life.

Thanks to my beta readers and everyone else who spent time with this story in its early forms. I wouldn't have made it without you.

My family has always given me their love and support despite my faults. I owe them everything. Everything. A special thanks to Grandma Cox, who always had lots of books and endless patience for an annoying, imaginative little girl.

And to Jeff, my motivator, teammate, anchor, plot helper, caretaker, entertainer, biggest fan, best friend, and amazing husband…thanks for teaching me about love.

About the Author

 Novelist and tattoo artist Celeste Easton was born in Ohio, where her first words were "Read me." When she isn't penning dark and delicious paranormal romances, she's busy collecting shoes and Victorian funerary photographs and chowing down on cake and sugar-free Red Bull. She blogs at www.onelifetwoinks .blogspot.com.

Kindle *Serials*

This book was originally released in episodes as a Kindle Serial. Kindle Serials launched in 2012 as a new way to experience serialized books. Kindle Serials allow readers to enjoy the story as the author creates it, purchasing once and receiving all existing episodes immediately, followed by future episodes as they are published. To find out more about Kindle Serials and to see the current selection of Serials titles, visit www.amazon.com/kindleserials.

8586923R00202

Made in the USA
San Bernardino, CA
14 February 2014